The Last Train to Barksville

Susan C. Daffron

An Alpine Grove Romantic Comedy

Book 12

 Published by Magic Fur Press
An imprint of Logical Expressions, Inc.
P.O. Box 383
Ponderay, ID 83852

The Last Train to Barksville

ISBN: 978-1-61038-069-0 (paperback)
        978-1-61038-070-6 (EPUB)

Like all of my books, *The Last Train to Barksville* is
dedicated to
my husband James Byrd,
my best friend and biggest supporter.
Thanks for everything!

<u>Books by Susan C. Daffron</u>
The Alpine Grove Romantic Comedies
Chez Stinky

Fuzzy Logic

The Art of Wag

Snow Furries

Bark to the Future

Howl at the Loon

The Good, the Bad, and the Pugly

The Treasure of the Hairy Cadre

The Luck of the Paw

Daydream Retriever

The Hound of Music

The Last Train to Barksville

The Jennings & O'Shea Mysteries
Sensing Trouble

Sensing Secrets

Sensing Truth

Chapter 1

Boldly Going

Carly Buchanan waved the pay stub in front of her dog Trixie. "Three hundred and forty-eight hours. Do you know how long it took to build up that much vacation time? *Years.* And now, after all my dedicated service and never taking any time off, they want to steal it from me. This is so unfair."

Trixie wagged uncertainly at the tirade. The dog was a brown-and–white, medium-sized mixed breed of uncertain heritage. One ear stood up and one flopped over, which gave her a perpetually perplexed expression.

Carly apologized for her outburst and stroked the fur between Trixie's ears. Who avoids taking vacation? No one thinks, "Gee, I hate rest and relaxation." What was wrong with her? Maybe Trixie's furrowed brow was warranted. And okay, holding your pay stub in front of your dog's face demanding answers might be a little unusual, but these were unusual times. If Carly didn't use at least two weeks of her accrued vacation time within the next month, the hours would be gone forever. The company let employees roll over vacation time from year to year, but only up to a point. Then all that fine print in the employee handbook kicked in, notably the use-it-or-lose-it policy. Because she was responsible for keeping the office running, there'd never been a good time to fit in a vacation. She'd always been too busy.

Carly scanned the small apartment where she and Trixie now lived. Boxes were stacked in neat rows throughout the living room, still sitting where she'd placed them a week ago when she'd moved out from the house she'd shared with her boyfriend, Stuart Patrick, for the last fifteen years. Everything was tidy, but when it comes to decor, there's only so much you can do when you have virtually no furniture.

Stuart had never been Stu, always Stuart. One Thanksgiving his mom had committed the ultimate sin by calling him "Stewie," and Carly had to stifle a laugh at his icy glare. She still couldn't quite believe they weren't a couple anymore. The breakup had been so sudden the whole thing seemed like a bad dream.

Stuart and Carly had shared everything except a marriage license. He'd always said they didn't need one. Because they loved each other, a piece of paper wasn't important. Being together was all that mattered. And after fifteen years, Carly had assumed she and Stuart had some kind of a common-law marriage. Everyone always said that if you lived together for seven years, you were married. Unfortunately, "everyone" was wrong, and "everyone" didn't have a law degree. Carly discovered the hard way that only a few states recognize common-law marriage. And California wasn't one of them.

The day Stuart asked her to move out was the worst day of Carly's life. The declaration felt like it had come out of nowhere. He'd announced he'd fallen in love with another woman and wanted Carly to leave the house immediately. Carly had cried and argued, but he was utterly unmoved by her entreaties. He'd calmly said, "The lease for Laurel's apartment is up next week, and I told her she could move in here."

Carly had stood in stunned silence as he'd continued in the same overly reasonable tone, "Laurel likes this house." As if Carly should care. That's when Carly knew he was serious, and it was over.

The only thing she'd managed to convince him to give up was Trixie. And that was probably only because the lovely Laurel was allergic to dog hair. The house was in Stuart's name, so Trixie and Carly were homeless virtually overnight. The year 1997 would go down in history as the year scientists cloned Dolly the sheep, and Stuart Patrick unceremoniously dumped Caroline E. Buchanan out of his life.

The plain white walls of the small studio apartment Carly had rented were barren. None of her favorite artwork graced the space because it remained on the walls of her now former home. Because Stuart earned more money, he'd paid for the furniture and almost everything else. The boxes stacked throughout Carly's apartment were filled with clothes, a few knickknacks, her art books, and various craft supplies. Carly had purchased a camping air mattress to sleep on and found a folding table and chairs at a thrift store. The environment in the apartment was depressing bordering on bleak. Here she was, thirty-six years old, and completely starting over. She didn't even have her own pots and pans. Not to mention plates and silverware.

Carly crumpled the pay stub in her fist. She'd dragged her feet, but if the powers that be in Human Resources insisted that she take a vacation, so be it. Maybe getting away would help her reboot her life. It was time to embark on My Life 2.0, featuring the new, improved Carly. The only question was where to go. Unfortunately, she wasn't great at making decisions, particularly spur-of-the-moment ones. It wasn't like she could run off to Paris and have a fling with some

European heartthrob. Although the idea had a lot of appeal, financially speaking, it wasn't feasible.

Carly gazed into Trixie's soulful brown eyes. "I bet you'd like to go somewhere that has lots of trees and fewer people, wouldn't you? With space for you to run around and play. What do you think? Where should we go?"

Trixie wagged and rolled over on her back so Carly could rub her tummy. She reached over to accede to the dog's wishes. "I don't want to go somewhere by myself. Maybe Lily and Ginger would be willing to take a trip with me. I can't just sit around here talking to you. That could make both of us crazy. I need some time with friends who knew me before I even met Stuart."

On the night of what Carly thought of as The Great Ousting, she'd stayed at a pet-friendly motel with Trixie and called her best friends, Lily Moore and Ginger Thomas, for moral support.

Both of her friends expressed suitable amounts of shock and outrage at Stuart's sudden change of heart. Ginger came up with a number of creative, catty names for his new girlfriend, Laurel, which made Carly feel a little better, at least temporarily. And Lily had decided that from now on she would only refer to Stuart as "Captain Prickard." Lily was a fan of *Star Trek Next Generation* and liked the play on words with Patrick Stewart's character.

Both women had even offered to come out and visit Carly. Although she had initially resisted the idea, now Carly was rethinking her decision. She picked up the phone and dialed the number of her sister Karen's veterinary clinic in Alpine Grove.

A woman who proclaimed that her name was Tracy answered, and transferred the call to the veterinarian.

Carly smiled at the sound of her sister's voice. Karen sounded so professional, yet Carly's mental image of her was of the tall gangly goofball that she'd sat around watching cartoons with on Saturday mornings. "Hey, it's me."

"How are you doing?" Karen said. "Did you get yourself set up in the new place? How is Trixie adjusting to apartment living?"

"We're fine, but I need to take a vacation."

"You *need* to?" Karen chuckled. "I need to win a million dollars. Could you work on that too?"

"I'm serious. If I don't use some of my vacation time this month, I lose it. But I don't know where to go."

"Do you want to visit here? My place is kind of small, but…"

"I don't want to impose on you, but I was wondering if there still are rental places like that cute cottage by the lake we stayed at when we were kids."

Karen said with a wry tone, "You're actually saying you want to return to the scene of the legendary ouchie pouchie incident?"

"The lake was so pretty. And for the ninety-fifth time, I was little. How was I supposed to know what you call a first-aid kit?"

"Little did we know then, that your need to rhyme would continue for the next thirty years. Anyway, I hate to be the bearer of bad news, but the summer rental market here is incredibly tight. Most of the lake houses get snapped up by people who have been renting the same places every summer for years."

Carly sighed and glanced down at Trixie. Maybe they could do something else. "Oh well, it was a nice idea. How's the best niece in the whole world doing?"

"Annie's fine. She's been busy trying to convince me how great sleep-away camp is going to be." Karen paused. "Wait. I have an idea. I was talking to someone a few minutes ago, and there might be a rental available after all. Hold on. I need to catch a guy with a golden retriever."

"What?" At the lack of response, Carly held the receiver in front of her face. The line was still open, so Karen hadn't hung up. Was some furry escapee running around the vet clinic? She picked at her chipped nail polish while she waited. Finally, Karen returned and said, "I have good news."

Carly said, "What happened? Was there a dog problem?"

"No, the dog is fine. His blood panel came back from the lab and he's quite healthy, in fact. But I think I have a line on a house for you."

"Really?" Carly's mood lifted for the first time in a week. "Where?"

"It's a gorgeous house right on the lake. While I was examining his golden, Ben was telling me how his rental tenant just flaked out on him. The house is available for two weeks, starting Sunday. Can you be here that soon?"

"Absolutely!"

"Great. Let me put you on hold. He's in the lobby paying his bill, and I need to tell him you want it before he goes and finds someone else. He said there's a waiting list, but he'd let me have it."

"So are you coming too? That's *wonderful*. You need a vacation even more than I do."

"I can't go, but it will be great to see you. Be right back."

Carly waited, petting Trixie. "How do you feel about a road trip?" Trixie wagged, but the sad truth was that Carly didn't want to stay at some opulent lake house all by herself, even if she could afford it, which she couldn't. They might be busy, but Ginger and Lily *had* to come with her on this vacation.

Karen returned, "Okay, it's all set up. Ben said he'll drop the key with me later this week."

"You should come too. When was the last time you took a vacation?"

"I can't take off work."

"Why not? The last time I saw you was when you went to that conference. You said you got a relief veterinarian. He sounded great."

"After a lot of campaigning on your niece's part, I grudgingly agreed to let her go to camp this year. And now we have a lot to do to get ready."

"When does she leave?"

"Sunday."

"That's perfect timing. Send her off to camp and then relax by the lake with me. I can tell by your voice that you're stressed."

"I'm fine. You're the one having the life crisis, not me."

"You work too hard." Carly paused. "And you didn't answer my question. When was the last time you took a vacation?"

"When Dave and I went to Hawaii."

"Are you serious? That was *years* ago, not too long before he died. I can't go on vacation by myself. Trixie and I are going to drag you out to this house forcibly if you don't agree."

"Oops." There was a pause and Karen continued, "I forgot about Trixie. The house doesn't allow pets."

"What kind of vet forgets that I have a dog?"

"You're hilarious."

"Well, I can't leave her here in this apartment, and I wouldn't want a pet sitter—or anyone else—to see this place. It's, well, never mind. I suppose I could take her to a kennel."

"There's a boarding kennel here that a lot of my clients use. I'll give you the number. Trixie will love it. The place is on eighty acres of forest and the dogs get lots of long walks. It's like doggie camp."

"I guess that would work. I'll miss Trixie, but knowing she's having a good time will help. The breakup with Stuart hasn't been great for her either. Her world has been turned upside down too, and I'm sure she wonders where he is. But you have to come with me on vacation. You can find a vet to cover for you, can't you? You know I can't afford to rent this house by myself. And with Annie at camp, you're going to be all alone. That will drive you insane."

"You're the one who hates being alone, not me." Karen sighed. "But I suppose I could make a few calls and see if I can find someone to fill in here."

Carly raised her fist in a victory sign. Successfully talking her sister into anything almost never happened. "This will be great. We *both* need some time off."

Carly looked down at Trixie, covered the phone receiver with her palm, and whispered into the dog's floppy ear, "It looks like you get to go to sleep-away camp like your cousin Annie. I think this will be good for us. We both need to boldly go somewhere far, far away from Captain Prickard."

~

After getting directions to the house and hanging up with Karen, Carly moved to the next step: convincing her friends to go on vacation with her. Carly had gone to college with Lily and Ginger, and they'd stayed close through the years. They'd met the first day of freshman year because they'd been assigned the same dorm suite at a small women's college in New England. Something about that communal living experience in the dorm had formed an enduring bond, and Carly knew that Ginger and Lily would always be there for her no matter what.

Carly called Lily first. Her friend was a self-proclaimed workaholic, so convincing Lily to take a vacation would be a hard sell. In fact, Carly couldn't remember Lily *ever* taking a vacation. Because she was an intellectual property lawyer, Lily spent a lot of time interpreting copyright, trademark, and patent law. Carly couldn't imagine doing that type of work, but Lily said she loved it. She worked for a huge law firm in Silicon Valley with lots of information technology clients that spent boatloads of money protecting their geeky assets.

Like Karen, Lily was focused intently on her career. After listening to Lily talk about her job for years, Carly thought some of Karen's clients who bit or scratched sounded more pleasant than the corporate weasels Lily had to deal with on a daily basis.

As soon as Carly called, Lily regaled her about the latest nut who was convinced a famous author had stolen the idea for his book from her. No matter how many times Lily pointed out that ideas can't be copyrighted, the nut was convinced that Michael Crichton had stolen the idea for *Jurassic Park* from her because her book had dinosaurs in it. The fact that the book had virtually no plot points in common with Crichton's didn't seem to matter.

Carly pointed out that dealing with lunatics was what made vacations necessary, and braced herself for the inevitable argument that legal work was important. But much to Carly's surprise, Lily retorted, "You know what? You're right. Why am I wasting my time trying to convince this idiot that she *shouldn't* hire me to sue some high falutin' author?"

"So does that mean I'll see you this Sunday?" Carly asked.

"I'll be there. You aren't the only one with a lot of vacation time. And like you've pointed out before, I've got the skunky flunky to help out. Life is short. Let him deal with it. My clients will just have to deal with him on their own because I'm outta here."

They said their goodbyes, and Carly squealed with delight when she hung up the phone. Lily was a brilliant lawyer and the skunky flunky was an associate she'd hired who had an unfortunate habit of dousing himself in cologne. When Carly had given him the moniker, Lily had roared with laughter. Although Carly was thrilled that Lily had agreed to come on vacation with her, it was out of character, and the note of anxiety in Lily's voice was equally unusual.

Next up was Ginger who, as it turned out, was having troubles of her own. At around the same time Carly had met Stuart, Ginger had met her husband, Nathan, and opted out of applying to medical school, derailing her potential career as a doctor. Although Ginger used to tutor kids in chemistry and biology part time, Carly couldn't remember the last time Ginger had mentioned anything related to her interest in science.

During the call, Ginger revealed in no uncertain terms that getting away from her brood of teenagers had a lot of appeal. She griped, "I'm tired of being chief cook, bottle washer, chauffeur, and general unpaid labor. I need a vacation too. Let's see how this family does without me for two weeks. As you would say, there's likely to be a mighty fighty, but see if I care."

After hanging up with Ginger, Carly pulled clothes out of boxes and put them in a suitcase. The fact that everything was working out so perfectly with her friends had to be some type of a sign from the universe that this vacation was meant to be. Tomorrow, she'd go into work and let everyone know she was taking two weeks off.

Unfortunately, telling a group of consultants that they would have no administrative assistance for an extended period of time ended up being about as well received as news of an impending apocalypse. Carly's announcement led to lots of whining and wailing about how the ever-beleaguered and overwhelmed consultants wouldn't be able to get their reports out on time.

Normally, Carly was accommodating to the point of being a squishy soft wimp. Although her job included trying to keep work flowing and everyone happy, in this instance, she found it extremely difficult to care about the consultants' protestations. It showed once again why it had been so easy for her to put off taking vacations. Everyone at work always made it sound like she was indispensable, and Carly enjoyed feeling needed. It didn't help that Stuart had never been able to get away, or so he'd claimed. At this point, Carly had to wonder what he was really doing on all those business trips. He probably packed a big box of lovie glovies so he could get some action with Lauren. Now Carly was glad she'd never looked in his suitcase. Eww.

After breaking the tragic news about her vacation to her coworkers, Carly tried to smile at the correct moments and explain that if she didn't take time off, she'd lose the hours, which was akin to throwing money away. But no one was even remotely interested in her potential financial losses or concerned about anything other than their precious reports.

Their lack of consideration grated on Carly. Why did she continue to work for such a bunch of self-absorbed jerks? Maybe rebooting her life should include rebooting her career, such as it was. Finally, she waved her hands and said, "I'm sorry, but I'm going on vacation whether you like it or not. While I'm gone, you'll have to figure things out all by yourselves. I've had a difficult week, and I think it would be easier for everyone if I start my vacation right now."

Amid the collective gasps and sputters of indignation, Carly grabbed her purse, pulled out Karen's business card, and slapped it on the desk. "If there's a massive crisis or emergency, this is the number of my sister's vet clinic. Someone there will probably know how to reach me. But unless it's a matter of life and death, like this building is on fire and in danger of burning down completely, please do *not* call me."

She retrieved her bagged lunch from her desk drawer and slammed it shut. "Good luck, and I'm serious: *no* ringy dingy! I'll see you in a couple of weeks."

Carly fumed through the entire drive back to her apartment. If she'd gone to law school like Lily, maybe she'd be working with grown-ups right now. But no, she'd met Stuart and taken this dead-end job creating a bunch of screamingly dull reports no one who wanted to remain awake would ever willingly read.

Carly almost never discussed her job with anyone because it was so mind-numbing and difficult to explain. Stories about working in admin at a high-technology consulting company were either too boring or too arcane for anyone else to be remotely interested in hearing about, so she kept quiet. But it was a paycheck. She'd had job security, good benefits, and an easy commute, which had been enough because she'd been more focused on other areas of her life. Namely Stuart.

Carly had always said she had great work-life balance because she wasn't stressed out performing a high-powered job like Lily's. But the truth was Carly had little interest in her work, so her balance was skewed in the other direction. Her life had revolved around Stuart, which in retrospect seemed pathetic. She was a smart, well-educated, intelligent woman who had let herself and her needs become subordinate to someone else's more interesting life. While it was happening, she hadn't really noticed. But the most pitiful thing was that she didn't even know what she *wanted* to do anymore.

When Carly arrived back at her apartment, the dog walker she'd hired was at the door getting ready to take Trixie out for her afternoon excursion. Carly thanked the young woman and said that she wouldn't need her services for two-and-a-half weeks because she and Trixie would be out of town.

Carly opened the door, went inside, and Trixie jumped out of her dog bed, leaping around the room in a display of exuberant canine joy about her impending outing. During their short walk around the apartment complex, Trixie embarked on walkie sniffies while Carly came to an obvious conclusion: there was absolutely no reason not to leave town immediately.

The idea of sitting alone in her dreary apartment was bleak, so why wait? When you have an apartment full of neatly arranged, yet utterly unpacked boxes, one more night in a motel on the road didn't seem too bad. Before she could change her mind and return to a state of mopey inertia, she packed her suitcase and loaded Trixie into the car.

Normally, Carly would have spent some time planning her trip, but not today. She had no idea how long it would take to get where she was going, so she opted to drive until she got tired and then find a motel. She had lots of time, so she could take the scenic route to Alpine Grove. If nothing else, logging so many hours behind the wheel would give her time to think.

It wasn't the first time Carly had been to Alpine Grove. Years before Karen had set up her veterinary practice in the town, their family had rented a house on the lake that was located south of Alpine Grove. Although the trip seemed like a lifetime ago, Carly remembered spending hours reading, swimming, and hanging out with her family. The experience had been fun and relaxing all at the same time. Carly couldn't wait to feel that way again. It had to be better than depressed and lonely.

The drive was long, but Carly passed the time listening to all her favorite CDs. She was able to enjoy songs she hadn't heard in years because Stuart had deemed the music bad or juvenile for some esoteric reason.

Carly arrived in Alpine Grove late Saturday. On weekends, Karen's veterinary clinic was open in the morning, so Carly drove straight through town and parked in the clinic lot. She turned to look at Trixie, who was on her doggie bed in the back seat. "We're here! I know it might look like we're at a veterinary hospital. That's because we are, but don't worry. You don't have to go inside."

Trixie offered her typical puzzled expression and Carly laughed. "You are the best traveling companion! No whining about the music or complaining about what I eat. I should have taken you on a trip with me a long time ago."

When Carly walked into the clinic, the blonde woman at the desk glanced at her, did a double take, and smiled. "You must be Carly."

"How did you know?"

"You look a lot like Dr. C. It's a little spooky." She held out her hand. "I'm Tracy Sullivan. I think we talked on the phone."

Carly knew that she didn't look much like her sister, but she volunteered a polite smile. "Nice to meet you. Is Karen around?"

Tracy stood up and walked around the desk. "I think she's in surgery, but I'll tell her you're here. You might need to wait a couple minutes while she finishes up."

Carly glanced at the glass door. "Okay. I need to get my dog out of the car. Could you ask Karen to meet me outside when she's done?"

"Sure." Tracy disappeared into the mysterious back room and Carly shuddered. The idea of holding a scalpel and cutting up dogs gave her the willies.

Carly returned to the parking lot and got Trixie out of the back seat. They spent some time wandering around the grassy "potty area," which was apparently filled with stimulating scents from the many dogs that had visited before. Trixie was practically hyperventilating from all the power sniffing.

A small flower garden lined the edge of the building, and the scent of roses wafted around Carly, reminding her of the last time she'd been to Alpine Grove so many years ago. The little garden was fenced off to keep out the inevitable parade of curious canines. From within their little fortress, the flowers bobbed in the breeze, their vibrant colors looking festive against the wood siding on the wall behind them.

Carly turned at the sound of the door opening and grinned at her sister as she walked toward her. Karen was taller than Carly, but had the same chestnut hair and hazel eyes. Carly often thought of herself as the "teapot" of the family because Karen was tall and lean while Carly was short and rounded. Together they looked like the female version of Laurel and Hardy or Abbott and Costello.

Karen was wearing a colorful lab coat and had a stethoscope hanging from her neck. She opened her arms wide and said, "Welcome to Alpine Grove."

Carly threw herself into the hug and squeezed tight. She let go and grinned at her sister. "I can't believe how happy I am to see you. It's been way too long."

"I know. Here are the directions to the boarding kennel and the key to the rental. Ben said the house will be cleaned and ready for us after three."

"That's perfect. I'll have time to drop off Trixie and go to the grocery store."

Karen wrapped her in another hug. "Yes, you will. I've got paperwork to do after we close and then I need to pack, so I'll be there around four."

"See you there."

Carly drove north back through the town of Alpine Grove and out toward what Karen referred to as the "toolies" where the boarding kennel was located. Karen had pointed out that although the place wasn't exactly convenient to town, it was in an extremely pretty location. After turning off the highway, Carly opened the windows wider to let the scent of warm grass and trees waft through the car's open windows. Taking long relaxing breaths, she made an effort to leave all thoughts of city life behind as she drove through the rolling countryside and into a deeply forested area.

Carly turned at a driveway that had a sign that read Wag On Inn. The gravel snaked through the woods, winding its way through huge cedar trees that created a mosaic of dappled shade.

The canopy of trees opened up to reveal a cleared area with kennels off to the left. A log house sat farther up the driveway behind a gate. A sign indicated that Carly should turn and park at the dog-boarding kennels. She followed the instructions and unloaded Trixie from her spot in the back seat. The whole area smelled like warm evergreen needles and Trixie raised her nose, sniffing appreciatively. Carly tilted her head back, breathing deeply to enjoy some of the pine-scented air herself.

She turned at the sound of a door slamming from the direction of the house. A petite woman walked down the steps from the front door of the log home, her long brunette braid swaying behind her back.

Bending down to pet Trixie, Carly said, "Karen was right. This *is* like doggie camp! I bet you're going to have lots of fun."

As the woman walked up, Carly told Trixie to sit and whispered, "I know you're squirrelly from so much time in the car, but be a good girl, okay?"

The woman said, "Hi, I'm Kat Stevens. It's nice to meet you." She extended her hand toward the dog. "What a pretty dog you are. And you're being so good."

Relieved that Trixie was behaving, Carly loosened her grip on the leash slightly. "I'm sure she's ready to do something other than stare out the car windows."

"Well, she'll get lots of exercise here. We go for long walks on the trails through the property. My husband is out there in the trees somewhere with loppers and saws, creating a new trail."

"That sounds wonderful. I was so upset when Karen told me the house we're renting doesn't accept dogs."

"Dr. Cassidy is a great vet. I don't know what we'd do without her." Kat leaned to ruffle Trixie's goofy ears. "Sorry you don't get to play at the lake, but this will be fun too."

"I've spent half the trip up here fuming about a few of the men where I work, and I'm looking forward to hanging out with a bunch of women for a change."

Kat laughed, "Yeah, I know what you mean. Any time she finds out that my husband isn't going to be around, a friend of mine demands to come over for a wine and whine party."

"I'm meeting my friends at the house and I can't wait to see them. We've known each other since we were in college. Even though it's a vacation, I warned them that they may have to listen to me whine. That reminds me. I should pick up some wine at the store."

Kat said, "It's great that you're still close to your friends from school."

"It was a small liberal arts college and we were roommates. Or suitemates, technically. I've had so many people ask me how I could stand going to a women's college, but it turned out to be the right decision for me, partly because I met Ginger and Lily, who ended up becoming my best friends."

Kat laughed, "I went to a woman's college for a year, and I used to get questions like that too. How could I stand going to school without any men? Why would I voluntarily do such a thing? How could I possibly manage to cope without the presence of men?"

"I know! What's the big deal? It was four years. The rest of my life is full of men, so who cares? Did you transfer to a coed school?"

"I was sick and barely made it through freshman year. That summer, I moved out of my parents' house and transferred to an in-state school because it was cheaper." Kat shrugged. "It's a long story with lots of drama, but mostly it relates to the fact that my mother and I don't get along."

"I was sick a lot when I was little, but not in college. That must have been hard."

"I thought that going to a women's college might help me get over my shyness. In high school, I never said a word in class unless the teacher called on me. Guys always talked over the girls in class, which didn't help." Kat shrugged. "I wish I could have stayed, but I'd slept through too many classes."

"I know what you mean. I was kind of shy too, partly because I felt like I was living in my sister's shadow. She was ahead of me in high school and a super brain."

Kat smiled. "Well, at least I didn't have *that* problem."

"The whole time I was in college, it was understood that women were absolutely as capable as men. I wish I could say I've seen that in my work life since then, but I haven't. Before I left the office the other day, I was so angry at the guys I work with, I wanted to scream. Normally I try to be nice, but they were being completely unreasonable and getting all churchy perchy on me."

"Do you mean preachy?"

"I'm sorry. My tendency to rhyme can get away from me when I get comfortable and start blabbing. My mother used to say I put too many croutons on my word salad. Fortunately, my friends are used to it." Carly waved her hands in exasperation. "You must be really easy to talk to because I shouldn't be dumping all this on you. It's way more than you needed to know about anything and everything. Maybe I've spent too much time in the car alone with my thoughts."

"Rhyming could come in handy if you're a poet." Kat took the leash from Carly. "Don't worry about it. I see a lot of people who have a lot going on before a trip. Sometimes they're concerned about catching a flight or whatever's going to happen at home while they're gone. Anyway, it's been nice chatting, and I promise we'll take good care of Trixie."

Carly gave Kat Trixie's veterinary records, hugged Trixie goodbye, and got back into her car.

The rental house was located on a peninsula on the lake near a landmark called Gray's Point. Karen had said the house was a gorgeous old Victorian that her client Ben Walsh had restored. Apparently, some people in town claimed the place was inhabited by the ghost of a woman named Miriam Gray. The rumor was that the ghost liked to sit in the branches of a tree near the beach, waiting for her lover to return from a fishing trip. There had been a storm and his fishing boat had sunk in the lake. The story was that Miriam continued to wait.

After stopping by the grocery store to collect supplies, Carly drove southward to the lake. She turned down the driveway, which unlike the meandering gravel trail to the kennels, was paved. The drive passed through some trees and then circled in front of the house, which was exactly as Karen had described: gorgeous. Ben must have spent a fortune restoring it and putting in the pristine landscaping. Stone walls snaked around the property, encircling the massive green lawn that stretched down to the lake. Karen hadn't said how much this place cost to rent, but Carly was pretty sure that even split four ways, she couldn't afford it. Oh well, it was too late now.

She grabbed her purse and a bag of groceries and got out of the car. The house had a huge, ornate wooden door with a metal lion's-head door knocker. She fumbled with the key in the lock and went inside. The massive entry area had an arched mahogany ceiling and immaculate stone floor. Thank goodness she'd boarded Trixie. Paw prints would stand out on the shiny polished surface.

Carly walked toward the back of the house past a room that had dark wood trim and was lined with bookshelves filled with sumptuous leather-bound hardbacks with gold trim. It had a huge wooden desk and table as well. Who had a valuable book collection who wasn't a count or an earl living in a castle? Maybe the books were fake to make Ben look smart. Carly was starting to wonder about this guy. Was he a millionaire? Kingpin of a drug cartel?

She set her grocery bag down in the kitchen and walked to a pair of French doors that led onto a patio and a path down to the lake beyond. A huge tree shaded an area on the right side of the lawn. It must be the one that Miriam sat in. The view was jaw-dropping, so who could blame Miriam for wanting to hang out? If you're going to haunt a house, you might as well haunt a beautiful one.

Carly jumped at the sound of a knock at the door. She ran back to the front of the house and spread her arms wide at the sight of Lily. "Dormie roomie!"

Lily dropped her suitcase, which landed on the stone floor with a resonant thud. She mirrored Carly's outstretched arms. "I made it. Hair, hide 'n all."

They hugged and Carly leaned back so she could see her friend's face. Lily had sleek, bleached blonde hair that was pulled back into a severe French twist. The dark circles below her light brown eyes weren't being camouflaged well by the heavy layer of concealer. Lily looked like she hadn't slept in months. Carly covered her surprise with a welcoming smile and gestured toward the back of the house. "Check out this place. Isn't it incredible?"

Lily tilted her head, examining the ornate woodwork on the ceiling. "No kidding. Are we going to need to perform an ad hoc bank heist to pay for this?"

"I'm hoping Karen got a deal on it because she knows the owner. But even if she didn't, as high-powered professional career woman, you can afford it." Carly turned at the sound of a car driving up the circular driveway.

Ginger hopped out and waved both hands frantically when she saw Carly and Lily standing in front of the open door to the opulent entryway. A grin spread across her round face and she jumped up and down, clapping.

All three women squealed and ran toward each other. Carly scampered down the steps with Lily and as they all went for a group hug, she proclaimed, "The three musketeers are reunited at last!"

Lily said, "Technically, in the book, there are four musketeers."

"Three Stooges, then?" Ginger said.

Carly shoved her shoulder. "Hey, speak for yourself, Curly."

Chapter 2

Unidentified Objects

After Carly left, Kat got Trixie settled in her kennel. The dog walker, Mia, opened the door and gathered up leashes for the late-afternoon walk.

Kat said, "Meet Trixie, our new guest. She's really sweet."

"And a little overweight." Mia gathered up a leash and went into the kennel to get the dog. "Maybe I should walk her with the little dogs. Okay, Trixie, let's see how you feel about Clyde."

"I'll be up at the house if you need anything." Kat left Mia to the dogs and made a conscious effort to return her mind to the article she was supposed to be writing. She had zero ideas for an introduction. It was difficult to get too excited about enterprise resource planning software, largely because she had only a vague idea what it was and the acronym, ERP, made her giggle. She knew ERP had something to do with supply chains. And maybe parts and manufacturing. Forms might be involved in some way too. Every time she tried to read about it, her mind wandered, desperately seeking something else to think about. Sadly, the Internet had become her go-to method of procrastinating. There was a fine line between "research" and avoidance, and Kat crossed that line on a daily basis. It wasn't her fault that there were so many interesting things to read out there in cyberspace.

When Kat walked into the house, she was greeted by a cacophony of barking from downstairs. In addition to the dogs in the boarding kennel, she had five dogs of her own, who were hanging out in the daylight basement. She shushed them and walked into the kitchen where her husband Joel was making a sandwich.

He sliced the bread in half and glanced at her. "How's the new dog?"

"Trixie seems like she'll be an easy keeper. Mellow and kind of fat."

"We like the slow ones."

"No kidding. It's the hyperactive border collies that wipe me out."

He set down the sandwich, "So I have some news that you may or may not like."

"Wow, that's quite a way to lead off a conversation. Almost as good as, 'don't get mad' before dropping some horrible bombshell." Kat crossed her arms. "Am I going to be mad?"

"I have an opportunity to make a lot of money."

"Money almost never makes me mad. Did you land a new programming client?"

"Not exactly. I've been asked to teach a programming course."

"Well, you're certainly qualified. Is it at the college in Gleasonville?"

"No, and this is where we get to the part you might not like. It's in Milwaukee. If I do a good job, then there's another one in Minneapolis next month. Then Atlanta the month after that."

"You're going to teach in *Milwaukee*? Why on earth would you want to do that?"

"It pays really well."

"How well?"

Joel handed her a piece of paper and Kat skimmed to the end. "Holy crap. They'll pay you that much to teach for a *week*?"

"I know. The money is incredible. I think it's too good to pass up."

"Have you taught before?" Kat pressed her palms to her chest. "I mean, I'd rather die than stand in front of a class full of programmers and teach. Even talking about something I know about, like writing, would be traumatic. Just walking across a stage with a dog for that charity show almost gave me a heart attack."

"I've done some presentations, and I know the subject inside and out, so I don't think it will be too bad. They sent me the instructor guides and the material is laid out well."

"That's a lot of people time too. And you won't be able to wander around in our forest to decompress."

"I know." He pulled the hair tie from his ponytail and ran his fingers back from his temples through his long, sandy blonde hair. "Crumpling myself into an airplane seat to get there isn't appealing either."

Kat grinned. "Are they going to make you shave and cut your hair?"

"No one cares. Long hair helps my stature in the geek realm. Half the programmers I know have ponytails longer than mine."

"Well that's good." Kat leaned against the counter. "But the idea of you being gone for a week out of every month makes me feel sort of sick. Except for that trip to visit your aunt, we've barely been apart since you moved in. I like it that way."

Joel stepped forward and put his arms around her. "I know. I do too."

She looked up into his eyes. The irises were deep green with flecks of hazel, rimmed with a darker green. The idea of not seeing Joel every day was heartbreaking. "We just got married a few months ago. Are you sure you want to do this?"

"We also just got a new car. Maybe we could pay it off early. No more payments would be nice."

"I suppose. Are you sure?"

"I'll try it. The worst thing that happens is they think I'm terrible and never ask me to teach again. Or I might find out I hate teaching."

"Or they love you and you're gone twenty-five percent of the time. Or more." Kat took a deep breath. "But if it's something you want to do, you should do it."

"I won't know unless I try." He hugged her tighter. "You've got help here now, so it shouldn't be too bad."

"How much do you want to bet that something in this place falls apart?" Kat gave him a wry smile. "It's like the house knows when you're not here and decides to return to the land like some kind of giant compost pile."

"I think you're exaggerating."

"While we were in Hawaii, the septic system self-destructed. Another time, the roof leaked." Kat waved her arms expansively. "I can't even remember all the things you've fixed anymore."

"Perhaps you need to put a handyman on speed-dial."

"I need *you*." She shook her head. "Wait. I'm sorry. That's not fair. This is me being a selfish worry wart and making up stories that might never happen. You should do what you want to do. Maybe you'll find out you love teaching."

"We'll see. In the short term, we could use the money thanks to expenses like the aforementioned septic disaster."

"I know. Life is expensive. We've had that conversation. What about your other work? Aren't they going to be annoyed if you disappear for a week?"

"I'm ahead of schedule on that project, so they can't really complain." Joel pushed her long dark braid behind her shoulder. "I'm going to miss you, you know."

"I know." Kat stood on her tiptoes and gave him a kiss. "I bet you'd be good at teaching. You're great at explaining things, and like you said, you'll never know if you don't do it. Maybe this is the first step toward becoming a world-famous professor. You could get a PhD in geekology and wear a tweed jacket."

Joel laughed. "That's unlikely. Tweed is not my style. We'll see if I can stand teaching in Milwaukee first and go from there."

"I know nothing about Milwaukee, other than Laverne and Shirley worked in a brewery there."

"Beer sounds good."

"Maybe you can find out what Hasenpfeffer Incorporated is. Or was."

He chuckled, "Yeah, we'll see. I'd rather not meet Lenny and Squiggy."

~

Carly, Lily, and Ginger gathered their things from their cars and dragged them inside. With five bedrooms and three bathrooms, the house provided plenty of room for the women to spread out.

Ginger selected a room and dropped her suitcase on the floor. She ran her fingers through her short, brunette hair to fluff up her pixie cut, and pointed at the bed. "I have no plans to do anything for the next two weeks except sleep, eat, drink, and sleep some more. My family has been warned that no one is to get in touch with me unless one of them is on the way to the hospital."

Carly giggled. "I said almost the same thing to the people I work with. I tried to be nice, but the fact that no one knows the telephone number here is kind of thrilling. It's like when we were in college. With only one pay phone on each floor, you didn't get a lot of pointless calls."

Lily pulled her cell phone out of her purse and flipped it open. "I have no signal." She closed it again and grinned. "As you would say, no ringy dingy. What a shame."

Carly said, "Like I told you on the phone, if someone truly has an emergency and needs to get in touch, they can call Karen's clinic, and they'll call us. She's got an answering service. No matter what a few of my coworkers may think, filing reports does not constitute a life-or-death emergency."

"Neither does a soccer mom melting down about car-pool assignments," Ginger added.

"Or a screwed-up trademark filing," Lily said. "There are thirty other lawyers who can deal with it."

After unpacking, the women reunited in the kitchen. Carly held up a bottle. "When I dropped off Trixie, the woman at the dog-boarding kennel said she has wine-and-whine parties with a girlfriend. I liked that idea, so I picked up some wine for us."

"That's awesome. I can provide some whining. No problem there." Ginger laughed. "I'll get the glasses."

Lily rummaged around the drawers, pulled out a corkscrew, and held it up. "Found it! We're in business."

Ginger set the glasses in a row on the long kitchen counter and Carly poured the wine. They settled in on barstools and swiveled around to face the glass doors that offered an expansive view of the lake. Carly's muscles relaxed for the first time in days, and she raised her glass, "Here's to best friends who are always there when you need them."

They clinked glasses and Ginger said, "Where's your sister? Didn't you say you talked Karen into coming?"

"She said she'd be here." Carly said with more confidence than she felt. Karen might decide she was too busy, had too many work responsibilities, or dream up some other excuse. Spontaneity was not her strong suit, and running off to the lake for vacation might be more than the overly conscientious veterinarian would be able to manage.

Ginger set her wine behind her on the counter and put her hand on Carly's shoulder. "So you need to tell us what *really* happened with the man with two first names."

"You do! What happened after Captain Prickard threw you out?" Lily said.

Ginger giggled. "Captain Prickard?"

Carly said, "That's Lily's new nickname for him."

Lily snorted and covered her mouth. "I can't believe none of us ever thought of that before. I mean Stuart Patrick, Patrick Stewart? Duh."

"Well, I didn't always think he was a complete prick. But all that's changed." Carly swiped at a tear on her cheek. "God, I wish I'd stop crying at nothing. This constant weary teary is stupid. He's the worst! Horrible! Evil!"

"And you still love him," Ginger said.

"I know. What is wrong with me? I haven't gotten a decent night's sleep since we broke up. I lie there awake, thinking about how much I miss him." Carly said, rubbing her eyes. "And now I look like a raccoon. If it's okay, I'd like to suggest that we don't bother with makeup for the rest of this trip. We'll be swimming and lying around. There's no one to impress here, and I know what you both look like after you've pulled an all-nighter studying for finals. And I still love you anyway."

"I respectfully decline that resolution," Lily said. "At twenty, I looked better after all-nighters than I do now during the day. Ergo, makeup shall be applied."

Carly glanced at Lily, wondering if she should say anything about how tired her friend looked. Maybe she'd recently recovered from the flu or something.

"You do look wrung out," Ginger said. "Have you been working late?"

Relieved that Ginger had brought it up, Carly added. "I noticed you look a little tired."

"I'm fine." Lily said and gulped down the rest of her glass of wine. "I sure hope you got more than one bottle."

At a knock on the door, Carly jumped off her bar stool. "That must be Karen." She threw open the front door and grinned at Karen. "Welcome to vacation, bossy sissy. Everyone's here."

Karen walked inside and turned her head to gaze around the huge entryway. She gazed up at the ceiling. "Holy *cow*. Ben didn't say this place was a palace."

Carly laughed. "I'm guessing this guy doesn't have trouble paying his veterinary bills."

"He doesn't, but I wasn't expecting this—he refers to this place as his *cabin*."

"Makes you wonder what his other house is like, doesn't it?" Carly grabbed her sister's hand and tugged her toward the kitchen. "You have to see the view out the back. We were just chatting and staring out at the lake. The sun's going to go down soon, and the sunset should be beautiful."

Ginger and Lily got up off the bar stools and greeted Karen. Lily poured more wine into her glass, walked to the French doors, and threw them open. "Howdy, nature. It's been a while."

Carly grabbed the wine bottle and followed everyone else onto the patio. A round glass table, surrounded by four chairs, sat off to one side. She set the wine on the table, and the women each claimed a seat.

Ginger placed an empty wine glass in front of Karen. "You need to join in on the wine and whine."

Karen raised her eyebrows. "What?"

"Tonight, you can whine about anything you want." Ginger poured some wine into the glass. "Accompanied by wine."

Lily said, "If I'm going to whine, I need to be able to whine freely. I vetoed the makeup motion, but I move that the next two weeks be a judgment-free zone."

"I like that idea," Carly said. "But I'm still going for no makeup until I stop crying at the drop of a hat."

"Me too," Ginger said. "I don't wear makeup at home, so it's not much of a sacrifice. I think my last tube of mascara expired during the Bush administration."

"Maybe you should throw it away," Karen said as she held up her glass in a toast. "Thank you to Carly for inviting me. I concur with the no judgments and no makeup. I'd like to add a motion for complete honesty. If you don't want to do something like go swimming, say so."

"Karen's saying that because she hates swimming," Carly said. "It messes up her hair."

"My hair is not the issue." Karen set down her glass. "Have you gone in the water yet? That lake is deep and the water is freezing at this time of year. I will not succumb to peer or sibling pressure. No way."

"I'm with Karen. I'll just stare out at the pretty water." Lily said. "Maybe skip some stones and ponder the meaning of life."

"There's a hiking trail near here that goes to an overlook high above the lake." Karen said. "It's supposed to be beautiful."

"Hiking sounds like something that would violate my primary goal of being a slug," Ginger said. "If I get ambitious, I might walk down to the beach and put my toes in the water."

Carly didn't say anything, simply enjoying the sound of the familiar voices. She gazed out at the sunset that was developing in front of their eyes. She might swim, or she might not.

The main thing that mattered was that somehow she'd managed to gather a group of her favorite people in the world together in spite of the fact that they were all incredibly busy with demanding jobs, families, and complicated lives. Right then, as she listened to the three women chat amiably, Carly couldn't imagine being happier anywhere else.

~

After the sun set, the temperature dropped, and the wine bottle was empty, so the group went back inside.

Carly said, "I wasn't sure what to buy at the store, so I'm making pasta for dinner. I hope that's okay."

"That always *was* one of your major food groups," Ginger said. "Do you still buy mac and cheese by the case? Or easy cheesy, as you used to call it."

"I've sworn off powdered cheese. Now I often make a Bolognese sauce. The recipe is from the *New York Times* and Stuart thinks it's delicious." Carly held up the package of spaghetti enthusiastically, then placed the box on the counter with a thump. "I suppose I thought of it because it's his favorite recipe, but I like it too."

"I'm sure it's great," Lily said, putting her arm around Carly's shoulder. "How can I help?"

Carly went to the refrigerator and handed Lily an onion, celery, and carrots. "Unlike the powdered cheese sauce from the box, this recipe requires the chopping of vegetables."

Ginger walked toward the living room and called over her shoulder, "Let's see if our rich benefactor has any tunes for this killer stereo."

Carly threw some oil into a big pot, took the onion off the cutting board Lily was using and placed it on her own. She began chopping and glanced at Karen, who was sitting on a bar stool, staring at the lake. "Annie is fine."

Karen looked over her shoulder. "I know. It's just so strange not to be cooking dinner for her."

"Relax. You deserve a break." Carly threw the onions into the pot and turned on the heat. "Annie is going to have a great time."

Karen didn't answer, and Carly could practically feel her sister brooding. Annie was a wonderful kid, but every mom deserved some time off. Ginger certainly wasn't having any trouble enjoying time away from her band of ruffians.

As if on cue, the Rolling Stones blasted from the living room. Apparently, Ginger had found Ben Walsh's stash of CDs.

For Carly, the lyrics to "You can't always get what you want" seemed appropriate for her current feelings toward Stuart, and she swayed to the music as she stirred the onions in the pot. Lily threw in the vegetables, and Carly sang into the wooden spoon.

Lily made a horrified face and covered her ears with her hands. "You still can't carry a tune. Oh my God, would you hum or something, woman? That's painful!"

Carly waved the spoon as if she were conducting, tossed the ground beef into the pot, and stirred. "I may not have a footloose man anymore, but at least I have a glass of wine in my hand."

"I hate to break it to you my friend, but no one ever described Captain Prickard as footloose," Lily said. "More like fossilized stuffed shirt, which is a lot more difficult to rhyme."

Carly paused her spoon waving in midair. "Stuart used to say I had a singsong mind because of my rhymes. At the time I thought it was a compliment. Now, I'm not so sure."

Ginger danced her way into the kitchen and held up a collection of CDs, splayed like oversized playing cards. "We have our own classic rock station! Someone help me pick the next album. There's so much great music here."

Carly shoved Lily away from the stove. "Go on. You're the music critic."

"I probably should have said something, but you shoulda dumped the Captain a long time ago. He didn't deserve you." Lily swayed over to Ginger holding her wine glass high and set it down so she could examine the CDs.

Carly added wine and tomatoes to the pot and turned down the heat so the sauce could simmer while she evaluated their musical choices. After a bit of discussion, they selected five CDs to put into the changer.

They walked back into the kitchen, and something outside the French doors caught Carly's eye. She shoved Ginger's arm, "What was that?"

Ginger turned. "What was what?"

"Outside. I saw something." Carly said.

Lily flipped the switch for the exterior light, and they all silently stared at the patio furniture for a moment.

Karen called from the kitchen, "Carly, I think you need to add more water or something. The sauce is smells like it's starting to burn."

Carly hustled into the kitchen, grabbed the wine bottle, and threw more wine into the pot. "The recipe doesn't use water. Wine."

Lily sat on a bar stool and turned to Karen. "I think Carly is going for more UFO sightings."

"Hey, that was *real!*" Carly protested. "I saw something in the sky."

"I think the sighting might have had more to do with consumption of what you referred to as 'risky whiskey,' than aliens," Ginger said as she settled onto the stool on the other side of Karen.

"It was probably the evil corporate-military establishment doing testing. For all we know, there's a secret base in Alpine Grove that is shooting things into the air to spy on you," Lily said.

"I didn't say it was a UFO, but I think I saw something outside. And it wasn't in the sky. It was at the door." Carly grinned. "Oh wait! Maybe it's the ghost."

"You're telling us *now* that you rented a haunted house? Thanks for the news flash," Ginger said.

Karen said, "I knew I shouldn't have told you that, Carly. There's no ghost. It's a small-town rumor. This house is on Gray's Point, and a woman named Miriam Gray lived here years ago. Her husband died in a boating accident."

"But she's still here. The locals say she sits in the big tree in the yard waiting for him to come home," Carly added.

Lily rolled her eyes melodramatically. "Yet another woman disappointed by a man. And y'all wonder why I never got married?"

Carly laughed at the emergence of Lily's southern heritage in her voice. When she had enough to drink, the fact that she'd grown up in Kentucky became more apparent. "You didn't get married because your high school *beau* threw you over for that woozy floozy after your coming-out party."

Lily waved her hand. "Pish-posh, as my dear grandmama would say. Ancient history."

"I don't buy it. You were never, ever going to get over him. The renowned beau engendered almost literal swooning,"

Ginger said. "It was nausea-inducing. He was a legend in your mind."

"Trey was most certainly *not* a legend to me," Lily said. "But I will admit that he was drop-dead gorgeous."

"Maybe in a preppy way," Carly said. "I'm sorry, but the golf pants he was wearing in that photo you had on your dresser were not attractive. The beau looked like he had walked off the set of *Caddyshack*. I was embarrassed for him."

"That was before the Derby party. All of the men were dressed like that. The ladies wore white lace dresses and hats." Lily sipped her wine. "Y'all don't understand because it's a southern thing."

Ginger reached for the wine bottle. "Okay people, we have a dead soldier. Where did you hide the wine, Carly?"

"I didn't hide it." She pointed at a door. "The pantry is over there. It's a walk-in pantry that's larger than my apartment."

Ginger disappeared behind the door and returned with another bottle. "Ladies, hold out your glasses."

"That sounds like the anti-alma mater song." Lily said.

Carly knew that the official song began by praising the school with, "We pay thee devotion..." but the alternative began, "We pay thee tuition..." and devolved into a description of staggering from barroom to bedroom and then staying up all night to finish an essay.

"I think that's the drinking song," Carly said. "That's the one that goes on about being the face upon the barroom floor."

"And it's better than being dull once more." Ginger said. "So let's all cheer and bring on the beer! Or wine in this case."

Karen jumped up off her bar stool and ran to the French doors. She'd been quietly ignoring the banter about collegiate overindulgences. She opened a door and peered outside.

The other three women followed her and Carly said, "Is it the ghost?"

"No, but you were right. There's something out there. I think it's a dog." Karen said.

Carly widened her eyes and stuck out her tongue at Lily. "See! I told you."

Ginger said, "You're a vet who spends all day poking around doggie innards. Are you sure you're not just overtired from work?"

"I'm sure it was a dog. I think she smelled the food." She turned to Carly. "Which I think might be trying to burn again."

Carly ran to the stove and threw more wine into the pot. "It's cooking down, so it will be extra savory. It will be great. I promise."

Karen opened a French door. "I'm going to sit out there for a couple minutes and see if the dog comes back."

"We'll call you when the pasta's done," Carly said.

As Karen slipped outside, Ginger said softly to Carly. "Is she okay?"

Carly made a wry face. "I hope so. She's probably just missing Annie. Or maybe she got sick of us going on and on about college."

Lily said, "Hey, it's not our fault if music and wine bring back some memories."

Carly put her arm around Lily's shoulder. "I know. Don't worry about it. She's a big girl. If something's bothering her, she'll tell me."

Maybe. Karen tended to keep her own counsel, and when it came to her sister, Carly was never completely sure what to think.

~

Once the pasta was drained, Carly went outside to retrieve Karen. "Have you found our UFO dog yet?"

"I saw her again, but she won't come to me." Karen said. "I'll set some food and water out for her."

"Right now, you can worry about your own food because dinner's ready." Carly patted her shoulder. "Come on. I'm sorry if you felt like the odd woman out. I know you don't know Ginger and Lily that well. We'll try to keep the college reminiscing to a minimum from now on."

Karen stood up and followed Carly inside. "Reminisce all you want. I know you haven't seen each other for a long time. It's going to take a while for me to relax. I'm out of practice."

Carly said, "More wine might help curb your overwhelming need to be responsible."

Karen smiled. "I suppose it wouldn't hurt."

The women sat around the table in the kitchen because the dining room was enormous. Ginger pointed out that it was so large they'd need bullhorns to talk to each other. Sitting in the kitchen also made it possible for Karen to keep an eye out for her stray dog.

Carly said, "What did the dog look like?"

"Maybe some type of small lab mix," Karen said. "I'm not sure. The lack of light made it hard to get a good look at her. But I could see her silhouette, and given her abdominal profile I think she might have had puppies recently. I hope they're okay."

"Well, if you can entice the flabby labby with some food, maybe she'll hang around long enough for you to ask her, Dr. Doolittle" Carly said with a smile.

Because of all the traveling and wine, exhaustion set in after dinner. The four women said their goodnights and retired to their rooms. And true to her word, Karen put out a bowl of water and food on the patio for the mystery dog.

Carly got ready for bed and crawled under the blankets, listening to the low hum of conversation as the other women chatted with each other on their trips to the bathroom. Her mind wandered as she stared blankly at the ceiling. Was Stuart crawling into bed with Laurel now? Was she changing out of her work clothes and taking off her makeup while she told him about her day? Was he complaining about his big trip to Los Angeles? The airline had undoubtedly committed yet another mortal sin. What was it this time?

She squeezed her eyes shut and flopped onto her side. Why did she keep thinking about these things? She needed to convince her brain to shut up and forget about Captain Prickard. Unfortunately, doing so was a lot easier said than done. He'd occupied the majority of her thoughts every single day for fifteen years. She knew his schedule and his mannerisms, down to the way he brushed his teeth in the morning. Constantly thinking about his needs and wants was a hard habit to break. And all this time telling herself not to think about him only made her think about him more.

Supposedly there were five stages of grief after a loss, and she was going through at least three of them at once.

Acceptance wasn't happening, and bargaining was definitely over. But denial and anger were getting a lot of air time, followed closely by depression. Carly flopped onto her back. How long was this going to last? Was she *ever* going to get a decent night's sleep again?

When Carly opened her eyes the next morning, sun was streaming through the window and the scents of yummy breakfast food were rising from downstairs. After tossing and turning for what felt like forever, she must have finally fallen asleep because she felt much better. She sat up and threw her legs over the side of the bed, smiling at the sound of Lily's distinctive musical laugh.

After donning an old pair of sweatpants and an oversized cozy sweatshirt, Carly went downstairs. Lily and Ginger were arguing about the right way to cook scrambled eggs and Karen was sitting outside on the patio, gazing out at the lake.

Lily said, "Hey sleepyhead. You need to settle an argument. I think that eggs should always be scrambled with a little milk mixed in."

"That's absurd," Ginger interjected. "They're perfectly fine without milk. I make them that way for my kids all the time. But I will say that all eggs are better with cheese. Lots of cheese."

Carly peered at contents of the frying pan. "What did you do here?"

"It was originally going to be an omelet, but I had a little accident," Lily said.

"Looks good to me." Carly held out her hands and made a gimme gesture. "I'll eat it while you debate."

Lily slid the eggs onto a plate and handed it to Carly. "I'm trying another omelet, but using a different procedure this time."

A yelp came from outside and they all turned to look. Karen was holding a small, dirty brown dog that was squirming wildly in her arms. Carly set down her plate and ran to the door. Karen had gained control of the dog and Carly mouthed, "Can I come out there?"

Karen nodded and Carly quietly opened the door. The dog jerked away, but Karen had a firm grasp on her and was whispering, "It's okay," repeatedly.

Carly sat at the table. "Is this our UFO girl? How is she doing?"

"She's dehydrated and hungry. And I was right. She's had puppies recently." Karen stroked the dog's head. "I think they must be close by, but she's so hungry, she couldn't resist the scent of our cooking. Poor baby. Look at how thin she is."

"*Puppies*? Where are they?" Carly said. "She wouldn't abandon them, would she?"

"She's malnourished and her milk has dried up. Let's give her some food and maybe she'll trust us enough to lead us to them."

"What should we give her?"

"What are those two making for breakfast? I thought I smelled eggs. I'm sure this little girl would like it if you got her a plate."

Carly nodded and ran inside to grab the doggie breakfast. She returned with a plate of eggs and placed it in front of Karen and the dog. Karen said softly to the dog, "Go ahead. I know you're hungry."

The dog looked at Karen, then Carly, paused for a nanosecond, and dove into the plate, gobbling down the food as if the women might change their minds about giving it to her.

Carly said, "She doesn't have a collar. Have you ever seen her at the clinic?"

Karen shook her head. "I don't think so. My guess is that someone stayed at one of these rentals and she got lost or was simply left behind."

"People do that?"

"Sometimes."

"How long do you think she's been around here?"

"Long enough to have puppies. Maybe she found the father out here too. Who knows? If vacationers have been feeding her, she could have been wandering for a while."

"What should we do?"

Karen said, "First, give her some food. Then I'll try to slowly and gently check her out. While I do that, you, Ginger, and Lily should go find the puppies. Then, assuming all of them are okay, we'll find homes for them."

Carly smiled. "There's a reason I call you bossy sissy. You're always so decisive and organized."

"It's part of the job." Karen stroked the dog's head. "Although I have to say that leaving work behind hasn't worked out so far."

After licking the plate, the dog looked up expectantly. Carly said, "Should I give her some more food?"

"Let's see how she does with this first. I'll just sit here and pet her for a while to see if she'll let me examine her. You should get out there and find her babies. There's no time to waste. I hope they're still alive."

"Okay, I'll round up the troops and we'll go puppy hunting." Carly shoved thoughts of discovering anything awful from her mind and bent to hug her sister. "I'm so glad you're here."

"Me too."

Chapter 3

Searching

Carly went back inside and clapped her hands to get everyone's attention. "Okay, put on your hiking shoes. Karen says we need to go find the puppies."

Lily scowled. "What puppies? Where?"

"I don't know. That's the problem." Carly gestured at the dog on the patio. "Karen said that our UFO dog had puppies recently and they are probably nearby. We need to find them."

Ginger started toward the stairs. "Oh no! Those poor little babies. I just need to run up and change. Put away the leftovers, Lily."

Lily bent to grab some plastic containers. "I should have brought hiking shoes. All I have is running shoes, and they're for running. They cost a fortune, with special arch supports."

"You can run if you want. But please hurry," Carly said as she grabbed a piece of toast and some eggs before Lily put them away.

Lily took a bite of toast. "Doesn't this dog know where her offspring are? This seems like a case of extremely bad parenting to me."

"She might, but Karen wants to examine her first. The poor dog is really skinny and hungry." Carly shrugged. "I think Karen wants to make sure the dog is okay. If the dog is sick, Karen might need to take her to the clinic. She wants us to look for the puppies as soon as possible."

"Well Karen is a vet, so I suppose she knows what she's talking about." Lily put a container in the refrigerator. "With all this food we're eating, I could use a little exercise anyway."

Once everyone was dressed and ready to roll, Lily, Ginger, and Carly exited the French doors to the patio. The momma dog was curled up in Karen's lap, taking a nap.

Carly whispered, "I think you have a new friend."

"She's exhausted," Karen said. "Motherhood is hard work."

"I know how she feels. Every mom needs a break from the kiddos once in a while," Ginger said. "Let's see if we can find her puppies. Do you have any suggestions as to where we should look?"

"Someplace sheltered, I'd imagine. Dogs like to make a den," Karen said. "I'm not sure where though. When she wakes up, I'll see if I can find a piece of rope, so I can make a little leash. Maybe she'll lead me to them."

"So you don't think she's sick?" Carly asked.

Karen said, "Without lab tests I can't be positive, but as far as I can tell, she's just hungry and tired. I think she's basically fine."

"Let's go that way," Ginger said, pointing toward a copse of pine trees. "I'm worried about the little puppies out there all by themselves."

Carly and Lily followed Ginger toward the woods. When she'd driven down the driveway, it hadn't occurred to Carly that the dense trees on either side of the house were what made the setting so private. Nestled between two mini-forests on its own peninsula, the house had no visible neighbors. If the stray dog were smart, she would have hidden her pups in these trees somewhere.

Carly ran toward the lake and whirled around like Julie Andrews in *The Sound of Music*. Lily put her fists on her hips. "What are you doing? We're supposed to look in the trees."

"Oh come on, you know you want to. The hills are alive!" Carly said.

"You're in a remarkably good mood," Ginger said. "Vacation agrees with you. I think I'm having trouble letting go of how pissed off I was at Nathan before I left. We had a huge fight, and I keep thinking about all the things I wish I'd said."

Carly stopped whirling. "Why didn't you say something? If it makes you feel better, I'm not actually in a good mood either. I can't make the little voice in my head stop chattering about Stuart. I was hoping that spinning my body around might make my brain stop spinning around. Honestly, I'll try anything at this point. It's driving me crazy. Everything I see reminds me of him. I can't sleep, and I'm exhausted."

Lily crouched down to tie her shoe. "It sounds like you both want to forget about men."

"*Yes!*" Carly shouted and raised her fist. "Tell me about how wonderful it is to be single and free."

"I'm with Carly. I'd like to live vicariously through you, Lily, because I'm sick of my life. I always imagine you like one of those women in *Friends*, getting all the action." Ginger said. "Meanwhile, at my house, I'm the taskmaster, making kids do their homework and clean their rooms. Then Nathan gets to be the fun one, coming home, making jokes, and being Mr. Nice Guy."

"I don't think you want to live vicariously through me because my life mostly consists of going to work. I haven't had a date in months. Those women in *Friends* aren't paying real New York City rent, I can tell you," Lily said as she stood up. "The last guy I went out with was either addicted to cocaine or had some type of horrible nasal disease. It was revolting."

They entered the woods, and a few minutes later a rustling noise came from nearby. Lily grabbed Ginger. "What was that?"

"How should I know?" Ginger shook her arm free. "Maybe it's a puppy. We're *heroines*."

"It's probably a squirrel," Carly said, moving slowly toward where she thought she'd heard the sound. "But don't you think we should check?"

"Maybe it's a bloodthirsty wolf. Or a bear. Are there bears here?" Lily said. "I don't have bear spray, do you?"

"Who brings bear spray to a lake house?" Carly asked.

"Maybe it's zombies," Ginger said. "Really scary ones with pieces of flesh falling off."

"Shut up," Lily said as she rock-hopped across a small stream. "If we get lost out here, it's your fault. And there's no toilet paper in the wilderness."

Carly followed Lily and carefully placed her foot on a rock in the stream, then lifted her foot and hesitated because there wasn't another rock. She stretched her leg out to reach another rock, so she was almost doing the splits. She flailed her arms like a demented seagull. "Help! I'm stuck. Somebody grab my hand."

Lily reached out and yanked Carly onto the opposite shore. "Graceful."

Ginger opted to use a different group of rocks to ford the small creek. When she made her final leap, her shirt caught on a low-hanging branch, ripping the shirt open. She yelped and tugged at the fabric, trying to pull it back together. "Ouch."

"Pretty bra. Magenta and lace. Very nice," Lily said with a smile.

"I wouldn't have expected you to have such a sexy breastie nestie," Carly added. "Nathan must like that one."

Ginger scowled at the commentary, and trudged on, clutching her shirt. As Lily turned back around she tripped, and her foot slid into a boggy area next to the stream with a splashy sucking sound. When she pulled her foot out, the running shoe was covered with brownish black mud. "Eww, what is that?"

"I don't know, but I think your shoe is doomed," Carly said.

"Well isn't that just perfect. These running shoes cost a fortune. Nature hates me. Let's keep moving. I can feel my toes squishing around in my sock." Lily pointed. "Go that way."

They walked for a while and didn't hear or see anything that resembled puppies or zombies. Finally Carly said, "Haven't we been by here before?"

"How can you tell? It's a bunch of trees." Lily retorted. "My toes are cold. Please don't tell me we're lost."

Carly shook her head. "Maybe…"

Ginger pointed behind her. "The lake is that way. If we follow the shore, we know we'll return to the house because it sits right on the beach."

"Thank goodness one of us is thinking," Carly said.

They turned and followed Ginger, who made a good show of acting confident about their location. They emerged from the trees, and she gestured toward the lake. "See! No problem."

Carly looked toward the right and hissed, "Hey! Naked guy at three o'clock."

Ginger and Lily quickly focused their attention on the man walking from the lake up the beach. Lily said, "Nice butt."

Ginger and Carly murmured their appreciation for the man's assets.

Apparently sensing he was being watched, the man stopped to appraise his environment. He pointed at them and yelled, "*Hey*! This is private property. Get out of here. You're trespassing."

Carly offered a friendly wave. "We're not trying to get a sneaky peeky. It feels like we've been walking for hours and I think we might be a little bit lost. Could you tell us which way to Gray's Point?"

The man picked up a towel from the ground and put it around his waist. He strolled up to them and gestured toward the beach. "I'm guessing you're renting the Walsh house?"

Carly nodded eagerly, trying to not to focus too much on the man's slim yet muscular and broad-shouldered build or his bluish-gray eyes. She was momentarily distracted by the drops of water dripping off his wet hair and sliding down his chest. Yowza. She smiled politely. "Yes, that's the one. How did you know?"

He pointed toward the trees. "You're *on* Gray's Point and you can see the roof of the Walsh house right there above the trees. It's next door."

~

The man said, "Now that you know where you are, please get off my property."

Carly placed her hand on her chest and said, "I'm Carly Buchanan and these are my friends, Lily and Ginger. We're trying to find a litter of puppies. Have you seen any around here?"

"Puppies?" He raised his eyebrows. "How do you *lose* a litter of puppies?"

Lily said, "Hey Mister, don't be a jerk. This is important. We found a female dog, and it looks like she had puppies recently, so we're trying to locate them."

The man gripped his towel more tightly. "Today, all I've seen is trespassers so far."

Ginger added, "We're worried about the babies. The momma dog's milk is dried up and they might be starving. I don't want to think about something bad happening to them. If you know this area, maybe you could help us look."

"My sister is back at the house. She's a veterinarian, and she thinks the pups are likely to be nearby. Please help us save them. It's an emergency," Carly said.

"I have to work and you need to leave. *Now*."

Carly put her palms together in prayer mode and widened her eyes in innocence. "You *have* to help us. They're little innocent puppies."

"I haven't seen any puppies. Get off my land. I mean it."

Lily said, "This is an emergency. I'm a lawyer, so if you call the police, I'll snow them with a bunch of legalese. Meanwhile, we're wasting time."

"The puppies could be hurt or they could *die*," Ginger added.

The man readjusted his grip on his towel and moved his shoulders slightly. "I suppose I could help you. But only for a little while. I have to get back to work."

"Maybe put on some clothes first," Lily suggested, crossing her arms across her chest. "You're getting all goose pimply. *Everywhere.* We'll wait."

"Thanks for helping us. What's your name?" Carly asked.

"Brent. I'll be back in a minute." He turned and ran back to a small, rustic cottage-style cabin. It was set back from the lake and surrounded by a cluster of huge pine trees. He trotted up the wooden steps to the deck and disappeared through a sliding glass door.

Carly grinned. "Well I gotta tell you that finding a naked guy who looks like *that* made all thoughts of Stuart vanish from my consciousness lickety splitety."

"Nathan who?" Ginger added with a giggle.

"He'd better help us find those puppies fast. I'm losing the feeling in the toes on my left foot. I probably have frostbite and my digits are going to fall off," Lily said.

"I don't have a medical degree, but it's seventy-five degrees out here, so I'm pretty sure your toes are safe from frostbite," Ginger said. "Don't be such a grump."

Clad in a faded tie-dye t-shirt and even more faded denim shorts, Brent ran back across the lawn and handed Carly a flashlight. "The puppies could be tucked down somewhere that's hard to see in the shade of the forest."

Carly thanked him and they turned back toward the trees. She said to Brent, "Could you please go first? We got totally turned around."

Brent obliged, and when they entered the treed area, he used his flashlight to investigate around fallen branches, logs, and various other hidey holes on the forest floor. Carly followed his lead, trying to consider what a dog might consider a safe place for her babies.

Ginger and Lily spread out so the group could cover a wider area. Everyone moved slowly in the direction of the house where they were staying. They were operating under the assumption that the dog wouldn't want her pups to be too far away.

Carly said, "If they aren't over here, do you think we should search the forest on the other side of the house too?"

"You won't get far," Brent said. "On that side of the peninsula, right past the trees there's a big rock outcropping. That's why there aren't houses on that side."

"We've been here less than twenty-four hours and haven't had time to meet the neighbors. Well, except you," Lily said. "Are you here on vacation too?"

"My family owns the cabin. Usually we rent it out, but I'm staying here for the summer," Brent said.

Carly raised her hand, "Shhh, you guys. Did you hear that?"

"Hear what?" Ginger said.

"I thought I heard a little squeaky noise," Carly said, tiptoeing as quietly as she could through the leaves and pine needles on the forest floor.

Ginger came up next to her and crouched down, cupping her ears with her hands. "I heard it! Over there."

Carly shined the light on the ground, scanning back and forth. All she saw was a lot of dirt, leaves, and branches.

Brent scanned the area to her right with his flashlight. "There's a hollow under this cedar root. Check it out."

Ginger got down on her hands and knees and crawled closer. "Move the light over here. I think I hear them!"

Carly got down next to her and shined the light in the hole. She pushed some branches aside, and the glow of her light reflected off several pairs of small round eyes. "Oh my goodness! Look at them. They're *adorable*."

Ginger cooed quietly and reached out to scoop a puppy out from under the cedar root. "Hey there, you." The puppy squirmed and whimpered, but then settled as Ginger cradled her furry bundle in the cloth from the edge of her torn shirt.

Carly lay on her stomach and scanned the light inside. "There are three more in there. I think I can reach one of them."

Ginger moved out of the way and Brent stretched out next to Carly. "I'll get that one."

Carly pulled her puppy out and moved away to give Brent more room. She sat cross-legged on the ground and tucked the pup into the bottom of her t-shirt. "Look at this tiny floofie woofie. He's so cute! And check out all those spots—he's like a little Appaloosa puppy."

Brent pulled out a puppy and sat up. He pointed at Lily, who was standing. "Could you take this one?"

She bent to grab the small dog under its front legs and held it out in front of her face. The puppy uttered a small yip and Lily's normally stern expression melted into compassion as she cuddled the puppy to her chest. "Oh you poor li'l dear. I got you. Don't you worry, honey, we're takin' you back to your momma now."

Brent pulled the last puppy out of the hole and sat back on his heels. "That's all of them."

"Let's take them to Karen," Ginger said as she stood up.

"Your house is that way," Brent said, pointing in the opposite direction Ginger was walking.

"Ginger! Come back here," Carly shouted.

"Lordie woman, you couldn't find your way out of a paper bag," Lily said. "Why in heaven's name were we following *you?*"

Carly giggled. "Note to self. Do not go hiking with Ginger without a compass."

Ginger returned to the group. "I was distracted by this little cutie. He's making the sweetest little noises. Lead on, Mr. Boy Scout."

Brent readjusted his hold on his puppy and moved through the forest. "Your house is right over there."

They emerged from the trees and found Karen sitting on the patio in a chaise lounge, reading a book. The small brown dog was still curled up in her lap, but jerked awake and stood up, startling Karen, who grabbed the rope before the dog could launch off the chair.

Carly waved at her sister and yelled, "We found them!"

Karen stood up and leaned over to readjust the rope on the dog's neck, so she wouldn't get loose.

Ginger, Lily, Carly, and Brent sat in a circle in front of the dog and let the puppies crawl out of their arms to see their mother. The brown dog was leaping for joy at the sight of her little brood.

The puppies swarmed around their mother and pushed toward her in a pile of wiggling fur. A tear streamed down

Carly's cheek, Ginger's eyes were wet, and even Lily seemed moved by the impromptu canine family reunion.

Karen sat on the ground across from them, hanging onto the rope. She pointed at Brent. "I don't want to be rude, but who are you?"

Carly said, "Oh sorry, Karen. This is Brent. He helped us find the puppies."

"Otherwise known as the naked guy who lives next door," Lily said.

"My name's Brent Michaelson." He put out his hand. "It's a pleasure to meet you."

"I'm Karen Cassidy. Thanks for putting on clothes before you stopped by."

"No problem."

~

Karen picked up the puppies one by one, examined them, and returned them to the canine group. She patted the mother dog's back. "It looks like she's done an excellent job keeping these little guys healthy. All four are males, and they seem fine."

"How old are they?" Carly asked.

"They appear to be about six weeks, which is probably why their mother has been weaning herself from them," Karen replied. "The poor thing was so starved she couldn't produce enough milk for these greedy little guys."

"I can relate. I'd like to wean my children from me," Ginger said. "Maybe my husband too."

Carly shoved Ginger's shoulder. "You've loved Nathan since forever. It's the perfect relationship that we all envied. And your kids are adorable."

"Yeah well, fast-forward fifteen years, and it's not quite so perfect." Ginger retorted as she reached for a puppy. "Get a load of this sweet puppy breath. They're so cute. What breed of dog do you think they are, Karen?"

"Well, their mother is definitely a Heinz 57 mutt." Karen ruffled the dog's ears. "I'm guessing there's some Labrador retriever in there, but it's hard to say what else. Given the black-and-white spots on the pups, their father might have been an Australian shepherd, cattle dog, or heeler."

"Well I think he's definitely a heel for knocking up our girl, here," Lily said. "Typical male. Slam, bam, thank you ma'am."

Karen stroked the fur on the dog's head. "I should go to town and get these little guys some puppy food. I also can stop by the clinic and get some vaccines. They seem healthy now, but puppies are susceptible to a number of serious diseases. And now that mom isn't producing milk, they aren't getting antibodies from her."

"What are we going to do with them? We can't keep them here," Carly said. "This place doesn't allow pets. That's why I had to board Trixie. Can you imagine what a litter of poopy puppies could do to this magnificent palace of a house?"

Ginger snuggled the pup she was holding closer to her body. "Well, we're certainly not putting them back where they were."

"Could they stay at your vet clinic?" Lily asked Karen.

Karen shook her head. "It would be best if they don't. The clinic isn't a good environment for them. Sometimes we've taken in orphaned or young puppies that needed to be bottle-fed, but once they're this age, they need space to move around and play."

Carly glanced at Brent, who had been quietly cuddling a puppy in his lap. "Could you take them to your house? Your family owns it, so you won't get in trouble."

He looked up, startled. "I'm not really in a great position to take on a litter of puppies right now. I have to work."

"We can help take care of them," Carly said. "Please! They need you."

Karen said, "A home environment would be better for them. I know the woman who runs the local dog-rescue group, and she'll be able to help us find them permanent homes once they're a little older. In two weeks, their puppy vaccines will have kicked in and they'll be safe to go to foster or permanent placements."

Brent shook his head. "I really don't think…"

"Please, they're just babies, and you *saved* them," Carly said, going for her best pleading voice.

"All right." He held the puppy up in front of his face. "But you need to promise to behave yourself. No eating paint, paintbrushes, or anything else, okay?"

"Hold on a minute. Is it safe for them there? Are you working on home repairs or something?" Lily turned to Karen. "I didn't consider that possibility—we didn't go inside the house."

"I can try to figure out a way to block them from my studio. The rest of the rooms should be fine." Brent said. "The rugs and furniture are already old and beat up. Unlike this place, it's more of a summer beach cabin. But I do need to work, so you have to promise to help. I don't have time to tend to them all day."

Karen said, "I'll bring an x-pen from the clinic, so you can round up the pups. That will be particularly important at night when you can't keep an eye on them. Puppies get into everything."

"I know. That old cabin has seen a lot of dogs in its day. My grandfather loved his hunting dogs." Brent said.

Carly reached out to pet the brown dog, who obviously was now completely devoted to Karen. "We need a name for our UFO dog. Calling her 'Mom' is too confusing when I'm staying at a place with my sister."

"I've been calling her Ripley," Karen said.

"You mean like 'Ripley's Believe It Or Not'?" Lily asked.

"No, Ripley from *Alien*, the sci-fi movie because she's the UFO dog," Karen said. At Lily's blank stare, she added, "Oh come on, you've seen it. Everyone's seen it."

Ginger laughed. "I'm sorry, but these puppies are nowhere near creepy enough for their momma to be Ripley. That alien thing coming out of Sigourney Weaver grossed me out."

"I think it's a cute name for a dog," Carly said. "Okay, Ripley, let's take you and your puppies over to Brent's house."

Ginger, Lily, Carly, and Brent each picked up a puppy.

Carly said, "Maybe you should bring Ripley, Karen. She likes you, and I'm not sure I can walk her and hold a puppy."

"I'll help you get everyone settled and then head to town for their shots and supplies," Karen replied.

They followed Brent through the woods and back to the clearing where his house was located. Because she'd been so focused on the naked man, Carly hadn't really paid much attention to the house. Brent wasn't exaggerating when he said it was old. The lake cottage had weathered cedar siding, and at the lakeshore, an old dock and slightly lopsided boat house had clearly seen their share of weather too.

The group tromped up the steps to the large wooden deck and Carly turned to look back at the lake. Although the landscaping wasn't perfectly manicured like the place they were staying, the view of the lake was equally stunning.

Brent handed his puppy to Carly so he could open the door and let everyone inside. "I'm not sure where to put them."

Karen walked in with Ripley, who sniffed at the old rag rug in front of the door. Karen turned her head to look around the space. "Maybe you could keep them in the kitchen, so they're on the linoleum and away from the rugs."

"When puppies gotta go, they gotta go," Ginger added, following Karen into the kitchen with her pup.

"Newspapers might be a good idea too," Brent said. "I'll see if I can find a piece of plywood to block the doorway and something to hold it up."

Carly sat on the floor and put her puppy down. The small canines started exploring the kitchen, and one of them immediately squatted. Carly said, "Could someone grab me a quicker picker-upper? Or maybe a bunch of them?"

Ginger grabbed a roll of paper towels off an under-cabinet dispenser with one hand and sat down next to Carly with her puppy. She handed the roll to Carly and looked up at Karen. "Maybe you could bring some puppy pads back from town too."

Karen laughed. "Yeah, we've got puppy stuff at the clinic. I'll stock up."

Brent returned with an old, brown metal box fan and a long piece of wood that was about two-and-a-half feet wide. He placed the wood across the kitchen doorway and set the fan against one end of the wood to hold it up. Pulling an old end table from the living room, he shoved it against the wood on the other side of the doorway.

Lily held her hand up to examine it and shook her index finger in front of a puppy nose. "Hey! No biting. I know you're little, but those teeth are sharp. Be a gentleman and try to be a bit more decorous in your behavior."

Karen stepped over the wood, heading for the sliding glass door out to the deck. "Okay, I'll be back in a couple of hours with lots of puppy supplies. Take good care of our little charges."

Ripley went to the wood across the doorway and whined at Karen's retreating form. Karen turned around and bent down to pet her new canine friend. "You need to stay here, Ripley. Keep an eye on everyone." Ripley wagged tentatively and sighed, turning back to the puppies, who were chasing each other around the humans and yipping merrily.

Ginger reached out to pet the brown dog. "It's okay. Sometimes you gotta be the mom even when you don't want to be."

Carly took her attention away from the puppy she was petting to glance at Ginger. What was going on with her? She'd always been devoted to her family.

Something was up with Ginger, and Carly was determined to find out what it was.

~

The kitchen had a lived-in look with golden knotty-pine cabinets and a big, round wooden table that was surrounded by ladder-back chairs. Brent sat in a chair and leaned forward with his elbows on his knees, watching the puppies roll around on the floor. His hair had dried and the light-brown curls stuck out every which way, giving him a slightly crazed appearance, like a cartoon character who had stuck his finger in an electric socket.

Carly pulled out a chair and sat next to him. She was bad at small talk and she barely knew this guy, but she mustered up her thanks. "I appreciate you letting these teenie weenies stay here. I know you don't know us, so it's sweet of you to help out."

"I could probably use a distraction anyway. I know I keep saying I have to work and I do. I'm supposed to be working, but in reality I'm not. So I may as well watch puppies." He sat up straight and smiled. "Plus, they sure are cute. How could I say no to these fuzzballs?"

"What kind of work do you do?"

"I paint. Or I did." He ran his fingers through his hair, which did not improve the unruly mess. "I'm kind of blocked at the moment."

Ginger pulled up a chair and sat on the other side of Brent. "Do you have any paintings here? I'd love to see them."

He gestured toward the doorway. "There's a bunch of unfinished stuff in my studio. It's all terrible though."

"Keep an eye on that furry monster over there. He's a wild thing. I'll be right back." Ginger got up and stepped over the wooden barricade. Lily stood and followed her out of the kitchen.

Although Carly was terribly curious and wanted to follow her friends to the studio, she thought it would be a little rude to ditch this guy she'd just met, leaving him alone in the kitchen with the litter of puppies they'd dumped on him. "I'm sure your paintings aren't terrible."

He waved off the comment. "I know you're trying to be nice, but forget I said anything. I'm trying to. Thinking too critically about art doesn't help creativity. In fact, it kills the muse stone dead."

Carly was a little taken aback by his vehemence. Apparently she'd struck a rather sensitive nerve. Time to change the subject. "I was thinking maybe we could play cards or a game while we wait for Karen to come back with the puppy food and supplies."

"Sure. There's a bunch of old games in a cabinet in the living room." He stood up. "I'll go see what we've got."

Carly stood at the kitchen doorway, checking out Brent's rear view as he crouched down in front of a cabinet. The way his t-shirt stretched across his shoulders as he rummaged through the cabinet was enjoyable to witness.

He opened up a box, closed it, and dropped it on the floor. "It looks like the dice are missing from Yahtzee so that's out."

Carly said, "Do you have better letters?"

"What's that? Is it a game?"

"Sorry. I mean Scrabble."

"Nope. And we've got twenty boxes of poker chips, but playing cards are MIA. They're probably around here somewhere. We've got a backgammon set."

"We need something four people can play."

"How about Monopoly?"

"That's fine with me." Carly shrugged. "I haven't played it in years."

Brent walked back to the kitchen, stepped over the wood, and handed her the battered game box. "I'm calling the race car."

Carly opened the lid and peered into the box. "All right, as long as I get the top hat."

Ginger walked up and stepped over the wood. "Are you getting dressed up?"

"Nope. Monopoly."

"I want the dog!" Ginger said.

Lily entered the kitchen and gazed down at the puppies. "You want to adopt one already? Which one? You have five choices."

"Oh please. I don't mean a real dog. The last thing I need is a dog right now. I mean the Monopoly token."

"I want the top hat!" Lily said.

"Too late," Carly said. "You can have the nimble thimble."

"The thimble sucks," Lily groused as she sat down. "No one wants the thimble."

Brent rummaged through the box. "The thimble appears to be more nimble than we thought. It's gone. How about the iron?"

"Even worse." Lily said as she slapped the iron onto the corner "Go" square on the board. "I nominate Carly to be the banker, since she's least likely to cheat."

"Hey, I wouldn't cheat." Ginger glanced down at the puppies. "Aww, look. I think they're getting sleepy. Oops. Maybe not all of them. Could you hand me those paper towels again?"

Carly passed the roll of towels over and they went around the table tossing the dice to see who got to go first.

Lily won the toss and started off by rolling a ten. "Well, hell's bells, I'm a jailbird already."

"Don't worry. It's probably only minimum security for white-collar criminals like yourself. And just like in the real world, if you're rich enough, you can buy your way out. Okay, my turn." Carly rolled a four. "Income tax. Figures. As if I didn't have enough financial problems right now."

"Throw your money into the pot, woman," Ginger said, and rolled a seven. "Ooh, look at me taking chances now." She pulled a Chance card from the stack. "Go to Jail – Go directly to Jail – Do not pass Go, do not collect $200."

Lily laughed. "Hey, cellmate!"

Brent grabbed the dice and rolled eleven. "St. Charles Place. I'm buying it."

Carly took his money and handed him the property card. "Slum lord."

"Embezzler," he retorted.

They continued to play and argue about rules. Much to Carly's surprise, there were different interpretations of the Free Parking space. In fact, quite a few of the Monopoly rules she'd assumed were actual rules, technically, weren't rules at all because they weren't listed in the instructions. She was a little worried that Lily and Ginger were going to come to blows about the Free Parking controversy. Officially, players weren't supposed to get the money from the pot when they landed on Free Parking. According to the official Hasbro rules, nothing happened when you landed on the square. *Nothing.*

After a protracted and somewhat heated discussion, a truce was declared, and they opted to use the "house rules" of receiving the money from the pot. Ginger pointed out that more money is always good, but Lily continued to maintain that *house rules* was a fancy way of saying, "We made up our own rules," which was tantamount to breaking the sacred laws of Monopoly land. Carly tried not to roll her eyes at the mini-lecture on board game jurisprudence. There was a reason Lily became a lawyer.

As it turned out, having multiple hotels on a property also wasn't included in the official rules, but everyone relented in the hope that it might end the game more quickly. All too soon, Brent was sporting three hotels on North Carolina Avenue and two on both Pacific and Pennsylvania. If anyone landed on the green streets, bankruptcy would be swift.

Ginger rolled a three and landed smack on Lily's hotel on Marvin Gardens. Lily smiled as she held out her hand. "Pay up, darlin'"

Ginger turned to Carly. "Excuse me, Ms. Banker lady. I need a loan."

"I'm sorry, but I can't do that," Carly responded. "It's not allowed. We already had this conversation."

"Well I can't afford to pay Lily, so I'm afraid I need to rob the bank," Ginger said. "Hand over some money, Ms. Banker."

Brent chuckled. "This is the most polite faux bank robbery I've ever seen."

"Hey be quiet, slum lord," Lily said. "Ginger is preparing to commit a federal offense here."

"I don't think she's robbing the bank because that would be cheating," Carly said. "And Ginger isn't a stealie stoolie. She's as honest as they come."

Ginger said, "I think you're confusing me with you. There's nothing in the rules that says I can't rob a bank. These are desperate times, and this is a stick up." She grabbed a five–hundred-dollar bill from the plastic banking tray and handed it to Lily.

Lily said, "Thank you," and rolled the dice. "Pacific Avenue. Uh oh."

"You owe me thirty thousand dollars," Brent said.

"That's impossible," Lily scanned the cluster of hotels. "You moved them all onto Pacific. You can't just *move* hotels. And even if you could, it wouldn't cost that much money."

"If she can rob a bank, I can move hotels and extort money. The cadmium red of the hotels complements the deep emerald hues of Pacific Avenue."

"Very Christmasy," Carly said.

"Give me a break. Who moves hotels based on color? That's absurd." Lily said.

Brent said, "Well, in that case, the neighborhood needed more high-density housing. As the local slum lord, I have decided to reposition my holdings in key locations and increase rates based on market demand."

There was a knock at the front door and Carly said, "That must be Karen."

Brent jumped up to answer it. "Thank God."

Ginger stood up and knocked the board over. "Oopsie. What a shame. It appears a ballistic missile has taken out the urban decay on Pacific Avenue."

The puppies woke up and ran to see what all the excitement was about near the table. Carly dropped to all fours to collect the hotels and game pieces before they ended up in curious puppy mouths. "No…hey, *you*. I mean it. That's not food."

One of the puppies scampered off with the five-hundred dollar bill Ginger had stolen, and she yanked it from his mouth as she picked him up. "You may not have my ill-gotten gains, little dog."

Lily picked up two puppies and held them while Ginger and Carly gathered the rest of the game pieces.

Karen and Brent stood by the wood across the entry to the kitchen. Karen asked, "What happened here?"

"Game's over." Carly snuggled a pup to her chest. "The puppies won."

Chapter 4

Join the Club

Karen stepped over the wood and handed two brown paper grocery bags full of pet supplies to Carly. "Toys, bowls, food, and a collar and leash for Ripley."

Carly peered in the bags. "You were busy."

Karen pulled out the puppy food and started preparing it. The puppies in Lily's arms began squirming and she set them down. "I think these guys are hungry."

Brent crouched down and reached out to stroke fuzzy puppy fur, "Calm down, little fella. It's coming."

Carly said, "While Karen feeds them, would it be okay if I look at your paintings?"

He straightened and turned toward the doorway with a wave. "Sure. This way."

Carly followed him down a hallway to a bedroom at the end. All of the furniture had been removed, replaced by dozens of canvases, several easels, a long folding table, cardboard boxes, palettes, and lots and lots of paint everywhere. Paintings were hanging, leaning against the wall, and lying on the floor. Photographs and pencil sketches were haphazardly tacked to the wall and strewn across the floor.

Brent waved toward the room. "Sorry it's kind of a mess. I wasn't expecting visitors."

Carly grinned, "It's wonderful. I've always wished I had gazillions of dollars so I could become an art collector."

"At this point, anyone can afford these worthless half-finished things."

Carly walked up close to the painting on the easel. It was an image of a moose among birch trees. "This is gorgeous."

"It might be, if I ever finish it."

"Why don't you? It looks like you're almost done. Well... sort of."

"It's not even close." He picked up a paintbrush and examined it, twirling it in his fingers as if it held answers. "It's hard to explain what's wrong. When I paint, it's intuitive. I can visualize in my mind what the image should look like, so I know what I need to do next. I think of it as being in a zone or a flow of creative energy. Have you ever been really focused like that, so you lose track of time?"

Carly shrugged. "Maybe. I don't know. If I have, it's been a while."

"It's what I have always loved most about art and painting. That feeling that the work itself is driving me. Almost as if the creativity is otherworldly and completely outside of myself. But that hasn't happened in a long time."

"Why not? Did something change?"

"I'm not sure. With a painting, sometimes you're working and you reach a turning point. You have to decide what to do next. I used to just know what the right choice was. It was some type of intuition I guess. I didn't even consciously think about it. But now when I reach that point, I'm paralyzed. When I step away and look at the piece, I feel as if it's the worst thing I've ever seen. The color, lighting, and placement are off and it feels like the whole mess is a giant mistake. Like every decision I made was wrong."

Carly gestured toward the moose painting. "But that's beautiful so far. The only thing that's wrong is that it's not finished."

"I look at it and the moose is positioned incorrectly. The color of the trees isn't right, the lighting is off, and the leaves are out of balance. All the excitement I had for it is gone. I can barely stand to look at it." He waved his arm toward the paintings leaning against the walls. "They're all like that. I get to a point and then I start second-guessing everything."

"Are any of them finished?" Carly asked.

He walked to a stack of canvases along the back wall, yanked one out, and set it in front. "I did this before my last show. It was left behind by accident, so I still have it."

Carly crouched in front of the painting, which was of a pair of wolves at sunrise with the light shimmering through pine trees. "How come it's not signed? Shouldn't it say Brent Michaelson in the corner?"

"I don't sign my paintings with my real name." He shrugged. "It's a drag when you share a name with a country singer. I don't want my stuff to be confused with his."

"So what name *do* you use?"

"Doesn't matter."

"Shouldn't you sign it? I studied art history in college, and I have a ton of art books. Your style seems familiar. Is it possible your paintings are *in* one of my books? That's so cool. At least tell me what letter your signature starts with."

"Why? What difference does it make?"

"Oh come on…"

"M." He smiled. "I guess you *do* like art."

"Well, Michelangelo, I don't care what you say. These are amazing." She sat down on the floor in front of the painting. "I was going to go to a show featuring a bunch of wildlife artists in Los Angeles, but my boyfriend bailed out on the trip at the last minute."

"This painting was supposed to go, but didn't attend either."

Carly ran her hand along the side of the canvas. "After you sign it, you should frame it and hang it up here in the house. Put it on display instead of hiding it this pile of canvases. Do you have a picture fixture for it?"

"You mean a frame?"

"Yes. Don't you have one?"

"Probably. Somewhere. I've been avoiding framing because it takes away from what I should be doing, which is painting. On the other hand, I'm not painting, so I suppose I could frame it. But why bother?" He pulled another unfinished painting from the pile. "At this rate, I'm never going to have another show, much less commissions. I worked on the last commission for months, until I finally gave up. I had to return the deposit and tell him I was hanging up my paintbrush for the time being."

Carly studied the eyes of the wolves in the painting. They were so expressive. And the detail in the fur made her want to reach out and touch the canvas, although she refrained. How could anyone so unbelievably talented give this up? "You make it sound like you're quitting."

He leaned another unfinished painting against the wall and sat down next to her. The image was of a bald eagle in flight over a lake, but it had no detail. Half of the canvas only had swashes of color that indicated where the lake would be. "Take my word for it. Unfinished paintings don't sell."

"Can't you add what's missing?"

"I have to see the color and how the light works in my mind first. It's not coming together." He leaned over and turned the canvas around, so the image was facing the wall. "I've tried to explain this to a lot of people and no one understands. Maybe whatever I had was a muse, creative mojo, or magical fairy dust. Who knows? But whatever it was, it's gone."

"Maybe you can get the magical artsy fairy to come back."

"Right now, the fairy is more antsy than artsy. That's why I'm here. I've given myself a break from anything to do with the business side of my work. This summer I don't have to do anything, except paint. I put all the shows, galleries, prints, licensing deals, and everything else on hold for three months."

Carly wrapped her arms around her knees, still admiring the wolf painting. "What happens at the end of the summer?"

"I either finish some paintings and keep working as an artist, or give up and find something else to do with my life."

"Aren't you putting a lot of pressure on yourself? That's kind of rough to impose a deadline like that."

"If I can't figure out what's wrong in three months with no distractions, I don't think I'll ever figure it out."

Carly gave him a wan smile. "Well, if it's any consolation, you're not the only one having an early mid-life crisis. My future is sort of up in the air too."

"Do you paint?"

"I have zero artistic talent. It sounds kind of pathetic to say it out loud, but I'm here because I spent so much of the last fifteen years worrying about someone else that now I don't know what to do about me. Who am I now that I'm not part of a couple? I have no idea, so I'm here with my friends, hoping they'll help me remember the person I was before I met Stuart."

"Is this the guy who didn't take you to the art show?"

"That's him. Stuart Patrick. He dumped me for a younger model named Laurel. My friends and I now refer to him as Captain Prickard. I really, *really* need to spend the next two weeks finding a way to forget about him."

Brent gave her a half smile, obviously amused by the sci-fi reference. "I hope you can make it so."

~

Brent and Carly returned to the kitchen where Karen, Lily, and Ginger were sitting around the table watching the puppies play with their new toys in the x-pen.

Karen said, "I gave the pups their shots, we fed them, and let them visit the grass for a few moments. Now I anticipate that after all the food and playtime, in about ten minutes they'll pass out."

Ginger looked at Brent and said, "Thanks for letting us invade your house like this and particularly your kitchen. Hopefully they'll figure out what the puppy pads are for."

Lily leaned toward Karen. "So now that the dogs are all set, it's okay for us to go home, isn't it?"

Karen nodded. "I'm volunteering to make dinner tonight."

Brent said, "While they sleep, I might be able to get some work done."

"I'll be back tomorrow morning," Carly said. "We promised to take care of them, and we will."

"We'll take turns," Ginger added as she pointed at a puppy. "That little guy seems to like me since I gave him his dinner. Like any other man, the way to his heart is through his stomach."

Lily stood up, "Okay, Mr. Slum Lord, I think it's time to give you your house back. We'll see you later."

Karen, Ginger, and Lily stepped over the wood and out of the kitchen. Carly went to follow them, but stopped and turned to face Brent again. "Thanks for showing me your work. I hope the artsy fairy smiles on you tonight. I'll see you tomorrow."

He chuckled. "Thanks for the support. I'll let you know how it goes."

Carly left the house and followed her friends through the woods, thinking about Brent. He was remarkably willing to talk, at least about art. Stuart had always mocked her for trying to ferret out his innermost feelings, making it sound like she was being pushy and a nosy parker, trying to invade his personal space. She'd been curious and interested in his life, but now she suspected he'd had quite a bit to hide. No wonder he resented her intrusions into his so-called privacy. His most intimate thoughts undoubtedly had been filled with the lovely Laurel. Gross.

The women went into the back of the house through the French doors and Lily said, "I'm starving. More importantly, I'm thirsty. Do we have more wine?"

"I picked up some at the store when I got the stuff for dinner," Karen said. "I figured we needed human supplies in addition to the puppy stuff. The wine is in the pantry. I'm going to go read for a while before I start dinner."

Lily said, "I feel like I smell like a dog. Or worse. I'm going to go take a shower."

Ginger said, "I'm going to sit on that chair on the patio and watch the sun set, while doing absolutely nothing else for anyone. *Nothing* I say!"

Carly poured two glasses of wine and followed Ginger out to the patio. She wanted to talk to her friend. Ginger was sprawled on the chaise lounge, and Carly handed her a glass of wine and sat down on one of the chairs at the table.

Carly held up the glass. "Here's to saving a litter of innocent puppies today. We did good, my friend."

Ginger raised her glass with a grin and took a sip. "You're right, Car. We saved lives. This might be the best thing I've done in years."

Carly set down her glass and leaned forward toward Ginger. "Is everything okay? You've said some things that have me a little worried about how you're doing."

"Don't worry about me. I have the perfect relationship, remember? Loving husband. Adorable children. That's what every woman wants, right?"

"You said you and Nathan had a fight. What happened?"

Ginger sat up. "Why are we talking about me? We're supposed to be here to support *you*. You're the one who went through a breakup."

"I know. And I'm so glad you're here. You and Lily are my best friends. I love you both. But Lily seems distracted and stressed and you seem...unhappy, or I don't know... different, somehow."

"Thank you for the pep talk. I feel much better now."

Carly took a sip of wine. This wasn't going well. "I mean you're not behaving like you. You've always been fun and snarky, and I mean that as a compliment. The whip-smart life of every smarty party. Watching you smack down pseudo-intellectual Amherst snots was a highlight of my college years."

Ginger laughed. "Yeah, some of those boys needed a good talking to."

"So what's going on with you?" Carly clutched her wine glass with both hands. "You don't seem like yourself."

Ginger sighed. "Have you ever wanted to take a break from your life? Just walk away and leave?"

"Isn't that what we're doing? It's called a vacation."

"I know, and your timing couldn't have been more perfect because I've been having these thoughts."

"What kind of thoughts?"

"Leaving."

Carly sat up straight. "Leaving? You mean leaving *Nathan*? You can't be serious. You love him. Well, I mean I thought you did. You *do*, right?"

"Yes. I do. I don't want to leave him permanently. I mean, I'm not *leaving him* leaving him like divorce or something. He still loves me and I love him, but I want a break. I want a break from marriage and children. I want a break from my life. A time out."

"I don't understand. I really don't. What's a *time out*?" Carly shook her head in disbelief. This couldn't be happening. "Making up words is *my* thing, not yours. Is a time out some new term for an affair? How could you do that to Nathan?"

"I haven't *done* anything."

"Then what are you talking about?"

Ginger set her glass down on the concrete. "I'm not sure exactly. Except that I want a break. Maybe it's that I don't know *what* I want anymore. That's what I hope to figure out while we're here."

"You and me both. I suppose I can understand that, given the recent turmoil in my life." Carly gulped down her wine. "This calls for more hooch. Please hand me your glass. We need reinforcements."

Ginger obliged and Carly went inside with the glasses. Lily came down the stairs, walked to the kitchen counter, and squinted at Carly. "What happened to you?"

"Have you talked to Ginger?"

Lily opened her eyes wide again. "Is she okay? She's not sick or anything, is she?"

"She wants a break. Pour yourself some wine and come out to the patio. We need to talk about this."

Lily did as instructed and followed Carly out to the patio. They sat at the table and stared at Ginger, who had her eyes closed. Lily finally said, "Okay, don't just sit there. What's Carly talking about? Spill it."

Ginger glanced at Carly. "Thanks, Miss Big Mouth."

"You want a *break*?" Lily said. "What's that supposed to mean?"

"A break from my life. I want to talk to adults. I'm tired of being the car-pool queen and the soccer mom. I'm so sick of it all I can barely stand it." Ginger waved her arms to both side. "Neither of you have kids, so you have no idea. But being a mom is the fullest of full-time jobs. It's all you do. There's no escape."

Lily said, "You escaped here, didn't you?"

"Sure, but you have no idea the fight I had to have to do it. Nathan is furious. And I'm furious that he's furious. Why shouldn't I have time to myself sometimes? What's so wrong with that? I don't even know who I am anymore."

Carly held up her palm like a crossing guard. "Hold on. Now you're in my territory. I keep wondering if I truly like certain things. Like that pasta sauce I made last night. Do I like it because it was something Stuart and I liked together? Or is it really that good? I don't even know, and what's *that* about? What's wrong with me?"

"When you spend so much time together, it's like you don't know where you end and the other person begins." Ginger gestured toward Carly. "Like you said, I was the woman who would fight about obscure scientific principles with smarty-pants Amherst jerks. But I don't know that woman anymore. It's like those experiences happened to someone else."

Lily said, "Back then, you were pre-med, spending all your time talking about biology and chemistry. Now you don't. You're at a different point in your life."

"But I want that life back! I want to be that person again. I want to be defined by something other than my capacity to produce small humans. And maybe using my brain for something more interesting than third-grade math homework." Ginger pointed at Carly again. "That's what I told Carly. All I want is a break. A time out. I'm not having an affair. I just want a break."

Lily sipped her wine. "I think everyone has times when they wish they could live a different life. Be Cinderella for a while. But life is life. And it beats the alternative."

Carly rolled her eyes. "Of course it does. But I think I understand what Ginger is saying. I'm tired of my own thoughts. All I think about is Stuart, Stuart, Stuart. Could I be any more boring? My brain is like a broken record. It's driving me nuts."

Lily smirked, "Well, you spent an awful long time in the artist's studio today. I'm guessing that took your mind off Captain Prickard. Was Mr. Slum Lord showing you his etchings?"

"His paintings actually. He's a wildlife artist and you saw his art. He's really good. Astonishing, really. I think I've seen his work before, like in a gallery or in books. He doesn't sign his real name, but he wouldn't tell me what he signs his paintings with. Only that it starts with the letter M. I wish I could check my art books. Did you recognize his work?"

Lily shook her head. "I've never been into art like you are. Maybe he's secretly Monet."

"Or Manet," Ginger added.

"You do know they're both dead, right? Whether or not Brent is famous, he's having trouble painting now. We were kidding around that we're both having early mid-life crises." Carly raised her eyebrows at Ginger. "Looks like you get to join our little club."

Ginger peered over her wine glass. "I'd rather not be a member of this club, but I'm afraid you're right."

Lily held up her wine glass. "To early mid-life crises!"

～

The next morning, Carly rolled over and groaned. Her mouth tasted like the inside of a jar of sauerkraut that had been rotting in a landfill for six months. Perhaps she'd had a bit too much wine last night. Reminiscing with her college friends about the poor decisions they'd made at frat parties might have been a bad idea. Karen had been wise to retire to her room before Ginger broke out the hard liquor.

Carly slipped on some sweatpants under her ratty nightshirt, brushed her teeth, and staggered downstairs, where Lily and Ginger were at the table hugging coffee mugs. Although they looked tired, they were speaking in complete sentences, so they had to be doing better than she was. Uttering monosyllables was about all Carly could muster.

Ginger raised a hand in greeting. "I hope you feel better than you look."

Carly shook her head and made a beeline for the coffee pot. She poured some coffee and collapsed into a chair at the table. "You *had* to bring tequila, didn't you?"

Ginger grinned. "I know how you enjoy it."

"Never again. This was almost as bad as the risky whiskey incident, but with a few screamie dreamies thrown in." Carly rested her forehead on the cool wood of the table and closed her eyes.

Lily said, "So what are we doing today? I got a bunch of brochures and I want to see the area. You can rent boats at the marina. Or there's a hike to a waterfall that sounds fun."

"I plan to do as little as possible," Ginger said. "I'm on vacation. Rest. Relaxation. Maybe reading a trashy romance novel with lots of gratuitous acrobatic sex scenes in it. Or maybe not. Even that sounds overly ambitious."

"We can't just sit around!" Lily said. "I haven't been on vacation in years, and I want to get out and explore this area. I mean, who knows when I'll ever be able to get away again? I may never have another opportunity to see this place."

Carly groaned and lifted her head. "Someone has to go tend to puppies. I'm sure there's cleanup to do."

"Not it!" Lily said.

"Carly, yesterday you volunteered to be first on the list. Remember?" Ginger said.

Carly raised her eyebrows. "What list? There's a list?"

"You volunteered to go over this morning. Now I'm writing it down." Ginger reached for a pad of paper and scribbled a note. "Look, there's your name, right there. It's a list."

"If I have to clean up puppy poo now, I promise I'll throw up, which our neighbor probably wouldn't appreciate," Carly said. "We've already saddled him with these dogs, so let's not rock the boat. I'll take the afternoon shift if one of you will go over there this morning. I swear."

"All right. Fine. Way to renege on your promise. But after I do doodie duty, I'm parking my butt on that lounge chair outside and not moving for the rest of the day," Ginger said.

Lily thumped her mug down on the table. "Aren't we going to go anywhere or do something today? I don't want to sit around here."

"Haven't you been listening? I don't feel well," Carly moaned. "Death by tequila."

Lily raised her mug and some coffee sloshed onto the table. "Oh come on, people! Life is short. We need to get out there and live it. This is like in school when you guys always wanted to stay in and study. If it weren't for me, we never would have gone anywhere."

"All that proves is that this isn't the only hangover I can blame on you," Carly said.

"Of course you wanted to go out. You never had to study," Ginger added. "The rest of us had to grind to get an A."

"Or a C," Carly added.

Lily waved her hand dismissively. "Oh please. Little Miss Goody Two Shoes never got a C."

"Did too! In Chemistry. I never should have taken that beaker-breaker class, but I had to take *some* science. Maybe biology would have been better." Carly crossed her arms on the table, put her head down, and closed her eyes again. "I don't know. It's too late now. Thank goodness I found art history. For a while, I was totally lost."

Ginger stood up. "Well maybe Mr. Monet isn't dressed yet. That might make taking the morning shift worthwhile."

Carly opened her eyes. "You're married. He might be married too, for all we know. Did anyone ask? Maybe he and his wife take separate vacations."

"It doesn't hurt to look," Ginger said with a wave as she headed for the stairs. "Go back to bed, Ms. Crankypants."

Lily grabbed her mug and stood up. "Well, I have no intention of wasting this day. I'm going to go see the sights."

After she finished her coffee, Carly took a shower and retreated to her bed to read until her hangover wore off. After eighty-six pages and a nap, she was better able to face the world, and she went back downstairs.

Karen sat at the kitchen table eating a piece of toast and looked up at Carly with a smile. "Ginger was wondering if you were still alive."

Carly sat across from her sister. "Where did everyone go?"

"Ginger took her lounge chair down to the beach and is working on developing skin cancer. She said Lily went to town. I just came back from a hike."

"Where did you go?"

"There's a trail that leads up to an overlook. I've heard about it from a bunch of locals and finally got to see it. The hike has a bit of elevation gain, but you should check it out. The view is amazing."

"Maybe later. I'm definitely not up for it today. Plus, I'm really out of shape," Carly placed her hand on her stomach, which was anything but flat. "I might need to start with more low-key walks before I graduate to going uphill."

"I stopped by Brent's place on the way back here. The puppies are eating and eliminating well."

"Only you would say *eliminating*."

"You'd say they don't have goopy poopy."

Carly grinned. "You know me so well. Okay, I'll go by there in a little while. Poor Brent probably isn't getting any work done."

"He looked pretty happy playing with the pups. Those little dogs could stand a bath though."

"If you want, I could do that when I go over there. It might be good for me to make myself scarce for a while, since Ginger and Lily both seem mad at me. They're acting funny and I'm wondering if they're regretting coming here."

"You seemed to be getting along famously last night before I went to bed."

"I think that was the alcohol. They're being nice like they always were in college. The two smart, gorgeous women dragging their sort of weird friend along with them to parties. This morning I think the vacation glow might have worn off."

"You've always been your own worst critic. Your friends love you. They're here, aren't they?"

"I suppose." Carly rested her elbow on the table and placed her chin on her palm. "But we're not twenty anymore. I was hoping that seeing them would give me some answers. I don't know. They seem to have some stuff of their own going on. Maybe we're too different now. Earlier, we were sniping at each other and I felt bad. Maybe this whole trip was a dumb idea."

"People argue. They're your friends and you'll talk it out. That's what friends do." Karen stood up, put her hand on Carly's shoulder, and gave it a squeeze. "Sisters too. I have to run into town and sign some checks at the clinic, so I'm going to take a shower. Don't worry. We just got here, and we're still settling in."

"You're right. Mom used to say I worry too much about what people think."

"Mom was right. Everything will be okay. Give it some time."

~

The phone rang, startling Karen and Carly from their conversation. Karen answered the phone, and Carly raised her eyebrows at her sister when she said, "I need to stop by the clinic, so I can come and get you. I'll meet you there in about a half an hour."

Karen hung up and Carly said, "Do you have a vet emergency?"

"It's Lily. She lost her purse somewhere in Alpine Grove. Her car keys were in her purse, so she can't get back here."

"*Lily?* She's always ultra organized. I can't remember her ever losing anything before. In college, she had special little color-coded areas set up on her bookshelf so her books and notebooks would be ready to go for each of her classes."

Karen shrugged. "I don't know what happened, but she's going to wait for me on the bench in front of the gift store."

Carly stood up. "Lily isn't good at waiting. She's going to be furious at herself and the universe in general. I'm feeling better about being next on the puppy-tending list."

"Coward." Karen grabbed her keys from a bowl on the table. "Lily sounded irritated, so I guess I'll skip the shower. I'll try helping her look for the purse, which might take a while. I'm sure Brent would appreciate it if you hosed down the stinky puppies."

"Maybe they'd like to go for a swim in the lake."

Karen stopped what she was doing. "That water is cold, and you need to be careful that the puppies stay warm. They're just babies. I brought some special puppy shampoo from the clinic that's extra mild."

"I was kidding! Don't go all mother-hen on me."

"Maybe you should wait to wash them. I could do it after I retrieve Lily. Or I guess you could go get Lily."

Karen had a habit of taking over, and Carly waved her hands in an erasing gesture. "No, you have to go into town anyway. I'll wash the puppies in nice warm, swishy swashy bath water. And I promise I'll be extremely gentle. Cross my heart."

"All right." Karen held up her keys. "If you're sure, then I'm heading out."

Carly made a shooing motion with her hands. "Go forth and find that purse before Lily has a nervous breakdown."

After Karen left, Carly changed into some clothes appropriate for puppy washing and walked over to Brent's house. After going back and forth between the two houses a few times, it was even more embarrassing that they'd managed to get lost in the trees the day before. It wasn't like the two structures were incredibly far away from each other.

She walked up the steps to the back deck of the cabin and tapped on the screen door. Brent peered around the doorway to the kitchen and said, "Come on in. The puppies are *really* awake and could use some company."

Carly strolled through the living room and stepped over the wood barrier into the kitchen. The room had been transformed into a gigantic puppy play pen with piddle pads, dog toys, and bowls strewn about. Ripley was lying in a corner curled up, trying to ignore a puppy that was bopping her nose with his little paw. She raised her head and tapped her tail on the floor in greeting. Another spotted puppy charged toward Carly, running headfirst into her ankles. After shaking his head a few times, he collapsed on her sandal and began nibbling at a strap. Carly sat cross-legged on the floor and extracted the wriggling pup from her shoe. "Hey little guy, that's not a chew toy. Neither are my fingers. Cut that out."

Brent handed the puppy a plastic bone that was lying on the floor in front of him. "Try this." The puppy took the toy in his mouth and sauntered off toward Ripley, looking pleased with his new prize.

Carly held her palms up to her nose. "Karen was right about these guys. They're filthy. She's assigned me to puppy-washing duty."

Brent scratched at his neck. "She mentioned that to me too. Unfortunately, this cabin doesn't have an ideal puppy-washing set up."

"Is there only the one bathroom down the hall next to your studio?"

"That's it."

"Washing puppies in that little shower stall could be difficult."

"The shower has some plumbing issues too. The pups are small, so it might be easier to do it in the sink." Brent gestured toward the metal double sink on the other side of the kitchen. "One side for washing. One side for rinsing."

Carly wrinkled her nose. "But that's where you wash your silverware and plates that you use for eating."

"I'll hose out the sink before I do the dishes again."

"Are you sure you don't mind?"

"These pups are getting ripe." Brent stood up and held out his hand to help her up. "I'll help."

"You're avoiding working, aren't you?"

"I prefer to think of this as facilitating improvements to my creative space."

Carly walked to the sink and started rinsing plates. "Should we wash and put everything away first in case the pups get rambunctious?"

Brent agreed that was a good idea and cleaned up the floor while Carly got started on dishes. He put the puppies back into their x-pen, walked over to the sink next to Carly, and reached for a dish towel.

Grabbing a dish from the drainer, he dried it and put it into a cabinet. "Ginger had an idea for puppy names, so we can call them something other than 'hey you' or 'stop that.'"

Carly put a plate into the dish drainer. "Uh oh."

"She suggested Porthos, Aramis, Athos, and D'Artagnan, but she couldn't figure out which puppy was which, so giving them names didn't help much."

Carly laughed. "From the *Three Musketeers*! That's perfect. Even though each puppy has different spots, it's still hard to tell them apart unless they're right next to each other."

"They need ID tags."

"They're kind of small for collars. Do you have any yarn? If you use different colors, it would be easier to identify them while we get to know them better."

"My grandmother used to knit, but that was years ago. I can take a look around."

Carly finished up the dishes while Brent wandered around the cabin pulling out drawers and searching in closets for yarn. She put a dish away and smiled at his exclamation of success from somewhere on the other side of the cabin. Grandma's yarn stash must have surfaced.

Carly walked out of the kitchen into the living room and followed the rustling noises to a bedroom off the hallway. Like the rest of the old dwelling, the room had wood paneling and looked like it had been lived in for a long time by a whole lot of people. Possibly entire armies. Knick knacks and old paintings hung on the walls and a vintage ceramic hurricane lamp was centered on a lacy doily that sat on a beat-up pine nightstand next to the double bed.

Brent held up a deck of Hoyle playing cards. "I know where the cards ended up."

"Good thing because I don't think anyone will be willing to play Monopoly ever again."

"That's for sure." He held a skein of yarn in each hand. "So far, I've got raw sienna, cinnabar green, and fifty balls of Portland gray. I don't know what my grandmother was making, but it was huge and ugly."

"If you can find one more color, we're all set."

Brent turned back to the closet, which was crammed full of old clothes, boxes, and bags. While he continued his archaeological dig through the debris, Carly scanned the paintings on the wall. It was obvious none of the works were Brent's because they bore no resemblance to his wildlife art. Maybe the artists were going for surrealism. Except hideous. The fantasy and dream imagery was reminiscent of Salvador Dalí or Rene Magritte, but without the skilled execution.

She moved closer to examine a sixteen-by-twenty painting in a huge oak frame that portrayed what might have been a farm or a circus because it sported quite a few pink cows and blue elephants cavorting around. But there also were white blobs that might be turnips, along with some carrots and other vegetables. Smaller objects appeared to be oddly shaped pies, fruits, and wine glasses. In the background was something that looked like a dented water tower, and surveying the mess was a twisted caricature of the Mona Lisa with her eyes bulging out. The whole canvas also was covered with some type of varnish that gave it a grotesque yellowish cast. The coating was cracked and peeling and Carly desperately wanted to pick off a chunk to see the true colors underneath the nasty glaze.

Brent held up a ball of yarn. "Finally! A dirty old ball of gold ochre."

"Rusty, dusty, oldie goldie works for me." Carly paused and pointed at the painting. "Do you know who the artist was?"

"My grandfather. That painting has been hanging there forever. I'd love to take it down. When I was a kid it gave me nightmares." Brent gathered up the yarn and stood next to Carly, gazing at the artwork. "Unfortunately, staying in the family cabin has some down sides. I've been warned that I'm not allowed to touch anything. If I do, people will yell at me."

Carly chuckled. "Yeah, family can be like that. You never know what's going to make your relatives lose their sense of humor. My sister is a case in point. Half the time I have no idea what's going on in her mind."

"My grandfather was the most easygoing guy you'd ever want to meet. He was the one who encouraged me to paint when I was a little kid. When I'd come out here, he'd set me up with a bunch of old acrylic paints and let me go to town."

"That's so sweet."

"Even though I think he did some vastly better work, this was his favorite painting." Brent shrugged. "It was incredibly special to him. Maybe it had sentimental value."

Carly pointed at a tendril of varnish. "You probably noticed it's peeling."

"I've asked about a hundred times if I can take it to be restored. No one will even consider it."

"That's a shame because it's falling apart."

"Well, what can you do?"

Carly smiled. "Family is complicated."

"Tell me about it."

Chapter 5

Washing and Tending

Carly helped Brent put the closet back together and he shoved the door closed. Getting it to stay shut required slamming his shoulder against the door so it would latch. "Someday, someone has got to go through all this crap."

"Fortunately, today is not that day," Carly said with a smile. "We've got stinky dinky dogs to wash."

"I'll get some towels."

Carly grabbed the puppy shampoo and placed it next to the sink, and Brent dropped a big stack of towels on the other side along with the balls of yarn.

He grinned at her. "Ready?"

"As ready as I'll ever be." She turned on the water and adjusted the temperature.

Brent handed her the filthiest puppy and Carly cooed at the small dog as she gently lowered him into the sink. The pup quickly became convinced that the water spraying from the faucet was an evil lethal deluge and began to whimper. Ripley came over to investigate, abruptly turned around, and curled up in her corner again.

Carly leaned over the sink and said in a syrupy voice, "Please don't cry. I'm a terrible softy and you're making me feel awful."

Brent said, "Be strong. He's playing you."

Carly began soaping up the pup, who continued to utter pathetic little yips and whines. "I know. I know. I'm *so* sorry about this, but I promise it will be okay. You were living under a tree, so you're dirty. I know you're adorable, but this has to be done. You're too stinky. I promise it will be fine."

The puppy tried several times to make a break for it and crawl out of the sink, but Brent pushed the little paws back in. Once Carly had finished scrubbing and rinsing, she picked up the puppy, placed him on a towel, wrapped him up like a burrito, and handed him to Brent. "One down, three to go."

Brent worked on drying the puppy and then put him into the x-pen and grabbed the second one. Carly repeated the process and before they knew it, four grumpy, damp but clean puppies were in the x-pen falling asleep. Apparently, being washed was exhausting.

Carly wiped the water off the counters and handed the crumpled mass of soggy towels to Brent. "If you throw these in the laundry, I'll help you clean up the kitchen."

He took the towels and disappeared from the room while Carly got down to scrubbing out the sink. Since she was on a roll, she moved all the canisters and appliances aside and scrubbed the counters as well.

Brent walked up behind her. "What are you doing?"

"What does it look like? Cleaning. I told you I'd help."

"The puppies weren't over here."

"I expanded my focus. It's therapeutic. Sometimes cleaning helps me think. And if I were to guess, I'd say the last time anyone cleaned behind this toaster oven was approximately 1987."

Brent made a face. "Unfortunately, that's possible."

"Not to mention the toaster oven itself. Look at the scatter platter. It's black, and that's got to be a fire hazard."

"I'm afraid to use it."

Carly stepped in front of the stove, opened the door to the oven, peeked inside, and gasped. "That's disgusting."

"I stick to using the microwave."

"I can see why." Carly opened the door to the microwave, which had been cleaned at some point, but wiped it out for good measure.

"You really don't have to do this."

"I want to." Carly pulled the tray out of the toaster oven and dropped it into the sink. "I don't want your house to burn down with these sweet little puppies in it."

"As you've probably guessed, I don't cook, so that's not a big risk. I'd have to turn on the oven for something to ignite." He took the sponge from her. "You're supposed to be on vacation, not cleaning my cabin."

"I know." Carly slumped her shoulders and leaned back against the counter. "I think my friends are mad at me. And when Lily comes back from town, she'll be livid because she lost her purse."

"Go home. Now that the puppies are finally crashed out, I need to paint."

"Thanks for helping clean them up." Carly surveyed the pile of fuzzy puppies and was overwhelmed by the cuteness. "Look at those cuddly snugglies! I just want to hug all that clean puppy fur."

"Don't you even think about waking them up. We can decide on the names and put the yarn on them tomorrow once they're dry."

Carly straightened. "Okay, well, I guess I'll let you get back to work. Good luck with your arty muse, Manet."

Brent grinned. "Good luck with your gloomy roomies."

Carly left the kitchen and reluctantly exited the cabin. Maybe Karen and Lily weren't back yet. She still had about one hundred and fifty pages left to go on her novel, and if she was lucky, she could finish it before they returned.

She emerged from the trees and gazed across the lawn. Ginger was lying on her stomach on the lounge chair next to the water's edge. Her arm was flopped over the side, indicating she was still taking her relaxing seriously. How long had she been lying there?

Carly changed her course and headed toward the lake instead of the house. As she drew closer, it became clear that Ginger had been outside for quite some time because her back was the color of boiled lobster tail.

Carly crouched down next to the chair and tapped the back of Ginger's hand. "Hey Ging, wake up."

Ginger moved her head to face Carly and groaned. "I fell asleep. Ow."

"I think maybe you should give up on sun worshiping for the time being."

"Ugh." Ginger sat up and put her palm to her temple. "I have a headache."

"You might have a bit of a sunburn. Let's go inside."

Carly walked with her friend up to the house. She resisted the impulse to give Ginger a hug. The gesture probably wouldn't go over well in her current crispy fried condition.

They went through the French doors to the dining area in the kitchen and Ginger made a beeline for the sink. She grabbed a glass and gulped down some water. "I was only going to lie there for fifteen minutes, then get Karen to put some sunscreen on my back."

"Karen went to town hours ago."

"I have to get out of this suit. It feels like sandpaper on my skin." Ginger set her glass down and started for the stairs.

"Maybe you should take an aspirin," Carly called after her.

"I know. My kids do stupid things like this all the time."

Carly got a drink of water for herself and sat down at the table, not sure what to do next. So far, she wasn't doing particularly well on the figure-out-the-rest-of-her-life program. And her friends had so many of their own issues going on that she didn't want to burden them. This gorgeous house was absolutely spotless, so there was nothing to clean. Even Trixie wasn't around to lend a sympathetic furry ear.

Carly took a another sip of water. Was Trixie enjoying doggie camp? From the description, it sounded like the dog would be getting a lot more exercise than usual. Pudgy little Trixie might not be appreciating all the extra exertion. Would it be weird to call and check in? Did people do that? Or was she being an overprotective doggie mommy?

Carly was distracted from her ruminations by the sound of Ginger's footsteps on the stairs. When she looked up, she giggled at Ginger's attire, "Are you heading for a toga party?"

"My clothes hurt. A sheet was the best I could come up with."

"Are you okay?"

"Yeah, although I feel like an idiot. With my kids, I usually put a cold compress on the burn." She held out a washcloth. "Could you do that? I can't reach around back there."

"Of course." Carly grabbed the cloth and gave Ginger's hand a squeeze. "Anything you need."

~

Ginger turned a chair around, straddled it, and Carly gently moved the sheet aside and laid the washcloth on her friend's sunburned back. Ginger moaned in appreciation. "Thank goodness Nathan and the kids aren't here to see this. After all my nagging about sunscreen, they'd never let me live this down."

"I guess you were tired."

"It's taken a couple days, but I think I'm finally relaxing. Being pissed at Nathan took longer to wear off than I expected."

"Maybe you had to burn the mad out of you. A sunburn U-turn."

Ginger offered a wry smile. "Maybe. That's one way to look at it. Did you go tend to the puppies and Michelangelo?"

"He helped me wash the puppies because he's avoiding painting. I love your idea for puppy names. He found some yarn so we can make them little collars and tell our musketeers apart."

"It's awfully quiet. Is it just us here?"

"Lily lost her purse and Karen went into town to pick her up."

"Uh oh."

"I know. Lily's mood is going to be ugly. Speaking of ugly, did you see the horrible painting in the bedroom at Brent's house? It's creepy."

"I thought you loved his paintings. And what were you doing in the bedroom?"

"Looking for yarn, and it's not Brent's painting or his bedroom. I guess his grandfather painted it. There are animals and vegetables, and, well, it's hard to describe. But it's icky."

"Icky? That's not the most eloquent art critique I've ever heard. Good thing you took all those art history classes."

"Okay then, to be more precise, it's surrealist ick. It's old and has this nasty varnish that's peeling off, which makes it worse." Carly pulled the washcloth off Ginger's back, wrung it out in the sink, and ran more cold water on it. "There's an awful warped Mona Lisa caricature and she watches you. I can't stop thinking about it. Brent said it gave him bad dreams when he was a kid."

"Maybe the peeling paint offended his artistic sensibilities."

"I've never seen paint peel like that. It's sad because I guess Brent's grandfather loved it."

"What kind of paint did he use?"

"I don't know, but Brent said his grandfather let him play with acrylics."

"Maybe the canvas was reused. Grandpa might have used paints that weren't chemically compatible. If he painted acrylic on top of oil, it would probably peel off. Acrylics have a different base than oils. Over time, the adhesion of the acrylic would separate from the oil underneath because the two types of paints would expand and contract at different rates."

Carly returned the washcloth to Ginger's back. "Once a chemistry nerd, always a chemistry nerd. Too bad science can't fix fugly, ugly art."

"Maybe the painting could be repaired with the right type of paint. Aren't there people who restore old paintings?"

"I think so, but Brent said he's asked about restoration and was told not to have it done."

The front door opened and Ginger moved to look. "Ouch."

Lily walked through the entryway into the kitchen and thumped her purse on the counter. "Where's the wine?"

Carly readjusted the washcloth on Ginger's back and stood up. "You found your purse!"

"I'm an idiot," Lily retorted as she made a beeline for the refrigerator. "And now most of the inhabitants of Alpine Grove also know I'm an idiot."

"What happened? Where's Karen?" Carly asked.

"After she found my purse, she went to the clinic." Lily grabbed a wine glass from a cabinet and poured a full glass of wine. "She was probably glad to be rid of me."

Ginger pulled the washcloth off her shoulders and rearranged her sheet. "Where was the purse?"

"Under a chair." Lily threw up her hands and slopped some wine on the counter. "Oops."

"Did someone take it?" Carly asked.

"I put it there. I was trying on some shoes and kicked it under the chair. I didn't like the shoes and I left. Then I went to a gift store and looked around. Then I went to a cafe and ordered a sandwich and realized I had no money because my purse was lost. It was so embarrassing. I don't know what's wrong with me. Who leaves her purse behind?"

"Did you go back and find it?" Ginger said.

"I retraced my steps, talked to everyone, and didn't find it." Lily took a long drink from her glass. "So I called Karen and then waited on a bench. I talked to the lady who owns the gift store. She was sympathetic, but I probably was being meaner than a snake, so she went back inside. Then I sat there by myself fuming for what seemed like forever."

"So how *did* you find your purse?" Ginger asked.

"Karen made me retrace my steps again. She looked under the seats where I tried on the shoes and there it was." Lily sighed. "Like I said, I'm an idiot."

"Well, the important thing is that you found the purse," Carly said.

"How are the puppies?" Lily sucked down the last of her wine and glanced at Ginger. "And why are you wearing a toga? Did I miss something?"

"The puppies are clean and probably ready for dinner by now. I went over there this afternoon while Ginger sunburned herself," Carly said.

"It's your turn for puppy clean up, Lily," Ginger said and made a gimme gesture with her hand. "But pour me some wine before you leave."

"All right." Lily filled a glass and handed it to her. "I'll be back in a few. Guard my purse."

Ginger and Carly watched as Lily exited through the French doors and wandered off toward the trees. Ginger turned to Carly. "What's with her? Everyone forgets stuff sometimes. It's just a purse."

"Well, it did have her keys and wallet in it."

The front door opened and Karen walked in. "What's for dinner? I'm starving."

Carly went to the refrigerator. "What do you want? There are a couple of options. I'm not sure what might be good for a speedy feedy."

Karen peered into the refrigerator. "How about a stir fry? I picked up a ton of veggies yesterday."

Ginger stood up and moaned. "I'll start some rice."

Karen gave her the once-over. "Did you get sunburned?"

"The sheet gives it away doesn't it?" Ginger twirled like a runway model. "I think it makes quite a fashion statement."

"Is it serious?" Karen leaned toward her. "Do you need to see a doctor?"

"Carly has been tending to me. If I have a little more wine, it won't hurt as much."

Karen shrugged and reached into the refrigerator and pulled some carrots out of the veggie drawer. "Well, drink lots of water. You're probably dehydrated."

Ginger went to the sink and got another glass of water. "Yes, Mom."

Carly gave her friend a theatrical eye roll in solidarity. Karen was everybody's mom.

~

That night, Carly spent her typical time awake tossing, turning, and working through fifteen thousand pointless ruminations related to Stuart. When she did finally fall asleep, she had weird dreams about farm animals and the Mona Lisa. It wasn't as bad as her alcohol-induced screamie dreamie, but when she opened her eyes, her first thought was that Brent wasn't kidding about that creepy painting. The last thing she needed was something else messing with her head.

She stumbled downstairs, made herself some coffee, and let Ginger cajole her into taking the first puppy-tending shift. With a shrug, she acquiesced. "Sure, you can play the sunburn card if you want. After spending all night dreaming about that horrible painting, I need to face it again and tell it to get out of my head."

Ginger grinned. "You're talking to art now?"

"Lack of sleep is getting to me."

After grabbing a piece of toast, Carly forged out into the world. It was a gorgeous morning, and the sunlight skittering across the surface of the lake looked like sparkles on the water. How could she still feel so glum in such a beautiful place? Maybe if she'd ever managed to talk Stuart into going on vacation, they'd still be together. He worked so hard, and they never seemed to take time out for themselves.

When they'd first started dating, they'd taken a whirlwind trip to Northern California and stopped in Yosemite. The whole trip had been fun. They'd laughed, hiked, and talked for hours. Memories of that fantastic trip had sustained Carly through some significantly less great times that transpired later.

Carly entered the wooded area and tilted her head to gaze up at the tree canopy. When she was a kid, she liked to sit in the crook of a tree in the backyard that she referred to as the beseeching beech. Something about the sound of the leaves whispering next to her had been soothing. Mom always used to call her in, saying, "Get out of that tree. It's time for dinner."

No matter how much Carly wanted to hate Stuart, she couldn't. Not completely. Stuart had been kind when Mom had gotten sick. At the time, even Karen had commented on how helpful he'd been. You didn't stay with a person for fifteen years for no reason, and they'd had lots in common. He was tidy, easy to live with, organized, and responsible.

The routines they'd established were comfortable, and Carly desperately missed that sense of order and security.

She walked up the steps to the house and tapped at the screen door. Brent didn't seem to be around, but she heard a playful puppy yip so she quietly stepped inside. As she dodged an easel lying in the living room floor, she called out, "Hello…I'm here. Please put on clothes if you aren't wearing any."

There was no response, so Carly walked into the kitchen, said hi to Ripley, and delved into the task of cleaning up. The puppies rolled around playing with each other and bumping into her as she collected soiled newspaper and puppy pads from within the x-pen. The little beasties were cute, but they generated a lot of oopsie poopsies.

Carly noted that the puppies already seemed to be latching onto the idea of using the puppy pads, which was encouraging. Once she was done cleaning and feeding the dogs, she sat on the floor and let the puppies clamber into her lap. "How are you guys doing? You sure smell better than you did yesterday." She snuggled a puppy into her arms and he squirmed and wriggled happily.

Carly looked up at Brent as he stepped over the wooden barricade into the kitchen. He smiled, "You got the morning shift, huh?"

"Ginger got extremely sunburned yesterday and wimped out." Carly set the puppy on the floor and he charged off to tackle another puppy. "Ouch. Be nice to your brother."

"Since you're here, could you help me with something?"

"Sure." Carly stood up and brushed her hands on her jeans. "Actually, this might sound silly, but I wanted to ask you if I could look at that painting in the bedroom again."

"How come?"

"Little kids aren't the only ones who have strange dreams about it."

He pointed to the door. "Maybe later. I found a roll of chicken wire in the shed and I want to make a makeshift fence outside for the puppies. I could use your help."

"I guess so."

"I'm hoping if they get more exercise outside, they'll sleep more at night inside."

Carly followed Brent and Ripley out the door to the deck and down the steps. "I guess I'm not the only one who is having trouble sleeping."

"Are your friends keeping you up?"

"They're fine. It's my brain that won't shut up. The mental chatter patter is making me crazy."

"You're supposed to be relaxing. It's a vacation. That's what you do."

"So far, vacation isn't helping my inability to get over Stuart."

"It sounds like your obsession with the Captain is sending you on a continuing mission to explore the strange new world of insomnia."

"Very funny. If you think of a way to get me to stop loving him, let me know."

Brent mumbled something that might have been an apology, picked up a tree branch, and opened the door of a weathered shed that was attached to the end of the boathouse. He waved the stick in front of him like a saber. "Watch out for spiders."

Carly crossed her arms. "I think I'll stay out here with Ripley, thanks."

Brent heaved a roll of chicken wire out the door, and it landed on the grass next to Carly with a *whump*. She stepped back a few paces while Ripley gave it a tentative sniff. Carly pointed at a suspicious white clump on the wire. "I think something is living in there. Or reproducing."

Brent emerged with some metal t-posts, which he tossed to the ground. The metal clattered and a large black spider scampered back toward its home in the shed. Brent shook out both hands and closed the door behind him. "Yuck. Talk about nightmares."

"Why don't you move the x-pen outside?"

"The puppies need more room to run around, and I want to paint outside for a while."

"Like plein air painting?"

"Exactly." Brent picked up the roll of chicken wire and dropped it on the ground a few times to encourage any inhabitants to vacate. "My studio is too depressing. Maybe if I get outside into nature, I'll feel more inspired. I'm tired of working from photos."

"That sounds reasonable."

"It does, doesn't it? But painting outside has never worked for me before. I get frustrated when I don't have all my paints and tools right there next to me. But at this point, I'll try anything."

"After tending to Ginger's back yesterday, I suggest you wear lots of sunscreen."

He picked up the chicken wire and the posts and strolled toward the house. "You want to join me?"

"I told you, I have no artistic skills. None. There's a reason I'm a viewer and not a painter. I appreciate art, but I have no illusions that I can produce it."

"Everyone has a creative side. Don't worry about it. Try doing something abstract."

"Easy for you to say. I'm going to waste a bunch of paint."

The fence was a makeshift affair. Because they didn't have any wire, Brent attached the chicken wire to the posts using some of the old gray yarn. It quickly became obvious to Carly that Brent wasn't exactly a master fence-builder. The posts were crooked and the chicken wire sagged and flopped over, but the puppies were small, so the enclosure was probably secure enough to keep them from running off and getting lost.

Brent and Carly carried the puppies out of the kitchen and placed them in their new space along with a water bowl and their mother. Ripley looked irritated that she was trapped with her obnoxious offspring again, but accepted her fate, spinning around a few times before lying down and settling in for a nap in a corner. The puppies seemed thrilled at their large grassy space and ran around chasing each other.

Brent gestured toward the house. "Ready to paint?"

"This is a bad idea. I truly can't paint. It's sad how awful I am."

"I don't care. Let's go grab the easels and paints."

"All right. After you, Mr. Matisse. But don't say I didn't warn you."

Chapter 6

Dragons

Brent set up one easel for Carly and another one for himself, and placed a card table between them. He threw an assortment of paints onto the table, as well as paint brushes and two glasses with water in them. "I haven't goofed around with acrylics in years."

Carly put her canvas on the easel. "This is going to be a huge waste of perfectly good paint."

"Don't worry about it. These tubes of paint have been sitting around here for ages."

Carly picked up a palette, grabbed a tube of cerulean blue, and squeezed some paint into one of the depressions. "I don't know what to paint."

"I'm the one who's blocked, not you. You picked up the blue. What were you thinking about when you picked up that tube?"

"It's a pretty color."

"What does it remind you of?"

"Sky, water, your shirt."

Brent looked down at the threadbare t-shirt he was wearing, which had a small, faded image of a sailboat with the words "Alpine Grove" below it. He ran his fingers through his hair. Rather than smoothing it down, the action riled it up, so hair stuck out of his head at bizarre angles. "I think you can come up with something more creative than a ten-year-old t-shirt."

Carly shrugged. "I can't think of anything."

"Look around you. My grandfather used to recommend starting with still life because it can't run away." He pointed at the ground. "That patch of dandelions isn't going anywhere."

"But I already have blue paint."

"Sky and water, remember? Use the blue for the background."

"This is silly. I told you I can't do this." She put down the paintbrush on the table. "What are you painting?"

"I'll think of something. Mix some paint." He turned back to his easel and gazed out at the lake for a few moments before picking up a pencil from the table and sketching an outline.

Carly leaned over. "What's that?"

"Nothing yet." He handed her the pencil. "Try drawing the basic shapes. Where do you want the dandelions to be in relation to the rest of the image?"

"I don't know."

"Yes, you do. Look at the shapes and their relationship to each other."

"I don't know what I'm doing." She threw up her hands. "What if it's wrong? You can't erase paint!"

"There is no wrong. It's how you see it. Try observing your subject from different angles. Up close. Far away. Upside down. Sideways. And if you don't like what you end up with, you can paint over it."

"Like your grandfather did on that creepy painting. Ginger told me that it's probably peeling because he put acrylics on oils."

"I have no idea why he would do that." He waved his paintbrush at her. "Go on. Listen to your intuition. This isn't a lifetime commitment. You're not getting married or something. Trust your gut and put some paint on the canvas. See what happens."

"The last time I trusted someone, it didn't work out too well." Carly jabbed her paintbrush into the blue she'd mixed. "Okay. Fine. This is me pledging my troth to a questionable and probably hideous mixture of cerulean blue and white."

"Good. Now be quiet and paint something."

They painted in silence for a while. Carly spent some time lying on the grass studying her dandelion patch up close. She splashed some yellow blobs on the canvas and some green swashes for the leaves. It was fun in a messy way. She swirled some darker yellow onto the flower to indicate petals and tried to make the petals seem like they were emerging from the center. Then she added some dandelion flowers that had gone to seed. That process didn't go too well, but if you squinted hard, the seed heads sort of looked like an exceptionally gray molting emu. After a few more swipes with the brush, she moved a few steps away from her canvas to get some perspective on her painting.

Brent glanced at her. "How's it going?"

Carly put her hand to her mouth. "Um…"

He walked in front of her canvas and smiled. "That's… interesting."

"I think I created dandelion porn." She glanced at his easel. "And next to your landscape, I can't even…oh my God, this is so embarrassing. Total creation mortification. And of course, your landscape is absolutely gorgeous."

"I forgot how much fun it is to paint with acrylics. I should do it more often." He pointed at one of the dandelion leaves. "I think that one may be in pain."

"Perhaps due to a fever." Carly said with a giggle. "Or a burning, itching sensation."

"That's gotta hurt." He pointed at another flower. "That one seems to have some especially, ah, fiery irritation going on right there."

Carly burst out laughing. "Your grandfather's painting is nothing compared to this. Now I can have nightmares about my own art."

"Only if you add some scary pink cows."

"And turnips. Or flying pies. Lots of pies. So *many* pies." Carly thumped back down onto the grass, laughing.

"Grandpa would be so proud." Brent sat next to her and patted her shoulder. "Maybe doing more painting will help with your insomnia."

"Is your grandfather still alive?"

Brent glanced at her. "No, he died a while ago. I guess it's been nine years now. My grandmother died last year. It's been strange being here without them. Half the time I go around a corner expecting to see my grandmother."

"I'm sorry. It sounds like you were close to them."

"I was. As you might have guessed from his art, my grandfather was kind of a character, but my grandmother was right there with him. They met in Paris during World War II. She was a war bride."

"Was she French?"

"Very." Brent leaned back on his elbows and gazed at the clouds. "She had a fabulous accent. I loved listening to her tell stories. And she teased my grandfather mercilessly about his paintings. They were always laughing. I bet that's why he painted that weird piece. It was probably to get a rise out of her."

Carly pointed up at her easel. "Maybe there's something about this house that inspires outlandish and sometimes grotesque artwork."

"Maybe you're right. I've been so wrapped up in work stress and trying to be a grown-up, serious artist that I haven't let my freak flag fly since I've been here." He stood up and grabbed a paintbrush. "I think this needs a dragon."

"Like Puff the magic dragon?"

"But in this case, he'll have to live by a lake instead of the sea."

From her spot on the grass, Carly watched as Brent painted a rainbow-hued dragon flying over the lake. She was captivated by how quickly he transformed a wash of color into a detailed, fantastical creature with iridescent scales.

He paused and stepped back from the easel. "Hey, I kinda like Puff."

Carly stood up to examine the dragon more closely. It was beautiful, and she start to hum the tune made famous by Peter, Paul, and Mary.

She grabbed Brent's hand and ducked under his arm, as if she were being twirled by Fred Astaire. "It may not be autumn, but we can pretend there's mist."

He laughed as he raised his arm for a better twirl. "Maybe I could add some noble kings and princes."

Once she was twirled out, Carly settled back onto the grass, gazing up at the easel. "I have to say, Mr. Magritte, that if the whole serious-wildlife-artist thing doesn't work out, you may have a future in children's book illustration."

Brent picked up his brush. "I suppose. I never really thought about that as an option."

"Why not? You don't *have* to paint wildlife. Why do you?" Carly wrapped her arms around her knees. "Like you said, you could paint anything. I bet your dandelions wouldn't resemble demented emus that have contracted some evil avian plague."

He set the brush aside. "I was one of those kids that loved to watch wildlife documentaries. Give me some *Mutual of Omaha's Wild Kingdom* on the TV and I was in heaven."

"I used to love that show. Marlin Perkins!"

"I thought he had the best job in the world. He got to travel around and watch animals. When my grandfather gave me paints, I started painting all the animals I wanted to see. I guess I kept going from there."

"It's a good thing you like animals so much, given that we dumped a whole litter of small critters on you." Carly looked behind her at the puppy pen, gasped, and jumped up. "There's only three. We're missing one. There's been a furry scurry. Where could he have gone?"

Brent followed her to the makeshift fence. Three puppies were curled up with their mom, enjoying a nap. "Ripley, where'd he go? Why didn't you say something?"

The dog lifted her head, blinked a few times, and offered a slow, sleepy wag, apparently indifferent to Carly's concern. A puppy stood up, yawned, and plopped back down into his spot next to Ripley's tummy.

Carly scanned the yard and didn't see the wayward spotted puppy anywhere. "We have to find him."

"I'll look over there." Brent started walking slowly toward the house. "You go that way."

Carly wailed, "The poor little thing doesn't even have a name yet!"

~

Carly felt sick to her stomach. She'd been given exactly one job: tending puppies. And she'd managed to screw it up. How could she *lose* a puppy? What if the little guy had wandered into the lake and drowned? Karen had warned her that the water was cold. What if he'd frozen to death? It was too horrible to contemplate.

Carly dropped down to all fours to get a puppy-level view of the situation. She crawled around on the grass toward the lake, but there was no sign of any puppy activity. If the little pup had gone this way, he hadn't needed to relieve himself. She stood up again and walked back to the enclosure. The dogs were still recumbent and sleepy, stretched out in the sun. They gave her a few curious looks as she crawled around the fence searching for evidence of escape.

Carly stopped at a bit of chicken wire that seemed to be bent outward. The little canine Houdini hadn't covered his tracks completely. She bent the fence back down and tried to smash it into the grass. She glared at Ripley, "Don't you dare let anybody else get out."

Carly turned to scan the direction the puppy might have gone. Maybe toward the trees or the house? There was no way to tell. Brent was wandering around the house whistling, but didn't appear to have run across the puppy. If something happened to this little dog, Carly would never forgive herself.

Carly made her way to the trees, scanning the ground for any evidence of fur or paw prints. Something, anything would help. Would they have heard an owl swoop down and grab a puppy? Probably. Owls were pretty big, weren't they? Brent probably knew their exact dimensions from painting them.

As if he'd been listening to her thoughts, Brent called out, "Carly! I found him."

Carly ran toward the house and found Brent sitting cross-legged next to the stairs up to the deck with a puppy cradled in his arms. Carly flopped down next to him and stroked the puppy's head. "You are in big trouble, mister."

"He was fast asleep under the stairs. I didn't see him the first time I walked around the house. When you're covered in spots, lying in dappled shade works well as camouflage."

Carly took the puppy from Brent and snuggled him close. "I was so worried. We should have been paying closer attention. Or made a better fence. Or something."

Brent stood up. "Let's put him back with his littermates."

"What if he gets out again? What will we do?"

"Find him again." He gestured toward the puppy in her arms who was squirming around, seemingly annoyed about being pulled from his nap spot. "We need to put the yarn on them, so we can assign names. Then we can do something other than whistle when they get out."

"You're just assuming they'll get out again? Why don't you fix the fence so they can't?"

"Why don't *you*?" Brent leaned over to unhook the wire from the t-post to open up the fence.

"I don't know how to build a fence."

"Do you think I do? Look at this mess. I improvised."

"Maybe you should have done some research first."

Brent took the puppy from her and put him on the ground. "I'm sorry, but the family lake cabin isn't stocked up on fence-building manuals."

Carly crossed her arms and waited for Brent to leave the enclosure and secure the fence again. She sighed. "You're right. I'm sorry. I have no room to complain. I'm not an expert or anything either."

"Apology accepted." He turned and walked back to the easel.

Carly followed him and giggled when she saw her painting again. "I can't ever show this to anybody. What should I do with it?"

"Take it inside." He glanced at her. "I'm going to grab another canvas and paint for a while. Maybe you could put the yarn on the pups before you go."

Taking the hint, Carly mumbled okay and grabbed her canvas. She went into the house and stopped by the bedroom to stare at Grandpa's painting. "Listen here. You need to stay out of my dreams, okay? I've brought you a friend, so you can be weird together." She set the painting on the floor and turned it to face the wall.

After a stop in the kitchen to grab the yarn and scissors, she went back outside and went through the laborious process of removing the chicken wire from the t-post again. It wasn't the easiest doorway to deal with.

Once she was inside and the makeshift door was secured , she carefully tied little pieces of yarn around the neck of each sleepy puppy. When she finished, she sat in the sun, enjoying petting the soft puppy fur. It was so peaceful listening to their little snorty snores.

Brent walked up and smiled down at her. "What did you decide? Which one is who?"

"I haven't decided yet. I was watching them sleep. What do you think?"

"You have a real problem with making decisions, don't you?"

Carly looked up in surprise, shading her eyes from the sun with her hand. "What?"

"Pick a puppy. Give him a name."

"Don't you think everyone should have input? We all found them."

Brent put his fists on his hips. "The next person who comes here to take care of them is going to ask me which puppy is named what. Just name them, for heaven's sake."

Carly stood up. "Fine. If you're going to be a jerk about it. D'Artagnan is green, Porthos is gray, Aramis is maroon, and Athos is gold. Happy now?"

"That wasn't so hard, was it?" He crouched down to open the fence for her.

Carly paused. Was she really that indecisive? "Hey, I make decisions all the time."

"Glad to hear it." Brent walked back to the easel and swapped the dragon out for a blank canvas. He paused to look at her. "Do you want to paint some more?"

"I probably should be getting back."

Brent didn't say anything and she stared at him for a moment before blurting, "I'm sorry I snapped at you. I was upset about losing little Aramis. And you've been so nice about letting the pups stay here."

"Why are you apologizing? You're right. I was a jerk."

"But you might be right too. I think I'm out of practice when it comes to making decisions. Karen always says I worry too much about what other people think."

Brent put down the brush, walked over and stood in front of her. "What difference does it make which puppy is named Aramis?"

"I don't know. I guess it doesn't matter."

He took her hand and gave it a squeeze. "It's like the blue paint. Sometimes you have to go with it and see what happens."

She gazed into his eyes. "The last time I committed to something...or someone...I ended up hurt, rejected, and miserable."

"I get that. I'm a master at relationship flameouts. As you pointed out, I can be a jerk, which is one of many reasons I'm still single. But being dumped by the Captain doesn't have to shape the rest of your life, does it? Give yourself a break."

"I spent years trying not to rock the boat, trying not to do or say the wrong thing. Being a fret cadet is a hard habit to break." She squeezed his hand again and let go. "But giving yourself a break goes for you too, you know. Maybe you should let Puff the magic dragon slip back out of his cave."

He pulled her into his arms and gave her a hug. "Thanks for staying and painting with me. It was fun. To be honest, it's the first time I've enjoyed painting in a long, long time."

Carly let go and grinned at him. "Any time you want me to waste some more paint and canvas, say the word. Maybe I'll go for some diseased daisies next time."

He laughed. "Okay, it's a deal."

~

As she strolled back through the trees, Carly reflected upon how Brent and Karen more or less both said the same thing about Carly's need to keep everyone happy, except herself. Brent figured it out pretty quickly and the guy barely knew her. And then he actually admitted to being a jerk.

In fifteen years, Stuart had always positioned himself as an exceptionally tolerant person who patiently dealt with what he referred to as Carly's "emotional outbursts." No wonder she'd spent so much time working to keep the peace. When they had arguments, she always felt like she'd lost, even when she got her way. There was a fine line between being accommodating and being a doormat. Over the years, had she really turned into that much of a sap?

She exited the forested area and strolled onto the sunny expanse of lawn. She could hear conversation through the screens and smiled at the sound of what she thought of as Karen's "professional" voice. When Karen was at work at the clinic, she always sounded so calm and rational, but she'd loosened up a little because of Lily's and Ginger's influence. Carly slowed her pace. Why was Karen's tone so formal? Was someone else there at the house?

She turned and walked toward the side of the house, instead of the back, so she could check out front. A car she didn't recognize was parked along the circular driveway behind hers. That was odd. They weren't expecting visitors.

As she got closer to the house, her chest tightened. She couldn't hear what was being said, but the sound of the voice was all too familiar. What was *Stuart* doing here? In response to his comment, Karen said stiffly, "Carly will be back soon. You are welcome to wait."

Stuart said, "I have important financial business to attend to and Carly needs to go with me."

"Sorry, but as Karen explained to you, Carly is otherwise engaged," Lily said. "And in no event shall I be required to entertain you."

"She'll be here when she gets here," Ginger added. "How about you take all your statistics and economic expansions into the dining room and leave us alone?"

Carly frowned at Ginger's words. Stuart had obviously said something her friends didn't like. And what business could he have here? The haughty tone in his voice brought back flashbacks to some of their worst arguments. The angrier he got, the more pedantic he became.

Carly squeezed her eyes shut and clenched her fists. She couldn't face seeing him right now. She turned and ran back toward the trees, wound her way through the forest, and burst out onto the sunny expanse of lawn behind Brent's cabin. The dogs stood up and barked at her as if she were a wanton criminal. She waved her hands and tried to shush them as she ran toward them. Brent put down his paintbrush, and when she reached him, she stopped short. What she really wanted to do was get another hug, but then he'd think she was even more of a hopeless case than he already did.

He grinned, "Back so soon? Were the sickly daisies and plague-ridden dandelions calling to you already?"

Carly clasped her hands in front of her. "No. I, well, I saw…I mean, I didn't want to."

"If you don't want to paint, what are you doing here?" He gestured toward the enclosure and the five wagging tails behind the chicken wire. "As you can see, everyone is present and accounted for. I'm keeping an eye on them, and they're fine."

"I know. There was someone at the house." She paused, and at his confused expression, exhaled a breath. "It was Stuart. I heard his voice and I ran away."

"I thought you were still in love with this guy. Maybe he's here to boldly win you back."

"I doubt that, given what I've heard about my replacement. He let me know in no uncertain terms that the lovely Laurel is everything I'm not. Apparently, she's brilliant, poised, willowy, and eloquent. Einstein Barbie."

"Maybe Barbie dumped him."

"Even if she did, I think I don't care anymore." Carly paused. Did she really mean that? Maybe she did. She shook her head. "When I heard his voice, all I wanted to do was get away from him. I think I've been daydreaming about the good times and letting myself forget what a horrible smirky, twerpy jerk he can be."

"You mean he's a bigger jerk than I am?" Brent said with a half-smile. "Say it isn't so."

Carly sank down to the grass and wrapped her arms around her knees. "You have no idea. Remember Major Winchester on the TV show *M*A*S*H*?"

"Yeah. He was the pompous guy who replaced Ferret Face."

"When Stuart gets angry he sounds exactly like Major Winchester. Maybe it's the accent. I don't know. But when I heard his voice, I freaked out a little."

Brent titled his head and raised his eyebrows. "That seems like an odd reaction to someone you're in love with."

"Maybe I didn't want to accept it before, but I don't want him back. Maybe I don't love him anymore. Maybe I never did. I don't know. All I know is I don't want to see him."

Brent sat down next to her on the grass. "So basically you're hiding here, hoping he'll go away?"

Carly glanced at him and said softly, "Yes."

"You do realize how ridiculous that sounds, right?"

"Yes."

"You need to find out what he wants. And then if you decide you want him to go away, you need to tell him that. No wimping out."

"I know."

Brent made a sweeping motion with both hands. "Get lost. I need to paint."

Carly stood up. "You're dangerously close to being a jerk again, you know."

"I don't care. It sounds like you have a far bigger jerk to deal with than me." He waved his hands again. "Leave."

Carly stood up slowly. "All right. Thanks for being here."

"You don't have to thank me. I live here, remember?"

Carly walked toward the trees taking small steps, so it would take longer to get back to the house. She stopped a few times to take deep breaths and to gaze up at the boughs gently swaying in the breeze. Talking to Stuart was likely to be completely awful.

Once again, she emerged from the trees into the sunlight. With a pause for one more deep breath, she marched across the lawn up to the patio and went through the French doors into the house.

Lily raised her water glass as if she were toasting. "Where in heaven's name have you been?"

"Your beloved ex-, the Captain, has docked his craft here," Ginger added and pointed to the dining room where Stuart stood in the doorway. "And look, there he is now. See! We told you she'd be back presently."

Carly turned away from Stuart and went to wash her hands at the sink. "What are you doing here?"

He moved toward her, taking long forceful strides. "I need to talk to you. It's important."

Lily and Ginger got up, and Lily said, "We'll be on the patio if you need us."

Stuart walked around the counter and stood next to Carly at the sink. "How are you?"

"What do you want?" Carly said quietly as blue paint swirled down the drain.

"You need to go to Gleasonville with me."

Carly glared at him. "You're wrong about that. I don't *need* to go anywhere with you. Nor do I want to."

"You have to because I need your signature. In person."

"What are you talking about?"

"The savings account we set up needs to be closed. We have to do it in person."

Carly dried her hands on a towel. "After you threw me out, we closed our bank account and I opened a new one."

"This is the vacation account."

Carly hadn't thought about that bank account in years. After the fantastic trip to Yosemite, they'd pledged to save for a great vacation and really splurge. Each of them had put in a contribution and promised that they'd keep adding to it every year on the anniversary of the trip. Of course, they never did.

Stuart said, "There's a branch of the bank in Gleasonville. I flew out here so we can get this done. If we leave now, we can get there before they close. Let's go."

Stunned from her flashback, she said, "I'll get my purse." She started for the stairs. How far away was Gleasonville anyway?

No matter how long the journey took, being trapped in a car with Stuart was not an experience she wanted to have. She stopped and said over her shoulder, "I'll follow you in my car."

~

On her way to Alpine Grove for vacation, Carly had driven through Gleasonville, so technically she'd been there before, although the place hadn't been particularly memorable. The community was south of Alpine Grove and featured lots of strip malls and big-box stores

Because Gleasonville had zero small-town ambiance, the drive to the bank was dull, and Carly had lots of time to think about her surprising reaction to seeing Stuart. Unlike her various fantasies, he hadn't come to Alpine Grove to tell her he was desperately wrong to throw her out and that she was the best thing that had ever happened to him. But she hadn't known why he was there when she'd first heard his voice.

Far from being elated at the potential for reconciliation, her reaction had been unexpectedly visceral. It was as if her physical being knew far better than her brain that she should do a flashy dashy away from this guy. She'd opted for the classic flight response. Deer and cottontail bunnies had nothing on her. See danger; run away. Too bad it had taken her fifteen years and a whole lot of heartache to figure out this little bit of truth.

The meeting at the bank was awkward, and Carly spoke as little as possible. When they were finished, Stuart tucked his share of the money into his wallet and said, "Well, I guess this is it. Nice to see you again."

"Goodbye, Stuart." Carly turned on her heel and left the bank without another word. She got into her car, started the ignition, turned on the stereo, and let the sense of relief and Aerosmith wash over her. Steven Tyler was suggesting that she "Walk This Way" at high volume as she drove out of the parking lot and turned north, back toward the lake.

Now that Carly really and truly had Stuart out of her head, it was time to get on with the rest of her vacation, not to mention the rest of her life. Fortunately, it seemed she was finally done crying. If she'd been compelled to cry on the drive back, she wouldn't be able to see, and wrecking the car would put a serious damper on her recreation. There'd be no more weary teary nonsense for this girl.

By the time Carly returned to the house, it was late in the afternoon. The moment she walked through the door, Lily, Ginger, and Karen were on her case, demanding to know what was going on.

Lily said, "What did he do? Where did you go?"

Carly explained about the bank account and Lily said, "You up and left here without a word. We thought that low-life had kidnapped you until we saw your car was gone."

Ginger added, "You should have said something."

"I wanted to get it over with," Carly replied.

"Are you okay?" Karen asked softly. "He didn't try to get back together, did he?"

Carly shook her head. "Quite the opposite." She sat down and explained how she'd been at Brent's, then when she'd heard Stuart, had run back to the cabin like a stricken chicken. "The moment I heard Stuart's voice, I felt sick. I didn't care what he wanted. All I knew was I didn't want to see him. Maybe I needed closure or something, but I'm done. What's more than done? Well done? Burnt? Crispy? Whatever it is, I'm hoping that tonight I'll be able to sleep, for a change."

Lily raised her eyebrows. "Well, this is a switch."

"About damn time," Ginger retorted. "You spent years dedicating your life to him and what did it get you?"

"Well…" Carly began.

"You were always there answering his every whim like a dutiful little wife. Trustworthy and reliable. Always home with dinner on the table when he arrived from work." Ginger smiled slightly. "I *am* a wife, and I don't let Nathan get away with that sexist drivel."

"You had the job of wife without any of the legal benefits," Lily added.

"Don't remind me," Carly said.

Lily continued, "I forgot what Stuart was like. When we were in college, I thought that preppy Boston accent was dreamy. Lordie, I must have been on drugs."

"I did too. I can't believe I…" Ginger stopped abruptly. "Wait. It's late enough for wine, isn't it?"

"I'm in, as long as you stay away from the hard liquor this time. I think it's time to toast to my improved mental health," Carly said as she pulled some wine glasses out of the cabinet.

Karen took the glass Carly handed to her and said, "I'm glad you're feeling better. You deserve a person who will appreciate you."

"I know. Why aren't there more guys like Dave? I still miss him," Carly said.

"Me too. Every single day," Karen said with a sad smile. "He was one in a million."

"You need to find your knight in shining armor." Ginger said as she picked up her glass. "A hot slayer of evil dragons."

Carly laughed, "Dragons must be the theme of the day. Brent added one to his painting."

"That's a little out of Michelangelo's artistic jurisdiction, isn't it?" Lily said.

"He said he was only goofing around, but I thought it was wonderful." Carly poured some wine into her glass and held it up. "Knowing for sure that I never want to see Stuart again is like a great weight that's been lifted off me. Breaking up with Captain Prickard might be the best thing that ever happened to me."

"Hear, hear!" Lily said. "You're better off without that albatross. It's time to start focusing on *you*."

Carly busied herself making dinner, and after they ate she volunteered for puppy duty.

Lily said, "I'm not complaining about missing out on cleanup, but you were at Monet's cabin almost all day. How come you want to go back?"

"Wait a minute," Ginger said, lifting her glass and tilting it toward Carly. "Do you have a thing for the artist? Is that why you're suddenly over Stuart?" "What exactly were you up to all that time? Did he go skinny dipping again? Did you go *with* him? If I missed out on more naked Monet, I'm going to be seriously disappointed."

"Sheesh, calm down, you guys. That's not it at all. I told you, we were painting, and well, I guess painting takes a while, particularly when you're as bad at it as I am. I want to take him some food to say thank you." Carly took her plate to the kitchen and set it down. "After I ran back there like a total chicken, he encouraged me to go face Stuart. We have tons of leftovers, and have either of you checked out the oven in that cabin? It's a thousand years old and completely filthy, so it's too scary to use. All he eats is frozen stuff he heats up in the microwave."

"Carly, you finally freed yourself from Stuart, who you catered to for the last fifteen years. This isn't you looking for someone to take care of again, is it?" Ginger asked.

"No! I promise it's not. I was only trying to be nice." Carly handed Ginger a plastic container. "If you're so worried, you take it to him. Tell him thank you for letting me stay and paint for a while."

Ginger grinned. "If I'm lucky, maybe he needed a shower after all that painting. Maybe he won't have a towel."

Lily poured the last of the wine into her glass. "You really have a one-track mind."

Ginger left with her plastic containers and everyone else retired to their rooms to read and relax. Carly didn't realize how exhausted she was until she crawled into bed. She closed her eyes and moments later was fast asleep.

Chapter 7

Family Lore

The next morning, Carly got up early. Even though she'd dreamed about the flying vegetables and farm animals in that stupid painting *again*, she hadn't lain awake thinking about Stuart. As a result, she felt better than she had in weeks and happily scampered downstairs to make coffee. The sun was shining and it was a beautiful day. How could her friends stand to be missing this?

After sipping her coffee and staring at the lake for a while, neither her sister nor her friends had emerged from their rooms. Carly was too keyed up to sit around any longer, and she had no outlet for her energy. With no one available to comment or complain, she opted to take the first round of puppy duty. And maybe clean the stove and toaster oven. She grabbed some cleansers, rags, and sponges and tossed them into a bucket.

She set out across the lawn and made her way through the trees. The early-morning air was invigorating, and the idea of hiking didn't sound as appalling as it had a few days ago. Maybe all this fresh air was doing some good. When she got back, she could call the dog-boarding kennel and see if it would be okay to take Trixie out for a hike. And if Brent was amenable, maybe he could take Ripley too. It would be cute having Trixie and Ripley go for a walk together. Ginger always said that when you're a mom, it's great to hang out with adults once in a while. Was that true for dogs? Sometimes it did seem like Ripley wouldn't mind a break from her band of puppy musketeers.

Carly tiptoed up the steps to the deck and tapped lightly on the screen door. Although it was early, by now Brent should be used to the puppy clean-up crew invading his cabin. As quietly as she could, Carly went into the house and shushed Ripley's bark. "It's just me. Let's go outside and then I'll clean up."

Carly took Ripley outside for a quick visit to a patch of grass and brought her back into the kitchen. After releasing the puppies from their confinement, Carly cleaned out the x-pen while the small fry and their mother ate their breakfast. Then she carried the puppies outside, one by one, to their makeshift enclosure. She sat outside with them and waited while they sniffed and relieved themselves. When all of the musketeers seemed content and empty, Carly took them back inside so they could play while she worked on cleaning the appliances.

As predicted, the oven was a nightmare. Apparently many pies had exploded or oozed upon its blackened ceramic surfaces. What a disaster. But with a whole lot of elbow grease, she was able to get the oven clean enough that someone might be willing to use the appliance again. While she worked on scrubbing, the tray and racks from the toaster oven soaked in the sink.

After dumping out approximately thirty years of bread crumbs and wiping off every possible surface, Carly reassembled the toaster oven and made herself a piece of toast as a reward for her efforts. She pulled an old cookbook off a shelf and flipped through the pages as she chewed. The toaster might be an antique, but it was still able to perform its primary function.

She tossed a piece of crust to Ripley and looked up as Brent staggered into the room. Clad in another threadbare t-shirt and torn gym shorts, he looked even more rumpled than usual, which was oddly endearing. No one would ever accuse him of being a clothes horse. Most of what he wore was either paint spattered or falling apart.

"What are you doing?" He ran his fingers through his hair, which worsened his tousled case of bed head. "I smelled something and thought the house was on fire."

"It's toast." Carly smiled. "I'm pleased to say that the toaster oven is not even a little bit scary anymore. I got all the desiccated bread crumbs and gunk off the scatter platter."

He walked over and opened the door. "Wow."

"The oven is clean too. You can use it without fear."

"I think you've gone way beyond puppy clean-up duty." He peered into the oven. "That's remarkable."

"I discovered that somebody in your family really likes pie."

"Liked. That was my grandmother. She loved baking." He leaned back against the counter. "I doubt the oven has been used since she died."

"You must miss her." Carly pointed at the cookbook. "She put tons of notes into this cookbook. I'm starting to feel like I know her a little bit. Some of the comments are funny. Like this one: 'Do not make this *ever* again! Tastes like *merde.*'"

Brent leaned over to look and chuckled. "Grandma limited her swearing to French, so kids wouldn't realize what a potty mouth she was."

"Some of the recipes sound good. Grandma said this one is *très bien*, which is promising. Then she's got some weird comments about turnips and beef."

"I hate turnips."

"Me too." Carly flipped a few pages. "Sounds like some other people do too. There are names listed next to the recipe. Maybe they complained."

"Yeah, who knows? My grandparents were incredibly gregarious and social. They threw lots of parties. I was usually hiding in the back bedroom, drawing or painting, to get away from the chaos."

Carly flipped a few more pages and then glanced at him. "You disguise it well, but you're kind of shy, aren't you?"

"I'm fine with one or two people, but not great with crowds." He shrugged. "There were lots of crowds back then. Before the Walsh family bought the place next door, tore it down, and built their palace, the old cabin was owned by friends of my grandparents. Between the two families, people were coming and going constantly. I spent the whole summer here when I was twelve. The summer of 1981 was one long party."

"You were twelve in 1981?" Carly frowned. "You're a lot younger than I thought."

He scratched the nape of his neck. "I suppose it's impolite to ask, but how old were you in 1981?"

"I graduated from college a year after you were hiding from partygoers."

Brent held up and folded down fingers. "So you're what… thirty-five or thirty-six now?"

"Thereabouts." Carly suddenly felt like an incredible failure. She was eight years older than this guy and he'd enjoyed worldwide success as an artist. Meanwhile, she'd done nothing except go to her crappy job every day and act as Stuart's live-in gofer. What a waste.

"Why do you suddenly look like you want to throw up?"

"I need to get my life together. Now. Yesterday would have been better, but my life is a mess. I have almost nothing to show for the last fifteen years. A boring, dead-end job, a studio apartment with no furniture, and a dog."

"The dog is good."

Carly couldn't help but laugh. "You're *right*. Trixie is by far the best thing in my life right now. In fact, I was thinking I could give her a break from the kennel and take her out for a hike."

"Have fun." He patted her on the shoulder. "I've gotta paint."

"More dragons?"

"I was thinking of great horned owls, but you never know what might happen." He stopped in the doorway and gestured toward the stove. "Thanks for cleaning up. See you later."

"Wait!"

He turned around. "Do you need something?"

"Would you like some toast? Or coffee?"

"I don't drink coffee, and you don't have to feed me," He stepped over the wood across the doorway. Before he disappeared into the living room, he turned back toward her and added, "If you thought the toaster oven was bad, you probably don't want to examine the coffeemaker too closely."

Carly shook her head in disbelief. Who didn't drink coffee? It was impossible to imagine starting her day without a cup of delicious life-affirming caffeine-laden goodness. She got up, rummaged through the cabinets, and pulled out an ancient, stained Mr. Coffee. With a tiny gasp of horror, she returned it to its resting place. Yuck.

Carly wanted to get another look at grandpa's creepy painting, so after she put the puppies back into their x-pen, she decided to take a quick detour into the bedroom before returning home.

Her ugly dandelion painting was still resting on the floor. Ignoring it, she stood in front of grandpa's work of weirdness with her arms folded across her chest. The image was still ugly, and dreaming about it was no fun at all. She leaned closer to the canvas and said, "You need to get out of my dreams, okay? I'm serious."

From behind her, Brent said, "When people say art speaks to them, they usually don't mean it literally."

With her hand pressed to her chest, she turned around. "Don't be all sneaky creepy like that. You almost gave me a heart attack."

"I live here. You're the one sneaking around."

"I'm not sneaking."

"Why are you in the bedroom then?"

"I can't get this painting out of my head. You need to tell me more about your grandfather."

"What do you want to know?"

"Everything."

~

Brent leaned against the door jamb and picked at the old wood with his fingernail. "How come you're so curious?"

"I don't know. I just am. Seeing the artwork and the cookbook makes me want to know more about your grandparents. They seem so charismatic."

He walked into the room, sat on the end of the bed, and looked up at the painting. "I suppose they were. At the risk of sounding like a nut, sometimes I forget they aren't here anymore. It's like their spirits are part of this place."

"What were their names?" Carly sat down next to him and leaned back on her elbows. "How did they meet? Tell me their story."

"Well, I don't know the whole story, but I do know they met during World War Two. My grandmother's name was Claudette Durand. She was a 20-year-old university student when she met my grandfather, Roger Michaelson, in Paris in 1944. As the story goes, they were outside of a Paris museum and he asked her for directions."

"I *knew* this would be romantic. So was it love at first sight?"

"She said his French was *merde*."

Carly giggled. "She was only twenty when they met?"

"Yes. She was fifteen years old when the war started in Europe. I guess she spent two years in the countryside during the German occupation of France and then worked with the French Resistance for while, then went back to Paris toward the end of the war."

"What did your grandfather...Roger...think about her being in the resistance?"

"I got the impression that he only found out about those activities later. Neither of them ever said much about it. Grandma did say that when they met, her first impression of the handsome American soldier was that he was clean and had good teeth. And like I said, she also used to harp on the fact that he didn't speak French. Fortunately, Grandma spoke English; otherwise I wouldn't exist."

Carly smiled. "I suppose not. Then what happened?"

"My grandfather was trying to find a bakery, which it turned out was owned by Claudette's father, aka my great-grandfather. Roger didn't speak French at all, so Claudette led him to the bakery and helped him get the bread he wanted."

"Who can blame him? If I were in Paris, I'd want some baguettes too. And cheese. Who could resist French cheese? Mmm. So I guess they started seeing each other?"

"My grandfather was stationed outside of Paris and had leave every Saturday. For two months, according to Grandma, he picked her up at the university, and they'd walk to her parents' apartment for lunch and have more of her father's fresh-baked bread."

"Aww. Love among the bakey cakey."

"I guess so. She said they couldn't go out to eat because they needed coupons to do that. After they had lunch, she showed him around Paris. They went to all the museums." He pointed at the painting on the wall. "As you know, Roger was an artist, and he and Claudette shared a love of art."

"Then what happened?"

Brent shrugged. "That's where Grandma started to get a little tight-lipped. I guess something happened and Roger disappeared for a while. She thought he'd been captured."

"Had he?"

"Apparently not. I guess he was on some special assignment. I've never been clear on exactly what he was up to, and he never talked about it. Maybe it was classified or something. But while he was gone, he wrote her lots of letters. At some point, Roger returned to Paris and proposed to Claudette. Sometime after that he was discharged, and he brought her to the United States with him."

"You mentioned she was a war bride." Carly flopped back onto the bed. "I know lots of people got married during the war, but how did they immigrate? Was it legal?"

"Grandpa wasn't the only one who fell in love. He said that in 1945, Congress passed the War Brides Act, which made it possible for my grandmother to immigrate to the United States with him."

"It must have been hard for her to leave her home and her family in France."

"I got the impression her family wasn't too excited about the idea. Although her parents liked Roger, they thought they'd never see their daughter again. Grandma always said that leaving her family was the most difficult part of the decision to come to the United States. Leaving them was worse than moving to a strange country where she didn't know anyone. But she said that after living through so many years of battle, she wanted to raise her children in a place without the constant threat of war."

"What happened after they got here?"

"They arrived in New York in 1946. My grandmother had finished her master's degree before coming to America, so she was able to get a job teaching French. She taught high school French for twenty years. My father used to say that although he loved his mother, my grandmother was an unbelievably strict teacher. He said she was the teacher no one wanted because taking her class was sure to trash your grade-point average."

Carly smiled. "That's easy to imagine, after reading her comments in the cookbook. She was a woman of strong opinions. I'm impressed she already had a master's degree at twenty-two. Who does that? Your family is filled with overachievers."

"I'm not sure how school works in France, but from my perspective, she was a softie."

"That's part of the job description for a grandma."

"I suppose, but after she got here, she sent money to her parents for a long time. I guess it took years for Europe to recover after the war."

"What did your grandfather do when he came back home?"

"After he was discharged, he used the GI Bill to get a master's degree in business administration. He worked for the Singer sewing machine company and later a company that manufactured irrigation systems for farms. He retired in 1985 and died a few years after that."

"How many kids did they have?"

"My dad, Arthur, and my Aunt Rose. Dad was born in 1947. Last month was his birthday, and the last time I saw Rose, she said he's having a midlife meltdown about turning fifty."

"Meltdowns seem to be going around." Carly did a little quickie mental math to figure out if she was actually closer in age to Brent's father than she was to him. Fourteen years versus eight. Hmm. She glanced up at Brent and a cradle-robbing thought skittered across her mind, but she quashed it immediately. "When was the last time you saw your aunt?"

"A few months ago. Rose landed on my doorstep, and we hung out for a few days. She's not a big believer in schedules—she claims they're too confining, so she tends to turn up unexpectedly."

"Was it good to see her?"

"It was, except that she also finds clothes confining. It's startling get up one morning and discover your aunt wandering around your kitchen in the nude."

Carly giggled. "I guess you're not the only nudist in the family."

"Hey, I thought I was *alone* on a private beach."

Carly ignored his protestations. "You said your grandparents both loved art. Was Claudette an artist too?"

"No, but she loved collecting paintings, and along with my grandfather encouraged me to pursue art. Before she died, I took her to my first major show in Los Angeles, and she was thrilled. Bringing your grandma is probably uncool, but she had a fantastic time, and everyone loved her."

Carly sat up and put her hand on his arm. "That's so sweet. She must have been incredibly proud of you."

He chuckled. "Now she'd be jumping down my throat for not painting. One of her favorite sayings was from Goethe: 'Whatever you can do, or dream you can do, begin it.' She'd be disgusted with my big pile of unfinished paintings and current lack of productivity."

"Maybe so, but I bet she'd bake you a pie." Carly giggled at his expression. "Oh come on, you know she would have."

Brent put his hand on hers and looked into her eyes. "I believe you're right. She would have said, 'pie fixes everything,' but with a really exotic French accent that I can't even pretend to imitate."

Carly squeezed his hand. "Thanks for sharing their story. I love happy endings. I wish I'd had the chance to meet them."

"I'm sure they would have liked you." He leaned over and kissed her lips softly.

Carly's thoughts retreated from far away places and people as his arms wrapped around her. Helplessly yielding to the warmth of his lips, the kiss was soft at first, but increased in intensity, shooting electricity throughout every last nerve ending in her body. Before she consciously realized what she was doing, she was kissing him back.

He released her and whispered, "My grandmother probably would have shared one of her other favorite Goethe quotes. 'As soon as you trust yourself, you will know how to live.'"

"Well, Mr. Magritte, I think we both need to work on that."

He ran a fingertip across her cheek and gently curled a wayward lock of hair behind her ear. "Yeah, I suppose you might be on to something."

～

Carly stared into Brent's gray-blue eyes for a moment, trying to discern what he thought of the kiss. Had he felt what she felt? But what on earth were they *doing*? She cleared her throat. "That was nice, but you realize it was a bad idea, right?"

"I suppose." He released her hand and stood up. "But you aren't the only sucker for romantic stories. My grandparents were devoted to each other."

Carly glanced up at the painting again. "Have you noticed that the frame is coming apart?"

"That's not a surprise. It's old. I should probably glue it back together before it crashes to the floor and wakes me up in the middle of the night." Brent reached up, pulled the painting off the wall, and laid it face down on the bed. "My father will kill me if anything happens to it."

"What's that marking mean?"

"I don't know."

"E-R-R. Like to make a mistake? To err is human. Did your grandmother write it? Maybe it's a word in French? I took Spanish in high school, so I'm no help."

"I picked up a little French from my grandmother, but most of it isn't suitable for polite company." He walked over to a bookshelf, pulled a book out, and handed it to her. "Here's a French-English dictionary."

Carly flipped through the pages. "I can't find anything, except the French verb *errer*, which means to wander."

"I don't know what to tell you."

"Maybe one of your grandfather's hunting dogs inspired it. The puppies say *err* all the time when they're playing." Carly handed the book back to him. "Well, I suppose I should get back."

"So about before—maybe we should forget that happened. I mean, you broke up with the Captain ten minutes ago."

"You're way too nice to be rebound guy, especially after I've already told you my life is a mess. But just so you know, it was nice to feel appreciated."

He smiled, "You're pretty easy to appreciate. Not to mention a good kisser."

"No one has said anything to me like that for years. Now I feel like even more of an idiot for staying with Stuart for so long. How could I have been so stupid?"

"You're not stupid. You trusted the wrong person." He shrugged. "These things happen."

"It sounds like there's another story there."

"Maybe some other time. I really need to get to work now."

Carly took the hint and said goodbye. She went back through the forest to the house, trying not to focus too much on how fantastic Brent's lips had felt on hers. She kept telling herself that it was a bad, bad idea, but he wasn't the only one who had enjoyed the kiss. She was only here for a short time and she'd barely gotten over Stuart. But the kiss had been *so* deliciously good.

When she walked in the French doors, everyone was gathered around the table eating breakfast.

Karen gestured hello with her coffee cup. "How are the pups?"

Carly sat in the chair next to her sister. "They're fine. All tidied up and happy. I also cleaned out the toaster oven and stove, so if you're over there and want to snack on something you're less likely to die."

Ginger said, "I knew you wouldn't be able to resist cleaning that filthy place."

"Thank the angels above you did something. That cabin is like a giant petri dish. I'm afraid to touch anything," Lily added. "It's dirty and falling apart. Home maintenance is obviously not Monet's forte."

"Or the forte of anyone in his family either, I don't think." Carly reached for a piece of bacon from the pile sitting on a place in the center of the table. "His family is interesting though."

"So what are we doing today?" Lily asked, clapping her hands together. "We need a plan."

"I'm going to call and see if I can take Trixie out for a hike. I miss her," Carly said.

"You have five dogs to play with, and you want to visit another one?" Ginger said. "That seems like canine overindulgence."

"But Trixie is *my* dog, so it's different. We've been through a lot together." Carly glanced toward the window. "The puppies are too small to hike with, and I'm afraid Ripley might run away."

Karen poured some more coffee into her mug. "Speaking of which, we need to call Brigid about getting these puppies homes or at least foster placements. That has to be lined up before we leave here at the end of next week."

"Give me the number and I'll call her." Carly said.

Lily stood up. "I'm up for hiking. Where is this place?"

"North of town. It's a bit of a drive," Carly said.

"Works for me." Lily started for the stairs. "Make your calls and then we're outta here."

Carly left a message for Brigid on the adoption group's answering machine and had a nice chat with Kat's answering machine to let them know she was coming by for a visit. The worst thing that could happen was that Kat would turn her away for some reason. But at least she'd get to see Trixie, so the poor dog wouldn't think Carly had abandoned her forever.

Lily followed Carly to her car and when she went to get in, launched into a cavalcade of dirty words.

"What's wrong?" Carly asked. "Why don't you get in the car? You're the one who's in a big rush."

Lily readjusted the fanny pack around her waist, turning it around front, and got into the passenger seat. "In addition to being hideous, this thing is poorly designed. How are you supposed to sit down?"

"I think they're designed for walking. If you think it's hideous, why did you buy it?"

"I refuse to lose my personal effects again, and it is impossible to lose them if they are physically attached to me."

Carly started the car. "Aren't you overreacting a little? Everyone loses stuff all the time."

"I am not everybody."

Carly took her eyes off the road for a moment to glance at her friend. "I know, but stupid things happen. How many people have left their coffee on top of the car, so it spews all over the place when they take off?"

Lily didn't respond. She was focused on extracting something from her fanny pack. "That's people not paying attention."

"What are you doing with your ringy dingy? I thought you said you didn't want to talk to anyone."

Lily held up her cell phone and flipped it open. "Looking for a signal."

"Are you expecting a call? You said all those lawyers have to figure out their patents for themselves."

"I said I don't want to talk to anyone from *work*. I'm expecting a call from someone else with...information."

"Information about what?"

"I'd rather not say."

Carly pulled over to the side of the two-lane road. "I'd rather you did say. What is going on? Everyone on this trip is having some sort of life crisis."

"That's an apt term."

"What are you talking about? What information are you expecting?" At Lily's stony silence, Carly widened her eyes and leaned toward her. "For heaven's sake, I'm your friend. *Tell me!*"

"Test results."

Carly moved back to her side of the car. "You mean like medical tests?"

"Unfortunately, yes."

~

Carly thumped her palm on the steering wheel. "Don't just sit there. Talk to me. What type of tests?"

"Every type. The doctors aren't sure what it is." Lily raised her cell phone again. "Could we get moving? There are only about three places where I can get a signal in this godforsaken place."

"Are you really sick?"

"I don't know. That's the problem. Doctors are a bunch of fools who seem to be more adept at guessing than anything else." Lily waved the cell phone in a swirling hurry-up gesture. "I'd rather not discuss it. Could we get going?"

Carly pulled back onto the road, unsure what to say next. "Well, what are the guesses?"

Lily fiddled with buttons on her phone, but didn't reply.

"Hey, I'm going to stop this car again and take that phone away from you if you don't start talking."

"Don't go all nuclear on me. It might be nothing. I was feeling extra tired and run down, so I went to the doctor."

"I thought you looked tired. Is that why you finally agreed to take a vacation? The doctors told you to, didn't they?"

"Well, not in so many words because they were talking about something else."

Carly looked at her. "What something? Do you mean something bad? You're scaring me here."

"Might be nothing, but there was a lump."

"What? Where?" At a stop sign, Carly slammed on the brakes a little too hard. "Oops. Sorry. Are you talking about cancer?"

"Well, Lord willing and the creek don't rise, it won't be. Like I said, it might be absolutely nothing and my boob is fine."

"But they found a lump? You're saying they did a breastie testie? Doesn't that mean cancer?"

Lily giggled. "I love how weird you are. Only you would come up with the words breastie testie in the face of life-threatening illness."

"I'm sorry." Carly felt a tear slide down her cheek. "But you can't have cancer. You just can't. You're way too young."

"Anyone can have cancer. But it could be a fibroadenoma."

"What's that?"

"A lump that isn't cancer."

Carly swiped away the tear. "Thanks for that scientific explanation. Where's Ginger, the science geek, when you need her? Did you tell her about this?"

"No, and I don't want you to either." Lily shook the cell phone at the window. "What I *want* is a signal."

"Karen says her phone usually works in town. Sometimes. But forget about that for a minute. I want you to tell me exactly what the doctor said. What test results are you waiting for?"

Lily gazed out the window. "So given all the time you've been next door lately, I'm thinking those must be some awfully clean puppies. Or you and Monet are getting up close and personal. You've been like two little peas in pod, which is suspicious. The fact is, you're way too big of a neat freak to be caught dead in that filthy place, unless you've got the hots for him."

"Don't change the subject."

"Don't *you* change the subject. What are you up to with the artist?"

Carly clenched her teeth. No one was as stubborn as Lily. If she didn't want to talk about her medical tests, she wouldn't. In college, Lily had been seeing some guy at Amherst and to this day Carly had no idea who he was. It was infuriating, and Carly refused to divulge anything that might or might or not be going on with Brent.

They rode in silence until they reached Alpine Grove and Carly had to slow down through the residential area. Lily said, "Stop! I have a signal. We need to pull over before I lose it."

Carly turned down a side street into a pretty, leafy neighborhood, parked in the shade of a huge maple tree, and waited while Lily poked at her phone. The expression on Lily's face was impassive as she listened to her messages.

When Lily closed the phone, Carly said, "Well?"

"My cohort Anthony is having a nervous breakdown about a patent. No word from any doctors. They said it would take about ten days to two weeks."

"Weeks? What are they doing? Writing it on parchment?"

"The specialist who is supposed to review everything is at a conference, which they said might delay the results."

"I can't believe you're so calm." Carly slammed her palm on the steering wheel. "Don't they understand you're waiting?"

"Believe me, I've already yelled, fumed, and sulked. I haven't had a good night's sleep in weeks. But the fact is I can't do anything except wait. That's why I came on this trip. I was hoping it would help take my mind off things. The puppies helped a little."

"I know they're cute, but I still can't believe you didn't say anything to me. Why didn't you tell us? Ginger and I are your friends."

"Because I knew you'd both freak out."

Carly wasn't sure what else to say, and they stared at the highway in silence as they passed by a big-box store and a motel and conference center. After that point, signs of commerce diminished so it was miles and miles of trees with a few farms and ranches interspersed between the tracts of forest.

When they finally turned off the highway. Lily said, "Where *is* this place?"

"Way off in the trees. I hope I don't get lost."

"Me too. They might never find us again out here."

After winding along back roads, Carly finally yelled, "There it is!" before turning into a driveway.

"I can't believe you found it."

"Well, I have been here before. And unlike our good friend Ginger, I have some sense of direction."

Lily tucked her phone back into her pack. "Remind me not to come here with her."

Carly parked in front of the kennels, and when they got out of the car, she and Lily were greeted by a cacophony of barking.

Lily shrieked and jumped back into the car, pointing frantically with her index finger at the windshield.

A gigantic brown, hairy dog was barreling toward the car, and Carly couldn't tell if he was friendly or not, so she followed Lily's lead and jumped back into the driver's seat.

Lily peered out at the dog, who was poking his nose on the window, leaving nostril prints. "What *is* that?"

Carly leaned over Lily. "It's an enormous dog. He's wagging his tail though, so I guess it's okay."

Carly opened the door and got out again. The dog trotted up and sat in front of her. "Nice doggie. How come you're out here all by yourself? Are you lost?"

The dog didn't seem to be sharing any secrets, but he leaned heavily on Carly in a silent request for affection. She obliged, hoping he wouldn't knock her over.

Lily got out of the car. "What are you doing?"

"Petting Chewbacca."

"I don't think so. This hairy thing is far more social than Chewbacca. Chewy always struck me as a bit of as a crank."

Carly giggled. "How come no one ever pointed out that Chewbacca is wandering around naked all the time? In all the movies, he's letting all his junk hang out there in the breeze. What's that about?"

"Oh honey, you do have it bad for the artist, don't you? When you start talking about nudity and man parts, it means you're horny. Ginger's the same way. She keeps fixating on going over there and walking in on Monet naked. The woman is obsessed."

"What about Nathan? She'd never cheat on him."

Lily shrugged her shoulders. "Hey, I call 'em like I see 'em."

A female voice shouted, "Linus, where are you?" and the giant dog launched away from Carly.

"Is that the owner?" Lily asked.

Carly nodded and waved to Kat. "I left a message on your machine. I hope it's okay to take out Trixie."

"That's fine. My husband is getting ready for a trip, so having one less dog to walk is great."

They went inside the kennel, where Trixie was beside herself with joy to see Carly. Her whirling exuberance made getting her leashed and ready to go somewhat complicated.

Once Carly was untangled, Kat directed the group toward the forest. "The trail is right down there. Follow Linus. He knows the way."

Carly, Lily and Trixie trailed behind the large dog as he trotted happily toward the massive trees. When they were away from Kat, Carly glanced at Lily. "I'm sorry, but this animal doesn't look like a Linus to me."

"You were right before. This walking carpet should be named Chewbacca. Then maybe we'd get the benefit of some Han Solo eye candy nearby too."

Chapter 8

Doubts

After Kat checked in on the dogs, she left the kennels and started back up the driveway toward the house. Joel emerged from the Tessa Hut hauling a large, black metal thing. The Tessa Hut was the nickname for the outbuilding in front of the house and had been given the designation because it was where Kat had initially confined her dog, Tessa, when Kat inherited the house.

The old outbuilding had been substantially rehabilitated since then and had been used to house boarding dogs before the kennels were constructed. When the wood-storage lean-to collapsed under heavy snow, Joel had removed the chain-link kennel from the Hut and rearranged the interior so it could house firewood for a while. After spring arrived and the firewood was relocated, Joel had proclaimed that after all the work he'd done on the Tessa Hut, he was claiming the space for himself. Figuring that every guy needed a man cave, Kat wasn't about to argue.

Joel stopped and set down a gleaming black treadle sewing-machine base when Kat walked up to him. She crouched beside it to take a look. "It's not rusty anymore. What did you do?"

"Cleaned seventy-plus years of grease, dirt, and lint off it, then sanded it and used a wire brush to deal with the rust. Then I painted it black."

"Well, now I know what you've been up to out there."

"Sanding is therapeutic. The wood cabinet is in better shape than I thought. Now that everything is back together, I think it will work. I oiled all the joints and the balance wheel. The action is really smooth now."

"But I don't know how to sew on one of these things. I know you use your feet, but do you have any idea how long it took me to figure out a clutch? Cars aren't supposed to make those kinds of noises."

"I can imagine." He put his arm around her shoulders and kissed her cheek. "But if people in 1925 could figure out how to use a treadle machine, so can we."

"You're doing all this work so you don't have to think about your trip."

Joel ignored the comment and hauled the cast-iron base up the stairs into the house. "I'm going to go put this together now. That machine-repair place in town had a leather treadle belt. I just need to put it on."

"You really want to sew something now?" Kat followed him into the living room, where the rest of the sewing-machine parts were lined up next to the window.

Joel put the base down. "This machine is seventy-two years old and still functions. I found out the other day that the thousands of lines of code I wrote for the Las Vegas project are being replaced. After only six months."

"You're kidding." Kat sat on the sofa. "But you worked on that project for a year."

Joel set the wooden cabinet on the cast-iron base and sat down on the floor. "Don't remind me."

"I suppose technology marches on and all that. At least the kennels are still standing, and the house hasn't fallen apart lately."

"There's something to be said for working in construction. If you're any good at all, what you build tends to last for more than six months." Joel fiddled with a screw and turned the balance wheel. "Check it out. Smooth as silk."

"It hardly makes any noise." Kat moved to sit next to him on the floor. "I remember Abigail using this when I was little. That whirring sound brings back memories."

"What did she make?"

"I'm not sure. I probably don't remember because I wasn't paying attention. Maybe she made all those colorful floppy skirts she wore."

"Or maybe it was the seventies."

Kat giggled. "Well yeah, there's that. Once you get this thing running, what do you plan to create?"

"I'm guessing Abigail made those curtains. Twenty years ago they might have been okay, but now they're falling apart."

"I think that pattern has always been ugly. My complete lack of interest in interior decorating is showing, but I'd be happy to help you select fabric."

He leaned over to give her a kiss. "Deal."

"By the way, Maria is coming over later after work. She has some beauty treatment she wants to try, and she claims it's not a single-person operation. Because it's also Friday night, I suspect she wants wine and to crash here."

"I'll make myself scarce. I have to read through the class materials again."

Kat stood up, leaving Joel to his reassembly task. She went downstairs and sat in front of her computer, willing the writing gods to speak to her about the article she was supposed to hand in the following week.

After staring at her monitor for quite some time, it was clear the gods continued to be sleeping on the job. She couldn't face going over her notes anymore, so she went back outside to the kennels to see if Trixie and her owner had returned yet. The trails were well marked, but sending people out into the forest was a little unsettling. Joel always said Kat was a worrywart, and he wasn't wrong.

She cruised through the kennels, which achieved nothing except waking up the dogs, so she went back inside the house. The sewing machine was back in one piece and was a lot prettier than Kat remembered it. She stroked the wood top, lifted it, and peered down at the sewing machine hiding below.

Joel emerged from the bathroom with a towel over his shoulders. "Does it seem to you like the water pressure is low?"

Kat gently closed the sewing machine lid and followed him into the bedroom. "Please tell me we're not having a water crisis eighteen hours before you're getting on a plane."

"That water filter attached to the pressure tank might be getting clogged with dirt. I'll change it before I leave."

The dogs hanging out downstairs in the daylight basement started barking as if the world were coming to an end, and Kat raised her eyebrows at Joel. "I think Maria has arrived."

"I'll be in my office."

Kat went to the top of the stairs and shushed the dogs, then walked to the windows in the kitchen that faced the front yard. She waved at Joel to indicate that he should come over. "You might want to see this."

He peered over her shoulder and down the driveway to the gate. Maria was attempting to unlatch it and obviously swearing at the mechanism. "Is that your old car?"

"It is. She got it painted."

"Magenta wouldn't have been my first choice."

"Me neither. I'm so glad I got a new car. For a long time, she threatened to give the Corolla back to me."

"I can't quite imagine you driving a magenta Toyota." He pointed at the window. "What is she doing to the gate?"

"Kicking it." Kat sighed. "I think she needs help again."

"How hard is it to open a gate?"

"She refers to it as our hermit barrier. Ever since she got her new fingernails, opening the gate has become problematic."

"I hesitate to ask this, but what do you mean *new* fingernails?"

"They're the cheap glue-on plastic ones you get at the drug store, and they fall off really easily. The last time she came over, Linus ate one before I could find it."

Joel wrinkled his nose. "Yuck."

"When spring runoff was too much for the culvert at the end of the driveway, she kept asking why we have a moat."

"Moats do have some advantages."

Kat looked over her shoulder and grinned at him as she opened the front door. "Hey, don't get any ideas."

~

Kat walked down the driveway to the gate that prevented dog-boarding clients from driving past the kennels and ending up at her front door.

Maria put her hands on her hips. "I don't understand why you had to turn this place into a fortress. I need to embark on my skin care makeover and getting to your house is hard now. Gates aren't welcoming."

"That's the idea." Kat leaned over, unlatched the gate, and walked it open. "Your skin isn't going anywhere, but to be honest, I'm having second thoughts about this idea."

Maria waved off the comment, got into her car, and pulled through the gate and up to the house.

Kat met her at the bottom of the steps. "I know it's supposed to have vitamins and antioxidants, but from what you told me, this skin-care treatment seems like a waste of perfectly good vegetables."

Linus came bounding out from behind the Tessa Hut and Maria put out both hands to ward him off. "Don't you dare stuff your stinky, smelly nose on my skirt. We've had this conversation. It's rude!"

"Hmm, I wonder where the rest of them are."

"Are you letting the dogs walk themselves now? That would sure save time. Not to mention wear and tear on your feet. Maybe you could get some more feminine shoes that don't make you look like a moose."

Kat turned at the sound of voices as Carly and Lily appeared from behind the house.

Carly waved. "I'm sorry. I didn't realize we'd end up in your backyard."

"That's okay. Linus was heading home." Kat took Trixie's leash from Carly. "This is my friend, Maria."

Everyone introduced themselves and Maria said, "I'm here to perform a critical skin-care treatment because living this rural lifestyle is hard on the complexion. I mean, would you take a gander at this woman?"

Carly and Lily gave Kat the once-over, and Carly smiled weakly.

Kat said, "One reason I work from home is so I can remain blissfully unaware of arbitrary rules about makeup and dress."

"We're on vacation, so we're a bit more casual than usual," Lily said.

"Lily vetoed my no-makeup decree though," Carly added.

Maria shook her head so vigorously that her curly brunette mane swept in front of her eyes. She brushed the curls back. "Working from home is no excuse to let yourself go."

"I think it's a great excuse. Even better was ditching my louse of a boss." Kat pointed at Maria. "And you, of all people, know why *that* was a good idea."

"You're right about that, girlfriend. Mark put the *hostile* in hostile work environment. While I admit to the truth of your statement, I still contend you need a makeover. The lumberjack motif isn't flattering."

"I think it would be nice to be able to work from home," Carly said in a not-too-subtle attempt to change the subject. "I can't believe how wonderful I feel being out of the office. I didn't realize how much my job had mentally beaten me down until I was away from it."

"I know exactly how you feel. I had cubicle PTSD for a long time," Kat said. "Never again."

"You're so lucky to have escaped the cubicle," Carly said. "I was thinking about getting a new job on the drive up here, but all anyone would hire me to do is more or less what I'm doing now, so it doesn't seem worth the effort."

"Carly called me from a Winding Road motel in the middle of nowhere and whined at me," Lily said. "But I had no advice. I'm a lawyer and, as such, I'm doomed to work in an office with arrogant lawyers forever."

"Maria has been banned from the entire Winding Road motel chain." Kat said with a sidelong grin at her friend.

"You know that wasn't my fault! I was unjustly accused of feeding the pigeons. And I absolutely didn't do that. It's not like I invited them in. They violated my room all by themselves." Maria put her fist on her hip. "Worst of all, they ate everything."

"And then crapped it out," Kat added. "All *over* the room."

"Twinkies don't smell so good after they've been through pigeon innards." Maria shrugged. "That sweet cakey goodness doesn't seem to agree with them."

Carly said, "Are you saying the pigeons were *inside* your motel room? How did they get in?"

"I might have left my box of Twinkies lying near an open window. The room was really stuffy, so I opened it up and then went out to dinner," Maria said.

Kat giggled, "That was your first mistake."

"My second mistake was coming back. If I'd known what I'd find when I returned to my room, I would have turned right around and gotten my butt out of town."

"What happened?" Lily asked.

"I opened the door to my room and found a flock of the biggest, ugliest gray pigeons you've ever seen. There must have been hundreds of them. They'd obviously busted through the window screen, then started fighting over the Twinkies. I think they were chowing down the whole time I was gone. But the second they saw me, they went berserk." Maria started flailing her arms. "They were screeching and flying around, crashing into stuff. There was a lot of flapping. Alfred Hitchcock should have been filming."

"Don't forget the screaming," Kat said. "Hitchcock would have appreciated that too."

"I may have screamed and uttered a few unladylike phrases. I was trying to get those nutso birds to get their disgusting selves back out the window. But they couldn't figure it out. You might not be aware of this, but pigeons are really dumb. So these pigeons are all flapping around losing their little bird brains, crashing around and flying into the closet and the bathroom. Some flew out the door into the hall, I think. I'm not sure exactly. But feathers and bird poop were going everywhere."

"I believe you referred to it as a pigeon tornado," Kat said with a giggle.

"Don't you dare laugh. I could have died in that room. It was *that* scary." Maria gestured toward the trees. "Some of the stupid birds finally figured out where to go after I took off my heel and threw it at one. I kinda only grazed him though, so my pretty red stiletto went out the window with the bird. I was so pissed."

"The guest the shoe landed on apparently wasn't too happy either." Kat glanced at Carly, who was staring at Maria in horror, and continued, "Because of all the flapping and screaming, people showed up and tracked down the birds that escaped into the building."

"The hotel management wasn't too pleased with me because during the melee the birds trashed the room. Lamps were busted, the curtains shredded, and bits of cardboard from the Twinkie box were everywhere," Maria said with a deep sigh.

"Don't forget the coating of pigeon excrement on everything." Kat shook her head. "Eww."

"Yeah, it was gross." Maria shrugged. "I never found my shoe either. Probably some pigeon ate it."

"And *that's* why she was banished from the chain forever," Kat said.

Maria opened her arms wide. "Here's the thing. If you're going get thrown out for trashing a room, it should be from something good. This was like some horrible, wild, pigeon party that I didn't even get to enjoy. And now my name is in the Winding Road motel computers somewhere. I've thought about trying to register, just to see if they're serious. They claim it's a lifetime ban, but that seems a bit extreme."

Lily seemed to awaken from her stunned silence. "You're lucky they didn't sue you."

"I explained where I was working, and they probably realized I had no money. It happened during an unfortunate phase during my early career in Las Vegas." Maria waved her hand toward Kat. "Okay, that's enough about that. Shouldn't we be getting on with our makeovers? You need help, girlfriend."

"We should be getting back to our house too. We've got puppies to tend," Carly said and crouched down in front of Trixie. "You be good."

"Since you're staying nearby, you're welcome to take her out for a hike whenever you like," Kat said. "There are lot of trails around here."

"I might take you up on that," Carly said. "But Lily hasn't been feeling well, so we're going to take it easy."

Lily raised her eyebrows. "Excuse me. What are you talking about? I'm fine."

"You're all wetty sweaty," Carly said. "We shouldn't have gone so far."

"I beg to differ. We women from the south don't sweat. We glow," Lily said. "And I'm fine. How many times do I have to tell you? I'm *fine*."

"We should be going," Carly said quickly and pulled a piece of paper out of her purse. "Please let me know if Trixie needs anything. We do have a phone, as it turns out."

"A phone that you can only use for local calls," Lily added with a small harrumphing noise.

Kat and Maria sat on the steps with Trixie and watched as Lily and Carly returned to their car and drove away.

Linus settled in next to Trixie at Kat's feet and she stroked his large furry head. "That was sort of odd. What do you think is up with Carly's friend?"

"I'm guessing she's sick."

"Why do you say that?"

"Remember when we stole the rhino? I think it's like that."

When Kat and Maria had worked together, a small rhino had been dubbed the company mascot. When an employee did something notable, their boss, Mark, would put the rhino on the person's desk with great pomp and circumstance. A recurring office gag had been to steal the rhino and dress it up.

Kat stopped petting the dog and looked at Maria. "Was that when we put Rocky in the tutu?"

"Yeah, and we put it on Jenny's desk, so it was sitting there when she got back from vacation. And then she got all weird about it." Maria leaned her head on Kat's shoulder. "Just like Carly 's friend."

"I felt awful. But how could we know Jenny wasn't really on vacation?"

"Going to the hospital for surgery isn't much of a vacation."

"We also didn't know she took ballet when she was a little girl and dreamed of being a professional dancer. I felt so mean."

"She was gonna do a bunch of physical therapy so she could get back to her ballroom classes. Maybe by now she's dancing again."

"I hope so."

"Yeah, me too, girlfriend. Me too."

〜

The next morning when Carly came downstairs, Lily and Ginger were sitting at the table drinking coffee in silence. Lily had dark circles under her eyes and appeared to be in dire need of a caffeine jolt. Maybe the walk with Trixie had been too much.

Carly grabbed a cup of coffee and sat down. "Where's Karen?"

"It's her turn for the morning puppy shift," Lily said.

Ginger gazed down at her mug as she swirled her coffee around. "Last night when I was there, Monet told me about his aunt. She sounds like quite the wild woman."

Carly nodded. "He mentioned his aunt Rose to me, but didn't say anything about her. What does she do?"

"Mostly writes songs and tries to stay sober. I guess she took the sixties pretty seriously. She traveled around with the Grateful Dead and Jefferson Airplane. She met everyone who was anyone in rock and roll."

"That guy has the most interesting family," Carly said. "He told me about his grandparents. They met in Paris during World War II."

"The impression I got is that Monet likes his aunt a lot better than he likes his father." Ginger took a sip from her mug. "Maybe it's because after she retired from music, she became a sculptor. He said she lives in Malibu and is a woman of strong opinions."

Lily chuckled, "That's the nice way of saying that she doesn't take crap from people."

"I guess she got that from her mother," Carly said. "From what he told me, Claudette sounds like she was quite the character. Oh, and while I was there, he took the creepy painting off the wall, and it has the letters *e-r-r* on the back. We were kidding around about how it's probably *err*, as in mistake."

"Is the painting from World War II?" Lily asked.

"I doubt it. Or, well, maybe it could be, I suppose. It's old and the paint is peeling." Carly got up and poured herself more coffee. "Ginger said the artist might have painted over an old canvas. Maybe grandpa did that, and whatever's underneath is older. Why?"

"The Nazis had a group called the Einsatzstab Reichsleiter Rosenberg that was charged with seizing cultural properties in occupied countries during World War II. The acronym is ERR," Lily said.

Carly's jaw dropped. "How do you remember stuff like that?"

"I was a history major, remember? My thesis was on World War II."

"I can barely remember what I had for dinner last night," Ginger quipped.

Carly waved her hand, "Oh stop it. That's not true. If it's about anything science-y or medical, you always remember. Lily, you need to talk to…"

"No, I don't," Lily interjected. "I *really* don't. Shut up Carly."

"What am I missing here?" Ginger cast her gaze from one woman to the other and back to Lily. "Ever since Brent told me about his aunt, I've been wondering if you're on something. Do we need to do an intervention? Because I'm okay with that. Are you with me, Carly?"

Carly clutched her mug. "I, um, I'm not sure…"

"I do not need an intervention and I resent the implication that I do," Lily said. "Sure, I had a few glasses of wine, but we all did."

"We're on vacation and you look like you haven't slept for a year," Ginger said. "What are you not telling me? If it's not booze, is it drugs? I have a friend who got hooked on pills. Should we take you to a meeting?"

Lily waved her hands in front of her. "I am not hooked on anything, and I'm not going to any meeting. I had some tests, that's all."

"Tests for what?" Ginger said.

"Cancer."

At the C-word, silence cloaked the women like a soggy woolen blanket, and they stared at one another for a few moments. Finally, Ginger softly asked for details, and Lily shared what she'd told Carly the day before. Carly cast her eyes down at her coffee, listening, glad that everything was out in the open at last. Keeping secrets always had consequences.

Finally, Lily stood up. "What are we doing today? I refuse to sit around here moping about my impending demise."

"That's not funny," Carly said. "Even if the tests show, well, something, there are treatments."

"I'm done discussing this topic. I need to take a shower, but after that, I vote we go harass Monet. I want to examine that painting," Lily said. "I'm curious now."

"Maybe we can convince Monet to scrape off some paint so we can see what's under the ugly cows and turnips in grandpa's work of weirdness," Ginger said. "That could be fascinating."

By the time they'd all showered and returned downstairs for breakfast, Karen was back from puppy duty and parked in her favorite lounge chair on the patio, reading. Carly went outside and sat at the table. "How are the pups?"

"Great. Did you talk to Brigid? Those little dogs need homes."

"I left a message for her, but we don't have an answering machine. Did she leave a message for you at the clinic?"

Karen indicated that as far as she knew, no one had called, so Carly figured her adoption duties were over for the moment. She accompanied Lily and Ginger through the trees to Brent's cabin.

Ginger brushed a wayward pine bough away. "Your sister doesn't have much of a sense of humor does she?"

"And I don't think she likes me," Lily added. "It's like going on vacation with your mom after you've been in trouble and she just chewed you out."

"Karen has always been a bit of a loner. I think dealing with so many people all day at the vet clinic is hard on her." Carly stepped over a log. "Everyone always thinks about how difficult it would be to work with animals, but I think she finds the people more annoying than any dog or cat."

"She told me how much she loves the diagnostic aspect and then went on and on about a fascinating case about a dog with unusual symptoms. We had a great conversation about the endocrine system and kidney function," Ginger said. "She said that in canines…"

"*No*," Carly yelped. "I don't want to hear this. I hate hearing medical stuff. Or thinking about sick dogs. I told Trixie, she can never, ever get sick."

"And people say lawyers are boring," Lily quipped. "You science geeks get all high falutin' with your Latin words."

"And lawyers don't? Give me a break. I think we need a *quid pro quo* agreement to disagree on that point," Ginger said.

Carly was the first to exit the trees, and as she stepped into the sunlight, she smiled at the sight of Brent standing in front of an easel near the puppy enclosure. As usual, his clothes and hair were rumpled, but he seemed so content standing in the sun, her stomach did a little happy flutter. He waved his paintbrush in greeting and she eagerly walked across the lawn toward him. Even though her brain kept telling her not to dwell how good it had felt to kiss him, the rest of her was ignoring anything resembling rational logic. What could she say? He was cute.

Within their lopsided enclosure, the puppies were wide awake, tumbling over each other and making little yipping noises as they rolled around on the grass. Carly crouched and stuck her fingers through the fence. "Hey, no biting, Porthos!"

Lily tilted her head to examine the painting on Brent's easel. "You're branching out to domesticated creatures."

"I have to watch them, and I can't go off into the forest to find wild critters."

Ginger pointed at the puppies. "These guys are acting pretty wild, if you ask me. Ouch, that's gotta hurt."

"We want to look at your grandfather's painting," Lily said. "We're intrigued by the historical and chemical potential."

Brent made a face. "I'm not sure what you mean by that, but sure. Look all you want."

The two women started toward the cabin, and Carly stood up to follow and was startled when Brent grabbed her arm. "Can I talk to you for a second?"

Carly nodded and turned to yell, "I'll be right in."

Ginger offered a backward wave in acknowledgment, and the door slammed behind her. Carly raised her eyebrows at Brent. "What's up? Are you tired of puppy duty? I can't blame you."

"It's fine, but I've had a change of heart."

"About your painting? I can see that, and I love this one. You really captured how playful they are. It's adorable. I was serious about children's book illustration. You'd be amazing at it."

"Thanks, but that isn't what I meant."

Carly pressed her palms together in mock prayer. "Wait! Please don't tell me you're throwing out the puppies. I promise it's only for another week. I haven't heard back from Brigid, the animal adoption woman yet. I'll try calling her again when we get back to the house."

Brent took her hands in his. "Calm down. The puppies are fine. I'm not evicting them."

"Then what?"

Pulling her so close to him that she could feel the sun-baked warmth of his skin, he said softly, "I changed my mind, and I've decided I'm okay with being rebound guy."

Carly paused and scanned his face. Was he kidding? Or was he saying what she thought he was saying? "Um, I thought we agreed to forget about the bliss kiss. I mean, I'm a lot older than you are. And I just broke up with Stuart. I don't live here. My life is a confusing mess."

"I don't care."

When he kissed her, Carly wasn't sure she did either.

~

By the time she came up for air, Carly was pretty sure her friends were going to wonder what she was up to outside. She glanced toward the door to the house and put her palm on Brent's chest. "Maybe I should go make sure the painting is okay."

"I'm sure it's fine." He slid his hand up her back to the nape of her neck and kissed her again. "You could volunteer for the next puppy-watching shift."

Carly pushed him away with a smile. "I *would* like to do some more plein air painting."

"That too."

Carly went into the house and back to the bedroom, where Lily and Ginger were discussing the ugly painting.

Lily said, "Have you ever noticed how European handwriting is different? I think this was scrawled by a German."

"That's hardly scientific," Ginger said.

Carly walked in and looked down at the painting lying on the bed. "You didn't do anything to the paint, did you? Brent said his grandfather loved this piece."

Ginger shook her head. "I'd have to use something to scrape it off and that would damage it. Even though it appears to be all peely in that corner, the paint is still attached."

"That's a relief," Carly said. "I'd hate to get Brent in trouble with his family. He's been so nice to us."

"I want to go to the library and look up some information," Lily said. "Karen said the Alpine Grove library is small, but the librarians love to do research."

"I'll take puppy duty," Carly said. "I want to paint out by the lake again," Carly said. "I know I'll never be good at it, but it's relaxing."

"Since I'm still crispy, I should stay out of the sun, so I guess I'll go to the library with you, Lily. I'm out of sexy romance novels to read," Ginger said. "I need more happy endings. And maybe we could find a restaurant somewhere."

After returning the painting to its spot on the wall, the three women went back outside. Carly waved to her friends as they disappeared down the path into the forest toward the house.

Brent put down his paintbrush and walked over to stand next to Carly. "Did anyone gain any deep insights into the painting?"

"Not really. Lily wants to go to the library and do some research. I told them I wanted to paint."

"Do you?" He put his arm around her and kissed her neck, which caused little shivers to skitter down her spine.

Carly gave herself a mental hand slap and stepped away. "You really shouldn't do that."

"Why not? We're consenting adults, and earlier you seemed to be consenting quite a bit. In fact, I'd say it went beyond consent and took the scenic route toward enthusiasm."

"I'm lonely. And you're..."

"Incredibly sexy?"

Carly giggled, "I was going to say available."

"Ouch."

"I didn't mean it like that. It's pretty obvious I find you attractive. But I'm only here for another week, then I take my dog and go back to my boring job and figure out my life. Vacation ends and I return to reality."

"Why?"

"What do you mean 'why'? Because I have to go home. Vacation is nice, but reality is, well, *real.* I have to work and make a living to pay for food and keep a roof over my head."

Brent ran his fingertip along her collarbone. "You keep saying you don't like your job. If you hate it so much, why don't you get a different one?"

"Doing what?" She grabbed his hand before it roamed anywhere else and her enthusiasm got the better of her again. "I don't know what else to do. I'm not qualified for anything. I don't even have a resume. I'm certainly not going to figure out a whole new career in a few days."

"Why not?"

Carly blinked in surprise. "Well, I'm not...I don't know. Why are we talking about this? Shouldn't we paint now?"

"All right. I'll go get the acrylics." He dropped her hand and headed for the house.

Carly turned and stared out at the lake. What was wrong with her? Why did she always have to be responsible all the time? So what if she had a summer fling with a cute guy while she was on vacation. Why did she always have to over think everything? What difference would it make if she had some fun? People had summer romances all the time. Why shouldn't she?

With a long sigh, Carly let her gaze cross the water to the evergreens and jagged gray rocks on the shoreline that protected the cove. It was easy to see why, after witnessing the horrors of war, Claudette and Roger had fallen in love with this peaceful little corner of paradise.

All the roughhousing and warm sun had a soporific effect on the puppies. Collapsed in a pile of fur in a corner of their enclosure with their mom, the pups had stopped yipping so the only sounds were the occasional chattering of a disgruntled squirrel and birds twittering at each other in the trees.

Here Carly was in her mid-thirties wondering what to do with her life, no closer to feeling like she'd "made it"—whatever that meant—than she'd been when she graduated from college. Lily was facing the real prospect of her life being over sooner rather than later, and Karen had lost her husband Dave years ago. Life was so short. What was Carly going to do with the rest of hers?

Brent walked to the folding table next to the easel, leaned a canvas against it, and set the box of acrylics down with a thud. "Here's the paint. I'll go get the easel."

Carly strode three steps to him and jumped into his arms, knocking him off balance. He stumbled and grabbed her around the waist to keep both of them from tumbling onto the grass. "What are you doing?"

"Giving you a big huggy wug."

"I noticed." He peeled her arms from him. "I thought you were figuring out your life, and I'm too available or something."

"I am and you are." A disturbing thought popped into Carly's head. "You're not attracted to Ginger, are you?"

"What? Now I'm not only too available, but I'm hitting on your friends as well?" He stepped over to the table, picked up his paintbrush, and pointed it at her. "I thought you wanted to paint. How about less hugging and more painting? I suggest a lot more painting, preferably in silence."

Carly put her hand on his arm. "I'm sorry. What I meant is that you've been so nice to us and the puppies. You've been incredibly kind, and I think Ginger has the hots for you. I was curious if the feeling was mutual."

"Why would you think that?"

"Historically speaking, men have a habit of falling all over themselves about Ginger and Lily. Not me."

"What about the Captain?"

"He was rejected by them first. Maybe he was getting desperate for a date. I didn't want to know, so I didn't ask a whole lot of questions." Carly waved her hands. "I don't want to think about him. What I was saying is that as usual, I've worried about everyone else. I like you. You like me—or you did. We're on vacation, so why not have a little fun?"

Brent gave her a half smile. "You really thought I'd be interested in Ginger? The woman is married and is always comparing me to her kids. Talk about not sexy."

"Well, you *are* a lot younger than we are."

"Sure, but I'm not in junior high school. You and your friends are all so hung up on age. It's bizarre. You grew up in the seventies like I did. It was just a few years earlier. We probably even had some of the same toys as kids. Every girl in my first-grade class wanted a Barbie Dream House. I bet you had one, didn't you?"

Carly laughed. "No, although I *really* wanted one. The Christmas I turned seven, I got the Barbie styling head and by New Year's I'd chopped off all her hair. Mom was furious. The fun's over when Barbie is bald."

"When I was seven, I got a Sit and Spin, which should really be called the swirl and hurl."

"I wanted one of those so bad! The commercials made it look amazing. I wanted a Hippity Hop too."

"My neighbor Joey had one of those, which was more or less the bounce and barf. And a Big Wheel, which was all about driving over ramps, wiping out, crying, and the occasional bout of vomiting."

"I'm sensing a theme here." Carly pulled some paints out of the box and set them on the table. "Did you have any artsy toys or any toys that didn't cause you to lose your cookies?"

"I wanted Super Elastic Bubble Plastic, but after I tried to perform surgery on Stretch Armstrong, my parents refused to get it for me."

"Ouch. Poor Stretch."

"He's probably hanging out with bald Barbie heads in toy purgatory, searching for his missing body parts."

"Did you have Spirograph or Etch A Sketch? Those were artsy."

"Nope. But my parents did go for some electronic games like handheld football and Simon."

Carly held up a paintbrush. "I remember Simon! Even the commercials were annoying!"

"It's a great way to start fights with your friends and get beat up. Rock'em Sock'em Robots weren't great for keeping the seven-year-old peace either." Brent smiled. "Did you have a Lite Brite?"

"I did and I loved it, although our dog ate some of the little pegs. He also ate a bunch of the plastic cherries from our Hi Ho Cherry-O game. When he got into the fakey cakey mix from the Easy-Bake Oven, it was a mess." She waved her paintbrush. "And let's not even talk about the time he got into the jar of Tang. That was one disgusting orange disaster."

"I'll bet, although I confess that one of my big regrets is that I never got to drink Tang as a kid. Maybe if I had, I'd be an astronaut now."

"Well, being an artist is pretty amazing. And every kid drank Tang in the seventies. What were you drinking instead?"

"Strawberry Nestle Quik, which was even more disgusting than Tang. My grandmother always insisted that I should drink the pink cow, or *vache rose*, as she referred to it. Maybe she liked that scary shade of radiant magenta. I don't know."

"Or she thought it matched the ugly painting well." Carly stepped closer to him and reached up to put her arms around his neck. "You know what? You're right. Age doesn't matter. And you may be too available, but you're also incredibly sexy."

"Well that's better." He pulled her close and kissed her. "So about that fun you were talking about. What did you have in mind?"

"I'm not sure, but definitely something less nausea-inducing than the swirl and hurl."

"Then I suggest no Tang or *vache rose* either."

Chapter 9

Still Smiling

By the time Carly returned to the house, she was feeling sappy and gooey about her summer romance. The chatting and painting with Brent had been so easy and enjoyable, and the hours flew by while she created another ugly flower painting to add to the cabin's bizarro art collection.

Brent added an image of her into his painting of the puppies by the lake. She was sitting cross-legged on the grass and obviously laughing at silly puppy antics. No one had ever put Carly in a painting, and her heart melted when she saw it. Being an unbelievably talented artist, he'd somehow managed to make her look prettier than she really was. The rendering looked like her, but a happier and more relaxed version than the person she saw in the mirror every morning.

During dinner Lily and Ginger made a lot of comments about her "afternoon with Monet," but Carly brushed them off, changing the subject to Ginger's children or the latest travails Lily had with one of her coworkers. Eventually Carly would have to tell them about her little fling, but for the time being, she wanted it to remain her secret.

The next morning, the women were sitting around the kitchen table when the phone rang, startling them out of their early-morning stupor. No one had heard the sound of the telephone for so long that Ginger jumped and almost fell off her chair.

Karen ran to the counter to answer it. "Yes, she's here. Is everything okay? All right, just a minute."

Karen waved at Carly. "It's the boarding kennel. And before you ask, yes, Trixie is fine."

Carly greeted Kat, who said, "I have a favor to ask you. If you can't, it's okay, but you mentioned you might want to take Trixie for the day, didn't you?"

"Yes, I'd like to take her for a hike."

"We have a little water problem here, so if you'd like to take her sooner, rather than later, I'd really appreciate it. I'll deduct the time off your bill."

"What happened?"

"Something is going on with our well. It's possible the pump has committed suicide. The fewer dogs we have here needing water and barking at plumbers, the better. If you can keep her for the day or, even better, today and tonight, I'm hoping the water situation will be resolved."

"I'll check and see if our neighbor can keep her overnight with the puppies, but I can definitely take her out today. I'll be by as soon as I get dressed." Carly hung up the phone. "Who has puppy duty this morning?"

"Me," Ginger said.

"Could you ask Brent if I can stop by there with Trixie in a couple of hours? I'd love to see what she thinks of the puppies and find out if she and Ripley get along. Maybe we can go hiking with both dogs."

Karen said, "Ripley would probably like that. She's probably tired of being cooped up with the pups. Oh, and don't forget to ask Kat about the puppy adoption person, Brigid. As far as I know, she still hasn't gotten back to us."

Carly gave her sister a mock salute. "I'm on it."

The drive out to the kennel was peaceful and sunny. Mid-June in Alpine Grove was glorious. The deciduous trees still had that bright-green freshly leafed look of spring, since the heat of summer hadn't set in yet. Carly let her mind wander back to painting with Brent. He was incredibly easy to talk to. Or maybe he simply listened well. She'd gone on and on about trivial details from her life and the consultants she worked with, which was probably boring, but he didn't seem to mind.

When Carly pulled up to the kennels, Kat was standing outside with her friend, Maria, a stout man clad in navy blue work clothes, and the gigantic dog, Linus. The man glanced at Carly's car, tugged his baseball hat further down on his forehead, and sauntered off.

Carly walked over to Kat and Maria, who both were decidedly orange. Did they know that? Maybe they'd used some kind of self-tanning lotion.

Kat said, "Thanks for coming by. Trixie will be thrilled to see you again so soon."

Carly rubbed at her jawline with her fingertips.

Maria put her hand on her hip. "I know what you're thinking, and you don't have to make that scrunchy face. We've got mirrors and we know we're orange. I blame the carrots."

"What carrots?" Carly asked.

"The ones we put on our face," Kat said. "There was a chemical reaction, I think. I'm not sure exactly. Maybe we did something wrong."

"Having no water didn't help. I still feel crusty," Maria scratched at her neck and examined her fingernails. "I knew we should have done the face mask at my apartment."

"You know I can't leave the dogs," Kat said. "I have responsibilities here and about a thousand things I have to do."

Carly had no interest in getting in the middle of what appeared to be an escalating argument between the orange-tinted people. "I'll take Trixie off your hands, so you'll have one less responsibility."

Kat gestured toward the kennel. "Follow me. Thanks for coming so quickly. I need to monitor what that well guy is up to. I can practically feel colossal sums of money flowing out of here like a waterfall."

Kat leashed Trixie, who, as predicted, was thrilled to see Carly, leaping around her kennel as gracefully as her rotund body would allow.

They went back outside, and Maria pointed at the man. "Why is it that plumbers can't find pants that fit? Even outdoorsy plumbers have no sense of decency. I don't need to see that hind-end view."

Carly giggled. "What is he doing?"

"I don't know, but I'm sure it's expensive," Kat grumbled. "I keep thinking that everything that can fall apart has already fallen apart, but then the house proves me wrong."

"I imagine when houses get to be a certain age, things start to wear out," Carly said. "The house I lived in with... oh never mind."

Maria raised her eyebrows. "Well, now you've piqued my interest. Are you living with someone or not?"

Carly shook her head. "I lived with someone for fifteen years, but we broke up recently. I still think of the house as mine, and I was going to say that it was new, so it didn't have enough time to fall apart."

"Lucky you," Kat said. "This place was built years ago and then not kept up particularly well. I loved my aunt, but since I inherited this house, I've learned she wasn't big into home maintenance."

"That's an understatement," Maria said with a snort. "Oh, and don't worry about that breakup. Now that you've boarded a dog here, you are destined to find love. Or at least sex."

Kat handed the leash to Carly with a theatrical sigh. "Oh please. Not this again."

Carly looked from Kat to Maria. Was it possible that someone had told them about Brent? Karen said that gossip raced through Alpine Grove like wildfire, but no one even knew, so this seemed a little extreme. "I'm not in love, but the next-door neighbor out at the lake has been very kind about taking care of the puppies for us. He's an artist, and I'm hoping that he'll take a break to go on the hike with me and Trixie."

"Told ya." Maria gave Kat a self-satisfied smile. "I *knew* it."

"You need to get over this thing," Kat said. "Or get a dog, if you're so worried about it."

"It's not a *thing*, girlfriend. It's inequality." Maria pointed her index finger at Kat's nose. "I'm outraged that you continue to discriminate against cats. It's just plain wrong. Why should I be excluded from love because I'm a cat lady?"

The burgeoning argument was interrupted by a man walking up to the group with a large black-and-brown dog. Linus and the new dog did a little wagging dance that included a play bow, and they galloped off toward the trees together.

Kat said, "Hi Jack. This is Carly and Trixie. Carly, Jack Sheridan, our favorite local forester and his dog, Frank."

"Jack is the former tenant of my fine residence in town," Maria added. "Until he moved out because he met a woman who boarded a dog here."

Kat's lips tightened, but she apparently thought better of reigniting Maria's rant. Instead, she turned to Jack. "Thanks for returning Joel's tools. He'll be happy to hear you fixed that hole. Let us know if anything else falls apart at the Shack. Disrepair seems to be going around."

"It was a lot easier to fix with the jointer. I saw the guy over at the well head. Is the pump dead?" Jack asked.

"The jury is still out," Kat said. "All I know is that we have no water."

Carly was mesmerized by Jack's eyes. The unusual shade of turquoise blue reminded her of the color of an icy mountain lake. Something about his calm gaze made Carly uncomfortable, and she looked down at his work boots instead. The tan canvas pants he was wearing had an extraordinary number of pockets. What was he carrying around?

Jack turned his attention to Carly. "Cute dog."

Carly could feel her cheeks heat up. He'd figured out she'd been staring at him, and she tried not to visibly squirm. How embarrassing. "Trixie and I are planning to go for a hike."

"With her artist boyfriend," Maria said.

"He's not my boyfriend, but he is an artist, and so was his grandfather. In fact, he's got a bizarre old painting in the cabin that my friends think might date back to World War II."

"Have you talked to Jan, the librarian at the library in town? She loves researching stuff like that," Kat turned to Jack. "Carly is staying out at the lake."

Jack scratched at his scruffy wanna-be beard. "I was looking into the history of some tracts of forestland by the lake and Jan told me that there was a forestry lookout tower there. Now the place is called Make-Out Point or Make-Out Rock by the locals. But apparently, during World War II, people didn't use the tower to look for forest fires or to make out. They were watching for enemy planes."

Carly said, "My sister may have taken that hike, but she didn't say anything about a tower."

"The tower is long gone, so that might have been the hike," Jack said.

"Make-Out Point is near where you're staying, I think," Kat said. "Aren't you near Gray's Point?"

"Yes, Miriam Gray's tree is in the back yard. I bet Brent would know about the tower. His family has owned his cabin for generations." Carly said.

"When are you moving in?" Maria asked.

"What?" Carly said.

"It's only a matter of time." Maria gestured toward Jack. "His girlfriend boarded a dog here. Then he and Becca spent a long weekend together during a snowstorm, and the rest is history."

Kat grumbled, "Would you let it go?"

Carly wasn't sure what the whole cat-versus-dog argument was about, but tempers definitely seemed to be running a little short. Time to move on. "I guess Trixie and I will be going now. Good luck with the well."

"Thanks," Kat said.

"Good luck with the new man," Maria said to Carly. "Not that you'll need it."

With an amused half-smile, Jack said, "Have a nice hike."

~

After Carly left, Maria announced that she wanted a shower, and she went home. Because a shower wouldn't be an option until the well problem was diagnosed, Kat walked the dogs instead. Afterward she was settling into lunch when the phone rang.

She greeted Joel with a smile. The first time she'd spoken to him on the telephone, she'd thought he should be a radio announcer with his fabulous voice, and her opinion hadn't changed since then. "Where are you?" she asked.

"Still at the airport. My flight is delayed, so getting here early was a big waste of time. How are you?"

"Orange."

"What?"

"Maria and I had a skin-care failure. Did you ever see the film "Willy Wonka and the Chocolate Factory"?

"I think so."

"Remember how the Oompa-Loompas had orange skin?"

"That must be, uh, interesting. You don't have green hair, do you?"

"Thankfully no, but when I look in the mirror, the impression is Oompa-Loompa-ish."

"You're a little taller though."

"Thanks. I feel pretty now. But that's not the worst thing."

He paused. "Something fell apart?"

"Bingo. And I *knew* this would happen. It's like the house knows the moment you set foot off this property. This time it's the well. We have no water. And I'm going to remain orange until the plumber figures it out or I get up the nerve to go next door and beg Mia to use her bathroom."

"And I thought sitting in the airport was bad. It's fun to watch the birds though."

"Why are there are birds at LAX?"

"I don't know. Maybe no one can catch them. They seem to be having a good time up there."

"By the way, Jack stopped by to return the thingie."

"The jointer?"

"Yeah, that." Kat traced her finger through the dust on the table. She blamed the dust on the dogs and the inevitable filth of rural living, but the fact was she wasn't much of a housekeeper either. The sight of this much dust would give her mother a heart attack, but not before she'd whipped out a can of Pledge. Kat drew an exclamation point in the dust. "By the way, your sister called. She wants you to look at her car."

"I thought she had a new one. Or new to her, anyway."

"I can't remember. They all start with M. She had Myrtle and she told me about one named Mabel too, I think. This one is Millie, and it's making a funny noise"

"Well, there's nothing I can do about Millie from Milwaukee."

"I told her that, but she's still pissed off."

"So what's new?"

Kat swirled a frownie face into the dust. Joel had taken care of his sister Cindy after their parents died in a car accident, and their sibling relationship was contentious at best. "I hope you'll be careful. I miss you."

"I'm in an airport, so I think I'm safe for the time being."

"I know, but the last time you went somewhere was when your aunt was sick. You had a concussion and I thought you were going to die."

"This time my nephew isn't around for me to trip over."

"Cindy says Johnny has gotten over his fireman phase. She couldn't take the screaming anymore and told him he's no longer allowed to pretend to drive anything that has a siren."

"Guess that means ambulance driver and cop are both out." Joel paused and Kat could hear the gate announcement for a United Airlines flight that was boarding. He continued, "Did Cindy say something to upset you?"

"Not really."

"Is it the water problem? I'm sure Ron will figure it out."

"Yeah, he's working on it. Carly asked me about taking Trixie for a hike and I called her to encourage her to do that today. I kind of feel like a loser for asking someone to take her dog back."

"Did she mind?"

"Not at all. She came right out and took Trixie. But Maria was getting all over my case about boarding cats. She kept telling Carly she would fall in love because Trixie is staying here. Poor Carly mentioned some neighbor who is helping with the puppies they found and then Maria started ranting. It was embarrassing."

"You should be used to that by now."

"I know, but I feel bad because I got pissed off at Maria. I'm orange, and I wasn't in the mood." Kat put her elbow on the table and placed her chin on her palm. "It's been a really long morning, and I miss you."

"I miss you too."

"It's so unfair. I mean, what terrible water demon have I offended? That well has probably lasted thirty years. Couldn't it wait one more week before crapping out?"

"Whoa, low-flying bird!"

"What? Are you okay?"

"Yeah, people are scattering, but the bird scored a direct hit on someone at Gate 22A. She's not happy about it."

"You don't expect a bird to take a dump on you when you're waiting for your flight."

Joel chuckled. "Life is full of surprises."

"Tell me about it." Kat paused, wondering if she should broach a delicate subject. "So do you have a few minutes before your flight?"

"According to the monitor flashing 'delayed' in big red letters, I have a lot of minutes."

"Okay, well, Cindy asked me something and I didn't know what to say, and I think I may have said something dumb."

"Are you saying she's mad at you too?"

Kat gazed down at Linus, made a face, and nodded vigorously. "I'm thinking yes, because she hung up on me."

"Welcome to my world."

Linus plopped his huge muzzle in Kat's lap and she rubbed his large brown ears. "I guess she was talking to one of her clients, who told her that she should be saving for

Johnny's college education. There's some new type of college saving account and her friend says she should set one up. So she was asking me about beneficiaries and stuff like that."

"We're in line to take care of Johnny if something happens to her. It makes sense that she'd ask us to be beneficiaries for this too."

"Without thinking, I said it was fine, but maybe she'd want his father to be the beneficiary instead. She yelled a string of bad words at me and hung up. I know you said Johnny's dad is out of the picture, but she totally lost it."

"I've learned to avoid that topic."

"What happened to the guy? She made it sound like he's still alive, although she'd like to kill him."

"Remember how I said your family didn't have a monopoly on running away and unplanned pregnancy?"

"Yes."

"Cindy took running away to a new level. She kept running away from our apartment in LA to Alpine Grove. I'd come up and drag her back. It was kind of crazy for a while. I spent so much time chasing after her, in retrospect I'm surprised I didn't get fired from my job."

"So she was meeting someone here?"

"Evidently. I never found out who it was, only that it was some guy in Alpine Grove. She'd steal money from me, grab a bus, and stay at the H12 motel. That's how I met Annette and Jon. They were nice about calling me and letting me know she was there again."

"How did it end?"

"Something happened, I guess. She wouldn't talk about it, and then several months later, she found out she was pregnant. When she turned eighteen, she took the insurance

settlement money from the car accident and bought her house in Alpine Grove."

"Her place is cute. Was it another dump that you spent a decade fixing up?"

"No, when I came up on weekends, I worked on my own place. I probably told you before, but when I bought it, The Shack was almost literally a shack. Making it livable took up all my time."

"It sounds like The Shack gave Chez Stinky a run for its money. Cindy must have gotten a killer deal on that cottage. It's adorable."

"Real estate was a lot cheaper then."

"Everything was. Anyway, I'm sorry I made Cindy angry. Maybe once you come back we can invite her and Johnny over for dinner or something."

"Do we have to?"

"She's your sister."

"Yeah." He sighed audibly. "Okay, the angry red letters are saying it's time to board now. I'll call you tonight from my hotel. I love you."

"I love you back. Fly safely."

∿

By the time Carly got to Brent's cabin, she had shaken off the residue of the tense interpersonal dynamics at the kennel. Being on vacation at the lake was so relaxing, it had been jarring to contend with people dealing with real life. Staying on vacation forever had a lot of appeal, even if it wasn't a financially viable life choice.

She unloaded Trixie from the car. The dog sniffed furiously at the green grass and did her best sled-dog imitation, yanking

Carly toward the lake and the puppy fence. The enclosure was empty, but Trixie was enthralled with the canine scents and dragged Carly around the perimeter sniffing audibly.

The door to the house opened and Brent and Ginger stepped out onto the deck. He was clad in a pair of well-used canvas shorts, clunky hiking boots, and a ratty t-shirt that had *Yosemite* printed on it. Perhaps Brent was more of a hiker than Carly had realized. Hmm.

Ginger laughed, lightly placed her hand on Brent's shoulder, and leaned toward him as if she were telling him a dirty secret. "You don't know this, but normally that dog is a slug—I'm talking a total couch potato. I don't what's gotten into her."

Carly's mouth opened then snapped shut as her mind flashed back to 1980. Reagan had been president and Ginger had been pulling those flirty moves on Nathan. Quite successfully in fact, given that they got married about five minutes after graduation. The poor guy had practically drooled whenever she was nearby. Ever-so-earnest, boring Carly, who was blessed with zero flirting skills, had been completely invisible by comparison.

Brent seemed unaware of Ginger's touchy-feely efforts and waved to Carly. "You ready to go for a hike?"

Carly tamped down her irritation and dragged Trixie away from the enticing puppy scents. "A guy at the kennel said there's a trail that goes to a rock where there was an old forestry tower. I'm wondering if it's the trail Karen hiked the other day."

Brent held out his hand to let Trixie sniff it. "The tower was old and rickety when I was a kid. Now it's long gone, but the view is still incredible."

"I'm not in the greatest shape." Carly nodded at Trixie. "Neither is she."

"We'll go slow." Brent gestured toward Ginger. "I'm going to go grab Ripley. You'll keep an eye on the puppies, right?"

Ginger agreed to the request, but Carly could tell she was disappointed that she was being ditched. How could Brent be so completely clueless?

Ginger followed Brent inside while Carly waited on the deck with Trixie. She crouched next to her dog. "Did you see that? Ginger was practically throwing herself at him. It was beyond flirty wirty. Didn't you think it was totally over the top?"

Trixie wagged, but didn't seem to have any other input on the matter. Brent opened the door and came back outside with Ripley, who was sporting her pretty new collar and leash.

Ripley glared at Trixie, who wagged tentatively. Ripley made a low growly noise and Brent said, "Hey, be nice. She's a guest."

Carly sighed. "Maybe this wasn't such a great idea. I don't think they like each other."

"They're on leashes, so it should be fine. Let's ignore them and see if they get used to each other. The trail is this way." Brent turned and strode off toward the driveway.

Carly followed, noting Brent's rather well-defined leg muscles. "How far away is it?"

"We need to go up to the road, then down a little ways. The trail crosses the old Thurston property and goes up into the National Forest."

"Won't the owners mind?"

"The Thurston family has let people use the trail forever. I'm not sure who actually owns the land anymore, but people have been hiking the trail for fifty or sixty years, so I don't think we need to worry about it." He reached to take her hand. "C'mon. Let's live dangerously."

Carly couldn't help smiling. It was silly, but she was thrilled that Brent was holding her hand. Maybe he was serious and truly was interested in her, and not Ginger. That would be a switch.

The dogs settled into a placid walk next to the humans and the group strolled up the driveway and onto the road. They walked past a few more driveways that presumably led to cabins nestled deep in the trees. At the end of the pavement, Brent said, "The trail goes this way."

They walked down a sun-dappled trail that ended at a massive rock outcropping. As Brent encouraged Ripley to start climbing up the first boulder, Carly recalled that Karen had mentioned the trail was somewhat challenging. Uh oh.

After a little coaxing, Ripley was up for the rock-climbing game, but Trixie was less enthusiastic. Carly climbed up and tried to pull Trixie up behind her. Brent climbed back down. "Maybe she needs a little boost."

He lifted up the dog and placed her on top of the rock. "I promise it's worth it."

"It better be."

They traversed the well-worn path through the rocky crags, which involved a lot more uphill activity than Carly or her dog were physically prepared to manage, so they took quite a few rest breaks.

Brent kept repeating that in the end, they'd be glad they made the climb. When they finally reached the top, Carly was gasping for breath. Brent moved aside so she could slip through the last craggy pass.

Carly stepped out onto a flat granite slab that jutted out over the lake several hundred feet above the water. She gripped the leash more tightly and yanked Trixie closer to her. "Oh my God!"

Brent put his arm around her. "I guess I should have asked if you're afraid of heights."

"Yes…no…well, not really." Carly took a deep breath, willing her heart rate to settle back down to a more normal pace. "This view is amazing."

"I've spent hours and hours up here, trying to figure out my life. I don't suggest that you try it right now, but I like to sit on the edge and look at the water."

"I think Trixie and I will stay back here *away* from the edge." Carly moved over to one side and sat on a rock that was shaped sort of like a chair. "This is good."

"Most people stop here, but the trail does keep going over to where the tower used to be. There's a pretty clearing."

"I'd like to rest for a few minutes. But I believe you now. Seeing the lake from this vantage point is worth it."

Brent sat next to her and Ripley settled in at his feet. "I told you."

"So what did you figure out when you were up here?"

"Lots of things." He leaned back against the rock and cast his gaze across the lake. "Looking out at the expanse of trees and water makes a guy contemplative."

"About what?"

He glanced at her. "My, aren't you curious."

"I am. You can't talk about figuring out your life to a woman who has no idea what to do with hers and not expect a little asky wasky to happen."

"Asky wasky?"

"What did you decide?"

"Well, one of the times I spent a lot of time up here was the summer after I graduated from high school, when I visited my grandparents."

"That must have been nice."

"At the time I wasn't doing well in school and wanted to get away. I'd barely graduated, and my parents were furious that I wasn't 'applying myself' and hadn't bothered trying to get into college. My father and I are like oil and water, which didn't help. It may be the family cabin, but Dad and I haven't been here at the same time since about 1978."

"That's a long time ago. You were what…nine or ten?"

"After that, he got into politics and he worked all the time. When he wasn't yelling at me for being a screw up, that is."

"Your father is a politician?"

"He's all about reducing taxes." Brent shrugged. "I was never clear how slashing programs and eliminating funding would help me get the education he was so desperate for me to focus on."

Carly put her hand on his. "I get the impression you're not quite over this, are you?"

"I suppose not. I'm a perpetual disappointment to him. We're never going to like each other, and holidays with family have been awkward since my grandmother died. The last few years I've managed to figure out ways to be on the road during the holidays."

"What about your mom?"

"It's politically expedient for my parents to remain married, but she got a job in New York, so they don't spend much time together. I rarely see Mom, except when I have shows in the city."

"Are you kidding me?" Carly turned to stare into his face. "Your paintings were in New York exhibitions? That is *such* a big deal. Are you saying your father doesn't think so?"

"He's not big into art." Brent stood up. "So are you ready to see where the tower was? It's an easy walk."

Carly looked down at Trixie. "What do you think? Easy sounds promising. Can you make it, girl?"

Trixie mustered to wag the tip of her tail, which Carly took as an affirmative.

~

Carly stood and stared out at the panoramic lake and mountain landscape for a moment, drinking in the view. It was like a postcard. The lake was enormous, and the blue water seemed to go on forever, the expanse interrupted only by a few small green islands. On the shoreline, outcroppings of granite jutted out toward the water. Interspersed among the swaths of forest were a few clearings that contained expensive lake homes like the place Carly was staying. Small cabins like Brent's were more difficult to spot in the dense trees.

Brent and Ripley started down the path, and Carly and Trixie followed them as they strolled along a narrow, tree-shaded pathway that curved away from the massive rocks along the ridge. Carly called from behind, "The trees up here are all leaning."

Brent looked over his shoulder. "That's probably from the wind and snow."

"Have you ever been here in the winter?"

"The cabin isn't winterized, but I've stayed in Alpine Grove a few times."

"It must be beautiful with the snow. Like *It's a Wonderful Life*, with people huddled together holding mittened hands, walking through the flurries down the main street and shopping for gifts."

"You like Christmas movies a lot, don't you?"

"I love everything about the holiday season. Don't you?"

"I think holidays at my house weren't quite as Currier and Ives as yours." As the trail widened, Brent slowed so Carly could walk alongside him. He shrugged. "The last couple years, I've spent Christmas Eve in New York with my mother. I meet Mom at Rockefeller Center, we watch the ice skaters for a little while, and go out to dinner. Then I fly home the next morning. There are lots of flights available if you travel on Christmas day."

Carly thought that except for the ice skaters, it sounded a little sad, but kept the sentiment to herself. "I just remembered today is Father's Day. Did you send your dad a card?"

"Nope." Brent stopped and pulled Ripley around. "Did you?"

"Of course! I can't believe you didn't."

"I already told you I have a not-so-great relationship with my dad. In addition to thinking I'm a slacker artist, he's hated pretty much every girlfriend I've ever had." He raised his eyebrows at her. "Happy now?"

"Not really, but I am curious about the girlfriends." Carly tugged Trixie away from a particularly exciting shrub. "After we met you, there was lots of speculation on your relationship status. Ginger said she pried the fact that you're unattached out of you. I would have loved to be a fly on that wall."

"It was an annoying conversation."

"She called you *reserved*. I thought it was an odd thing to say, because you've always seemed pretty talkative to me."

"I don't talk to your friends as much as I do to you."

Carly stopped to wait for Trixie. "How come?"

He paused to observe Trixie's complicated sniffing routine. "You're easier to talk to, I guess."

"That's the nice way of saying I'm nosy, isn't it?"

"No, it's not that exactly. Ginger always seems like she wants something. And Lily makes me feel like I'm being cross-examined. Your sister seems kind of distracted, like she's thinking about something else."

Carly resumed walking. "What about me?"

"You act like you're interested in what I'm saying. You have this way of focusing all your attention when you listen." He shrugged. "I'm not explaining this well, but it's unusual."

Carly's cheeks were warm and it wasn't only from the exercise. That had to be one of the nicest things anyone had ever said to her. "I'm not sure what to say, other than thank you. And I truly *am* interested in what you're saying."

The trees along the trail thinned, revealing a clearing with a large, square concrete slab in the middle. Carly walked up to the edge and turned to face the lake. The view was mostly obscured by trees. She gestured toward the water. "I bet from the top of the tower, you were able to see for miles."

"It was cool, although also probably dangerous, since it was falling apart."

Carly left the slab and walked toward the tree line so she could get a better view of the lake. "Hey, people have carved their initials into a tree over here."

"They're on a lot of the trees."

Carly moved to examine another pine. "This one says TS plus RC. That's so sweet."

"They don't call it Make-Out Point for nothing."

"I thought it was Make-Out Rock."

"Depends on who you ask." Brent grinned. "The make-out part is always consistent though."

Carly walked around examining the carvings. Some of them were obviously old, and a few even included dates. "Check it out. This one is from 1975!"

"I've never really spent much time looking at these before." Brent ran his hand across a trunk. "This one says *La Joconde a le sourire*. That's strange."

"Maybe some French tourists stopped by to make out." Carly giggled. "Oooh, la, la. Amour."

"It's possible tourists carved it, but maybe not. It's something my grandparents used to say to each other."

"What does it mean?"

"The Mona Lisa is still smiling." He traced a fingertip across the letters carved into the wood. "It was like an inside joke with them, I think. One or the other would say that phrase and then they'd both laugh."

"How come?"

"I have no idea. They never told me what was so funny."

"They *must* have been the ones who carved it into the tree, then." Carly moved to stand beside him. "How wonderful that you've found a piece of your family history up here."

"Knowing my grandmother, it might relate to some dirty joke." He chuckled. "I was a little kid, so maybe they didn't want me to hear the x-rated explanation."

Carly turned to face him. "When do you think they might have come up here? The carving looks old."

He pulled her close, passing Ripley's leash to his other hand and lifting her arms up around his neck. He slid his hands to her back and dipped his head to kiss her collarbone. When he moved to kiss her lips, Carly's last rational thought was that Brent was all kinds of hot and she yanked him closer. She stepped backward, stumbling over Ripley, who barked once in annoyance, but got out of the way. Carly pulled Brent toward her so her back was pressed against the tree. Her hands moved from his neck to his chest, running her palms under his t-shirt. She leaned her head back, so she could see his face. "I'm starting to get a much better understanding of the make-out aspect of this place."

Brent laughed. "I told you so."

A pleasurable few minutes later, Carly felt Trixie tug on the leash and looked down. "Did you need something? I'm sorry, but I was busy."

Brent groaned and took a step back. "Maybe we should get out of here before we end up rolling around on the grass with a canine audience."

"That sounds uncomfortable." Carly grabbed the front of his shirt and pulled him close again. "But I'd like to pick up where we left off. Indoors. Behind a door. And without an audience."

He grinned. "For you, that's a downright decisive statement."

"I'm inspired."

"Hiking is a lot faster going downhill."

Carly grabbed his hand. "Let's go."

They followed the trail back to the overlook and made their way down the rocky incline. Carly felt like her hormones were helping to propel her down the hill. Something about how Brent felt was irresistible, and she wanted to spend more time touching him. Lots more. It was past time to get this summer romance in gear.

By the time they made it down to the road, Carly was exhausted. It was unlikely she'd be able to move the next day. Every muscle was screaming from the exertion, and she couldn't wait to get her aching feet out of her shoes.

Brent said, "I have to say, going to Make-Out Rock with you is a whole lot more fun than going by myself."

Carly giggled and before she could think up a suitable reply, she was on the ground sitting on the leash. "Ouch. What did I do?"

Brent crouched down next to her. "You went sideways. Did you step wrong on that rock?"

"Maybe. I think I twisted my ankle."

Brent stood and held out both hands to her. "Can you walk?"

Carly grabbed his hands and let him pull her up. "I think so. Before I landed on my butt, I was thinking that when I went out the kennel, I forgot to ask Kat about her friend who will help us find the puppies new homes."

"Well, you have other things to worry about right now. Let's get back to my place and put some ice on that ankle. Maybe Karen can take a look at it."

"She's a vet."

"Close enough. She can probably tell if a bone is broken in a human too."

"I'm sure it's not broken. I can't believe we hiked over all those huge boulders and I managed to trip on the road."

Brent put his arm around her shoulder. "Come on, Hop-a-long. We're almost there."

She put her arm around his waist. "Even if I'm wounded, it was still worth it."

"I agree."

Chapter 10

Secret Poker

When Carly hobbled into the cabin, the puppies initiated a chorus of barking and yipping. Ripley ran around Carly to get to her offspring, followed by Trixie, who seemed to want to know what all the fuss was about.

Holding Brent's hand for support, Carly stepped over the plywood and entered the kitchen. Lily and Ginger were sitting at the table playing cards and supervising the puppies, who were milling around the two adult dogs.

Lily glanced up from her hand. "What happened to you?"

"I tripped and twisted my ankle," Carly said, letting go of Brent's hand. "It's no big deal."

Ginger narrowed her eyes. "How was the hike?"

"Great," Carly said a little too quickly. "The overlook is amazing, and then we went a little farther down the trail where there used to be a tower. The trees had carvings in them."

Ginger turned her attention to Brent. "Did you enjoy it?"

"I've been there many times," he replied.

Carly pulled out a chair and sat down with a sigh of relief. "We might have found something Brent's grandparents carved in the tree. It's in French."

"What did it say?" Lily said.

Carly glanced at Brent and he volunteered, "*La Joconde a le sourire*, which means the Mona Lisa is still smiling."

Lily laid her hand of cards on the table. "You didn't tell us your grandparents were museum curators."

Carly touched Brent's forearm. "You said your grandmother was a member of the French Resistance, but she didn't work in a museum, did she?"

"No, neither of them did," Brent said. "What are you talking about?"

"When we were at the library, I read about that phrase. During World War II, curators removed the Mona Lisa from the Louvre and moved it around hiding places all over France. They sent messages over the BBC saying *La Joconde a le sourire*, which meant the painting had arrived safely at its new clandestine destination."

Ginger put down her cards and looked up at Brent. "Are you sure your grandparents weren't curators?"

"I doubt it. When they met, my grandmother was still in school and my grandfather was fighting in the war."

"Maybe they stole artwork," Lily said. "If Grandma was in the Resistance, who knows what they were into. The Mona Lisa could be a metaphor for other stolen art."

"I'm sure they didn't steal anything. It was some kind of inside joke with them." He walked to the sink, grabbed a glass, and filled it with water. "Everyone listened to the BBC back then."

"I think artwork was moved all over the place during the war," Ginger said. "Did you ever see that old Burt Lancaster movie called *The Train*? This bad Nazi guy is attempting to move stolen art masterpieces by train to Germany. Burt is a Resistance leader and there's this whole complicated plot where they reroute the train away from Germany and back to Paris, but no one can tell because they temporarily change all the train station signs so it seems like they're going to Germany. Supposedly it was based on a true story."

"Maybe your grandparents were smugglers," Lily said. "Lots of artwork stolen during the war is still missing, you know."

"I don't…" Carly said.

"Or…wait, even better, maybe grandpa forged some masterpieces. The weird painting is a ruse to throw people off the trail. What if he was a brilliant forgery artist? I mean, Monet's talent probably comes from somewhere." Lily smiled smugly as if she'd won over a jury. "And fencing paintings is how they got the money to buy a place on the lake. Mystery solved."

Brent placed his glass on the counter. "I've got to get to work."

As he left the kitchen, Carly went to stand up and make sure he was okay. She winced. "Ouch. I think my ankle is swelling up."

"Don't get up. I'll go make sure we didn't piss him off," Ginger said. "Way to be hypersensitive."

"Why don't you take off your shoes?" Lily said. "And I'll get you an ice pack."

"Thanks." Carly glanced over her shoulder at the doorway, worried that Brent was upset. His grandparents were important to him, and Lily had called them everything from art thieves to smugglers. "You don't really think they forged paintings, do you?"

Lily handed her a plastic bag filled with ice cubes. "I don't know. I'm simply speculating. There's a Nazi marking on the back of that ugly painting. We have to assume it was stolen by Germans. Maybe grandpa painted over it with acrylic on purpose, so it's not obvious that it's valuable."

"I don't know…" Carly began.

"Ginger will apologize." Lily started scooping up the cards from the table. "Honestly though, I wish she'd stop throwing herself at that guy."

"Do you think that's what she's doing?" Carly paused. She *hadn't* been imagining it. "I'm not sure he'd be interested in something like that."

"Something like *what*? Women? Wait. Do you know something I don't? While you were painting, did he tell you he's gay?"

"No, I mean having an affair. He might not be interested in Ginger, that's all. He mentioned that she's married."

"Well good for him." Lily thumped the deck of cards on edge to square them up. "But when Ginger sets her mind on something, or someone, she can be pretty persuasive. You saw what happened to Nathan. She had him wrapped around her dainty little pinkie. The poor guy was head over heels."

"I remember."

"I don't understand what she sees in Matisse anyway. Hasn't she already done the whole spoiled-rich-kid thing?"

"You think Brent is spoiled?" Carly shook her head. "I didn't get that impression. Mostly he strikes me as a kind person." She wasn't going to mention that he also was sexy and an exceptionally good kisser.

"You always think the best of people." Lily shuffled the cards. "Nathan was completely out of touch with reality. I mean, we all know that I was a debutante with a preppy high school boyfriend and all that, but Nathan flew first class to

Italy to visit his family every summer and sometimes twice a year. He lived in a mansion in some highfalutin' California zip code and his parents bought him whatever he wanted, including a convertible BMW for his sixteenth birthday."

"I never really thought about it. All I knew was that Nathan was gorgeous, and every male in his family went to Amherst. Oh, and that he was way, *way* out of my league."

"You didn't miss much back then. He's improved over time thanks to Ginger's influence. She loves him. I don't know what is wrong with her, chasing around after that artist. She's got kids, a house, a whole life with Nathan. They have a fight and now she wants to throw it all away? It's nuts. I'd give my eye-teeth for what she's got."

"You would?" Carly was surprised. Lily always seemed to revel in her career and her single independent status. This was new.

"Well, don't you ever think about having children?" Lily shuffled the cards, pulled one out of the stack, and held it up. "We're getting to be at that age when time's running out. At this point, Lady Luck isn't likely to smile on me in the offspring department."

"You haven't heard anything about the tests, have you?"

"It's Sunday, honey."

"Oh. Well, I'm sure everything will be fine. And you're not too old to have children if that's what you want."

"A date might be a good first step."

"Well, you don't even need that anymore. You can adopt or go to a sperm bank. Or something. You have a lot of options."

"Always looking on the bright side, aren't you? Well, maybe I'm an old-fashioned Kentucky girl, but I'd kind of like to have kids the traditional way."

Carly smiled across the table at her friend, "I know what you mean. I feel the same way."

~

Ginger managed to drag Brent back out from his studio. "You can work later. We need you. Playing cards is more fun with four people."

From the expression on his face, Carly was pretty sure he was irritated. If nothing else, she was sure he didn't want to play cards. She smiled weakly at him in silent apology.

Lily shuffled the cards like a Vegas dealer, with elaborate hand motions and flourishes. "The game is poker. Five-card draw. But we're not playing for money."

"Please don't say we're playing strip poker," Carly said. "Please, *no*."

"Nope. This is secret poker. You win a round, you get to ask everyone a question, and each person has to reveal a deep, dark secret."

Ginger laughed. "You people already know all my secrets."

"I doubt that," Lily retorted. "And I know you stink at cards, so this could be fun."

Brent caught Carly's eye and she moved her shoulders slightly to mutely indicate that she had no idea what Lily was up to.

"I'm confused," Carly said. "You're supposed to bet first, aren't you?"

"We've got thousands of poker chips here," Lily said. "But let's start with twenty. Take your chips and use them wisely."

"Even though they're not worth money, you can still use the chips to ante up," Lily said as she dealt the cards face down.

Everyone threw a chip into the pot and took up their cards. Carly examined her hand, which was pathetic. She made an effort not to whimper, but it was a sad lineup. No one would ever accuse her of having a good poker face either. She was doomed.

Lily said, "Carly, how many cards do you want?"

"Three." Carly discarded the worst of the worst and examined the replacements. She would have to bluff hard, or she'd be forced to reveal a whole lot of information she'd rather not share.

Somehow Carly bluffed her way into winning the hand. It was a miracle. But then Lily demanded that she come up with a question. Carly had nothing. "Um. I don't know."

"Oh, come on. Think, woman," Lily said. "What do you want to know? This is your big chance to embarrass us."

Carly didn't want to make anyone feel bad, and her mind was a blank.

Ginger said, "It's not the SATs, Carly. There's no wrong answer. Ask us something."

Carly finally blurted, "All right, all right. I've got one. What color panty wanties...or, wait...I guess I mean *underwear* do you have on today?"

"Thanks for clarifying," Brent said with a chuckle. "White."

Carly said, "Tighty whities?" and Brent gave her a half-smile in response.

"Shocker," Lily said. "Mine are pink."

Ginger pulled the waistband of her stretchy pants, looked down, and said, "Black and lacy, thank you very much."

Carly dealt, but apparently after only one round, everyone had figured out her bluffing tells and she lost egregiously.

Brent asked, "What 'As seen on TV' product do you secretly want to buy?"

Carly laughed. "Oh that's easy! I wanted a Bedazzler so bad when I was a kid."

"What's that?" he asked.

"Don't you remember? You could put plastic rhinestones and gems onto anything."

Brent fingered a poker chip. "Why would you want to do that?"

"Now I wouldn't. But what can I say? It was the seventies, and everything was glittery." Carly shrugged. "Maybe it was disco fever."

"Unlike Liberace over here, I wanted Ginsu knives." Lily said.

"Because who doesn't want to chop up tin cans?" Ginger said. "If you must know, I wanted a Chia Pet. I actually got one and found out that the furry plants don't grow as fast as they do on TV."

"Shocker," Brent retorted sarcastically, echoing Lily's phrase.

The next round ended with Ginger asking a question about imaginary friends. No one admitted to having one. Carly was glad Karen wasn't there to bring up the topic of

Carly's imaginary cat, Monroe. But that was different, wasn't it?

Lily won the next round and demanded to know about everyone's first kiss.

With a heavy sigh, Carly said, "Donny Childs in seventh grade. It was disgusting."

Ginger admitted to kissing her cousin Arnold when she was three. "I was precocious."

Brent said, "A girl named Joanne Glass. It was sweet."

The women cooed a collective "aww" so enthusiastically that Brent got up to get a glass of water in a largely unsuccessful effort to hide the fact that he was blushing.

Ginger won another round and asked, "If you could go back in time and erase one thing you said or did, what would it be?"

Carly had trouble deciding. She'd made so many mistakes, it was tough settling on only one. After going through a few what-if scenarios in her head, she answered, "I think I would have said no when Stuart asked me to move in with him."

"Interesting choice." Ginger got up, grabbed the puppy water bowl, and took it to the sink to refill it. "I thought for sure you'd say going out with him in the first place."

"No, because we would have been fine dating casually. It was only after we moved in together that I thought it meant we'd be together forever." Carly sighed. "Boy, was I naive."

"Fifteen years was a good run," Ginger offered as she sat back down. "Okay, what about you, Lily?"

Lily squirmed in her seat. "I made an error in judgment in college."

Carly said, "Oh, come on. That's lame. Everyone made errors in judgment then. What was the error?"

"I slept with Nathan." Lily said quietly.

"*My* Nathan?" Ginger demanded. "When?"

Lily mumbled, "That's not relevant," then took up the cards and shuffled them repeatedly.

Ginger pressed her lips together, apparently deciding that getting into details about past transgressions might not be wise at this point in time. She turned to Brent, "Well, what have you got, Monet?"

"I, um, I guess I wouldn't have said the things to my father that I did when he sent me off to school." He looked down at his cards and shook his head slightly, "I didn't want to go."

"Where did he send you?" Carly asked.

"London."

"Big hardship," Lily snapped as she dealt cards onto the table, "Okay. Moving on. Last round."

"Hey, this was *your* idea," Ginger said as she picked up her cards. "I need to get back to the house. Nathan is supposed to call. I need to be near the phone so I can have a long, long conversation with my husband."

Carly suspected there might have been some stealth cheating when Lily quickly won the next hand.

Lily slapped her cards on the table and demanded, "Have you ever fallen in love with someone you shouldn't have? Have you ever loved the wrong person?"

Carly said, "Yes. Duh. I think everyone is well aware of my mistake in that area."

Ginger stood up and threw her cards at Lily, "Well, after all these years, it sure looks like *I* fell in love with the wrong person, doesn't it?"

Lily exclaimed, "That's not what I meant." She pushed back her chair and followed Ginger out the door, leaving Brent and Carly sitting in the kitchen alone.

"Gee, that was fun." Carly gave him a feeble smile, "I suppose I should ask. How about you? Have you been unlucky in love?"

"I have, so I guess it's unanimous. That's why Dad was so intent on sending me to London."

"Where did you go to school?"

"Central Saint Martins, which is a big-deal school for art and design in Europe."

"I thought he wasn't into your art."

"He liked that idea more than me running off with my girlfriend. We thought we were Romeo and Juliet and played that Dire Straits song a million times on repeat."

"Aww, that's adorable."

"Not really. We were both mad at our parents and we both liked to draw. I can safely say that was the extent of what we had in common."

"It's something. And it's more than a lot of people have going for them."

"Mostly we had hormones going for us. We argued constantly. When we weren't having sex, we could barely hold a civil conversation."

"I suppose that might be a problem."

"At the time it would have killed me to admit it, but Dad did the right thing. Going to school in London was the best thing that could have happened to me."

Carly took his hand. "Sometimes things work out the way they're supposed to, I guess."

He squeezed her hand gently, "Maybe you should go see if your friends are okay."

"I hate to ask this, but could you take care of Trixie tonight without me? She's really tired from the hike, so she'll probably sleep the whole time."

"Sure. What's one more dog? I'll see you tomorrow."

∿

By the time Carly hobbled back to the house, Lily and Ginger had locked themselves in Ginger's bedroom and were hashing out college infidelities in emphatic, hushed whispers. So much for consoling her friends.

She hopped over to the table and sat with Karen, who lifted her wine glass toward the ceiling. "What is going on with them? Why did those two women storm through here without even saying hello to me? And why are you hopping?"

"I twisted my ankle. And it turns out Lily slept with Nathan."

"You mean Ginger's husband? When?"

"That's him. It was in college, and now all these years later, Lily inexplicably decided to spill the beanie weanies."

"Wow." Karen set down her glass. "I might be the only one actually relaxing on this vacation."

"Hanging out reading books is a good idea. I should read more." Carly paused. She hadn't been reading because she'd been painting and hiking with Brent, which hadn't exactly been much of a hardship.

Karen pointed at Carly's foot. "Are you sure your ankle is okay? Did you put ice on it?"

"I did and it's fine." Carly set her elbows on the table and rested her chin in her hands. "Friendships are so tricky. I mean, you know I love Lily and Ginger, but there's so much history with us. And then they were grilling Brent about his family. You know how Lily can get."

"Like a lawyer?"

"Exactly. They ambushed the poor guy. It got so bad he left the room."

"How did you feel?"

"Me? What does that matter? I was worried about him. He has all these great memories of his grandparents and then Lily and Ginger started going on about how they might have been art thieves or forgers."

"Maybe they were. You don't know much about him or his family."

"Anything's possible I suppose, but I don't think so. From his description, it doesn't seem likely."

Karen shook her head. "You never know. People can surprise you."

"I think Lily asked a question about loving the wrong person to get Ginger to confess to having the hots for Brent. But it didn't work out too well."

"This must have been some conversation."

"We played secret poker, so revealing secrets is part of the game. Like Truth or Dare, minus the dare."

Karen sipped her wine. "I'm glad I missed it."

"Me too. You would have called me on one of my answers."

"Are you admitting that you cheated? You *never* cheat."

Carly rested her foot on the chair next to her. "It was more like I opted for a narrow interpretation of the question."

They chatted about the adventures of Carly's imaginary cat, Monroe, while Karen microwaved some leftovers. After they ate, Karen stood up and put her hand on Carly's shoulder. "It sounds like it was a rough evening. Are you sure you're okay?"

Carly reached up and patted Karen's hand. "I'm fine. And now I know I wasn't getting anywhere near as much action in college as everyone else was."

Karen laughed. "See you in the morning."

When she woke up, Carly was acutely aware that her ankle remained displeased about the hiking mishap the day before. Nobody was ever going to confuse her with an athlete, that was for sure.

After hopping her way through her morning routine, she carefully went downstairs and slowly made her way to Brent's cabin. With any luck he'd be awake, and Trixie had behaved herself overnight.

When Carly arrived at the clearing behind the cabin, she was greeted by a whole lot of barking and yipping. Six dogs could really make a racket. Brent had already relocated the puppies to their outdoor pen and the musketeers fell over each other with glee at the sight of her. Even though it was deafening, it was nice having such an enthusiastic welcoming committee.

Trixie was barking inside the house, and when the door opened, the dog charged outside followed by Brent, who moved at a more sedate pace. However, he was smiling, so at least he seemed pleased to see her. After all the drama of the prior evening, Carly wasn't sure what he might be thinking.

She smiled in return. "You look happy."

"I'm glad to see you."

Carly stepped closer. "Really? Then maybe it's a good time to ask you a favor. I need to take Trixie back to the kennel this morning and my foot hurts. Would you be willing to drive me?"

"Although I think Trixie is looking forward to getting out of here, I'm sorry, but I can't. I have to do something in town."

Carly frowned and crouched in front of her dog. "Did you do something bad?"

Brent shook his head. "She was good, but I think she's a little afraid of Ripley. They don't hate each other, but I wouldn't call them best buddies either, so I put Trixie in the second bedroom. She was a little stressed out, I think."

Carly ruffled Trixie's ears. "I guess she's used to having her own space. She might be relieved to go back to the kennel."

"I need to ask you a favor, even though it might not be the greatest time since I just turned you down."

"What is it?"

"I need to take a quick trip to Los Angeles. Would you be willing to stay here overnight and watch the puppies?"

Carly paused for a moment to assimilate the news. "I guess so. Are you sure you trust me to stay here?"

"You're not planning to run off with all my valuables are you? Because if you are, good luck finding any."

"I guess stealing weird art and your collection of old t-shirts isn't going to set me up for an early retirement in Aruba, is it?"

"A bunch of unfinished paintings aren't going to net you much either." He reached out to pull her into a hug. "I'd really appreciate it. When I came up here, I wasn't expecting to be responsible for so many animals."

Carly put her hands around his waist and tilted back her head to look into his eyes. "That's sort of my fault, so this is the least I can do. Can I ask what the trip is about?"

He gave her a bone-melting kiss. "It might be nothing, but if it works out, we can celebrate when I get back."

"While you're gone, I can spend some time thinking of ways to celebrate." She let go of him and stepped back. "But first I should get someone else to drive Trixie and me back out to her woodsy doggie retreat."

"Are any of your friends still talking to each other?"

"I don't know. They weren't downstairs when I skedaddled out of there. Last night there was a lot of talking behind closed doors, so I'm hoping maybe they worked it out."

"Ever the optimist."

Carly shrugged. "Well, this whole trip is another thing that's basically my fault. At this rate, I may end up having no friends, so maybe staying here isn't such a bad idea."

He took her hand. "Promise me you won't spend the whole time cleaning, okay? Just relax and hang out."

"I'll try to control myself. But if a spidey widey crawls out of the cobwebs and starts crawling on me, all bets are off."

"All right. I suppose that's fair."

~

Back at the house, Carly convinced Ginger to drive her out to the kennel. They stopped by Brent's cabin, picked up Trixie, and hit the road. Carly had desperately wanted to give Brent a kiss goodbye, but refrained. Ginger was clearly already in a bad mood. And Lily had apparently decided to forego breakfast and remained holed up in her room.

In the back seat, Trixie had a good time poking her snout out the window, sniffing the breezes. Ginger was driving silently and Carly cast about for something to say. Should she address the elephant in the front seat?

Carly cleared her throat. "So did you talk to Nathan?"

"Yes."

"What did he say?"

Ginger glanced away from the road at Carly. "That it's true. He and Lily had a fling and neither of them ever mentioned it. In *all* these years."

"Well, what does it matter now?"

"It matters. They both lied to me. I feel like I can't trust either of them. These are supposed to be the people I'm closest to in my life."

"They're still the same people."

"But my feelings about them aren't. How did you feel when you heard about me and Stuart?"

"What about you and Stuart?" Carly widened her eyes. "Wait. Did you and Stuart…?"

"Oh, come on." Ginger glanced at her again. "You knew about this. Before you guys got together, Stuart and I had a fling."

"He said you and Lily both rejected him."

"Well then he lied. We had a whirlwind night at a cheesy motel in lovely Chicopee, near all the strip malls."

"*When?*"

"It was after a frat party. Lily wasn't the only one who made errors in judgment, you know. Don't you remember when I went through my frat-boy phase sophomore year?"

"I remember." Carly put her face in her palms. "But, wow. I can't believe this. I mean, was everyone sleeping with everyone, except me?"

"Well, there wasn't that much sleeping."

Carly lifted her head. "That's not funny at all, and you know it."

"Sorry. But what does it matter? You're done with Stuart anyway. I, on the other hand, have to return to my lying spouse in a few days. Maybe I'll get even first."

"*No*...I mean, you shouldn't do that. You can't do that to Nathan." At Ginger's startled glance, Carly said more evenly, "Anyway, Brent is going out of town. He asked me to stay over there and watch the puppies."

Ginger didn't respond, and they spent the rest of the drive in sulky silence. Carly couldn't stop thinking about the revelations of the past twenty-four hours. Maybe if Ginger was so dead set on having some big fling with Brent, Carly should get out of the way. Obviously, Carly was every man's last pathetic desperate choice. Worse, if she'd known Stuart had lied way back when, she wouldn't have wasted fifteen years with the loser. Who knows how many other things he lied about? She was such an idiot. And men were disgusting.

By the time they got to the kennel, Carly had decided she was done with men entirely. Better to be a grumpy old spinster than to have some lying scum-sucking low-life male break her heart again.

They got out of the car and Carly unloaded Trixie. She rang the buzzer, and they all turned at the sickly sound of an elderly car wheezing up the driveway. It was an old silver hatchback with rusty highlights that could have been a refugee from a scrap yard.

The car sputtered to a stop and a door slammed from the direction of the house. Kat descended the stairs, her long braid swinging behind her as she walked.

A tall woman with short sandy-blonde hair got out of the rustmobile and a young boy exited the passenger side. Without looking back at the child, the woman immediately strode purposefully up the driveway toward Kat.

With a wide wave of her arms, she yelled, "Don't you *ever* answer your phone?"

Kat said something Carly didn't hear and pointed at her and Ginger. Carly waved the tips of her fingers slightly. Whoever the tall woman was, she definitely wasn't happy.

The little boy walked over to Carly and held out his hand. "I'm Johnny. Who are you?"

"My name is Carly and this is my friend, Ginger."

"Can I pet your dog? She's really fat."

"I know, and yes you may, Johnny. Thank you for asking." Carly smiled at the dog, who was wagging eagerly. "Her name is Trixie, and she loves little boys."

"I'm not *little*," he said with the unique arrogance of the young. "I'm *eight* now. I'm not allowed to scream anymore."

"I think that's a good rule," Carly said.

Kat and the tall woman joined the group, and given the expression on Kat's face, Carly was pretty sure Kat would be happier if she were on another planet.

Kat said, "This is my sister-in-law, Cindy. It looks like you've already met Johnny."

"Kat is my aunt now," Johnny said. "She married my uncle Joel, but Mommy said they'll be getting divorced soon."

Cindy jerked her index finger toward the forest. "Could you go sit over there on that cinder block, please? And don't move from that spot until I say so."

Johnny remained motionless and she pointed more emphatically at the block, "*Now!*"

He gave Trixie one last pat, stomped over to the cinder block, and made a big show of sitting on it.

Carly smiled. "What a sweet boy."

"Want to babysit him?" Cindy said. "I don't know you and you might think I'm kidding, but trust me, I'm not."

Carly glanced at Ginger, who said, "We're only visiting Alpine Grove for a few more days."

Kat said, "Let me take Trixie for you. Thanks again for taking her. Everything is fixed, and we have water again."

Kat was less orange today, which Carly figured meant she'd been able to wash her face. "By the way, we haven't heard from your friend Brigid yet. Could you ask her to call Dr. Cassidy? The puppies are doing great, and they need to go to their foster homes. We want to make arrangements and get them settled before we leave."

"Sure. I'll send her an email."

"So if I *email* you, will I get an answer to my question?" Cindy demanded.

Kat bit her lip, closed her eyes, and said softly, "I told you, I'll talk to Joel about it tonight. He's going to call at seven thirty, and I'll explain that you need a babysitter."

"It's important! I never get to take vacations, and my friend has an all-expense-paid spa vacation that she won. I *have* to go. There are hardly any babysitters in this godforsaken town. Or we've been blacklisted. It's not fair."

Carly glanced at Ginger again, who raised her eyebrows and mouthed a silent "Wow."

Perhaps little Johnny was sitting in a time out for good reason. It was probably time to leave. Carly handed Kat Trixie's leash. "We should be going."

Kat smiled apologetically. "Thanks again."

Cindy said, "It was nice to meet you," then turned back to Kat. "Make sure you tell Joel what I said."

"I will. At seven thirty," Kat said.

"Of course. Mr. Schedule. How could I forget?"

Carly and Ginger waved goodbye and hustled back to the car. Ginger started the engine. "That was like a flashback to my family, complete with a bratty kid no one wants to babysit. I'm glad we've got some more days of vacation left. I'm not ready to go back. Not *even* ready."

Carly laughed, "Lily was telling me how she envies you because you have kids. The ole biological clock is ticking."

"What do you think about kids? Your clock is running out too."

"Don't remind me. I always thought for sure I'd be the one of us who'd be married with seven kids. But maybe the clock running out isn't the worst thing either."

Ginger took her hand off the steering wheel and put it on Carly's. "You know you'd be a great mom, don't you?"

"Thanks for saying that. I don't know if I would be, but I guess we'll have to see what happens."

Chapter 11

Coming and Going

With a death grip on Trixie's leash, Kat stood and watched as Cindy's car sputtered down the driveway. She looked down at the dog, whose eyes were round and filled with concern.

Kat crouched down and stroked the fur on the dog's chest. "I'm sorry Trix. It's not you. I'm starting to understand why Joel gets so angry with his sister. I don't usually lose my temper like that, but she was being mean."

Trixie wagged tentatively, and Kat put her back in the kennel to sleep off her worries about strange human conflicts. Even though Cindy was probably miles away by now, Kat's hands were still shaking when she walked into the kitchen. After brewing a calming cup of chamomile tea, she sat at the table, cradling the mug and staring at nothing.

She glanced up at the clock, then leaned forward, resting her forehead on the cool wood of the table and staring down at her sneakers. It was only eight o'clock and she'd already managed to cause a family incident. Joel was going to *kill* her.

She sat up, grabbed a piece of paper with his hotel phone number from the table, and walked to the wall phone. Joel's class didn't start until ten, so he might still be sitting around his room going over his lesson plans.

Kat exhaled a sigh of relief and settled back into her chair when Joel answered the phone.

He sound startled to hear from her, which probably wasn't unreasonable. "Are you okay? Did something happen to the dogs or cats?"

Kat tugged at the phone cord, watching it stretch and contract. "I'm fine. Everybody's fine."

"Then how come you're calling? I have to teach a class soon, and you know I'll call you tonight."

"I know." Kat coiled the cord around her index finger. "I did something that I think you're not going to like."

There was a long pause, and he said, "That doesn't sound good. What did you do?"

"Your sister showed up here this morning."

"Uh-oh. Why?"

Kat slumped into the chair. "I didn't return her call quickly enough. I guess she left a voice mail while we were talking last night."

"What did she want?"

"For us to babysit Johnny for a week in mid-July."

"I hope you said no."

"Well, I was going to…"

"You didn't tell her we *would*, did you?"

Kat tugged the coil of cord off her finger. "When Cindy came out here I might have gotten a little angry."

Joel sighed heavily. "Unfortunately, that's awfully easy for me to imagine."

"She kept haranguing me about how you and I are going to get divorced, but before we do she should get free babysitting services."

"Oh jeez."

"The conversation went downhill from there. At least Carly left before it got really ugly."

"How far downhill did it go?"

"I got angry at Cindy and before I realized what I was saying, I said 'Fine, we'll do it' so she'd shut up."

"Let me guess. She stopped yelling, gave you a satisfied smile, and left."

"I'm so, *so* sorry."

Joel didn't say anything for a long moment and Kat could imagine the distressed expression on his face.

She said quickly, "I can call her and tell her that I talked to you, and well, I don't know. We could make up a lie, I guess. I don't suppose you need to schedule an elective surgery or some kind of minor outpatient procedure, do you?"

"No, don't do that. If we lie, I promise you, she'll find out somehow, and we'll never hear the end of it. I'm thinking."

Kat wrapped the cord around two fingers. "I can't be responsible for that kid for a week. He's out of school and I could lose my mind dealing with him twenty-four-seven. Without a teacher to deflect and absorb some of Johnny's energy, he'll be unstoppable. I mean, he was supposed to be on a time out, but while Cindy and I were standing there arguing, he asked twenty-five questions in a row without even waiting for a response. She grabbed him before he succeeded in disappearing down a trail into the forest."

"At least she caught him before he escaped."

"That week in July, I have article deadlines and the kennel is beyond full. We've actually got a waiting list of people who want to board dogs. It's like everyone woke up after the long freezing journey of winter and decided to go on vacation at the same time."

"Maybe we can use that to our advantage."

"How?"

"Boot camp."

Kat yanked on the cord, disentangling her fingers again. "What are you talking about? You think Cindy is going to agree to let us enlist her eight-year-old in the military?"

"You always say 'a tired dog is a good dog.' What if we apply the same principle to Johnny?"

"You mean tire him out? Is that even possible?"

"Maybe. What if the kid has to go on all of the dog walks? If the kennel is busy, between you, me, and Mia walking dogs, we could take a lot of walks. Maybe Mia could convince her boyfriend to go on a few too."

"Chris might not mind that, but we don't need that many people. We only walk dogs three times a day."

"There's no reason you couldn't do more walks. The dogs would love it." Joel chuckled. "I'd certainly be motivated to help. Maybe when I get home, I'll extend some of the trails, so they're longer."

"You really think we can tire that kid out?"

"We can try, and he'll hate it. We'll never have to babysit again."

Kat smiled. "You know, you can be kind of devious in an analytical way."

"I have my moments."

"I also have a better understanding of why you do everything Cindy asks you to do. It's to get her to stop yelling at you, isn't it?"

"Pretty much."

Kat glanced at the clock. "I know you have to go teach, but thanks for talking to me. I feel better."

"I'm glad. I should get organized here."

"I'll spend some time plotting out all the incredibly healthy vegan meals we can make for boot-camp week. I'm thinking tofu, lentils, and every green leafy vegetable we can find at the grocery store. It will be like our life, but exaggerated. That kid is gonna be craving ice cream, potato chips, and burgers *so* bad by time he gets home."

Joel laughed. "There's the spirit."

"Good luck with the nerd class. I love you."

"I love you back. I'll call you tonight and let you know how it went."

Kat hung up the phone and grinned. Time to figure out how to create the most healthy, outdoorsy, sugar-free boot camp, ever. Maybe they could throw in some educational time while walking in the forest.

After all, what eight-year-old didn't love hearing about programming theory? Having just taught a class, Joel could probably wax poetic on all kinds of stuff that would put an eight-year-old to sleep. Or Johnny would become the world's youngest authority on database design. Either way, it would be okay. If nothing else, they had a plan.

∿

Carly asked Ginger to drop her at Brent's cabin because she needed to talk to him about the arrangements for her foray into cabin- and puppy-sitting. She didn't mention to Ginger that she also simply wanted to see him.

She'd always used the trail to visit the cabin, so it felt odd to go up to the front door. She walked around the side of the cabin, walked up the steps to the deck, and tapped on the screen door.

The puppies started barking, yipping, and carrying on. While she was house-sitting, she certainly wouldn't have problems with any surprise intruders sneaking up on her.

Brent appeared from one of the bedrooms in the back of the house wearing nothing except old blue jeans and a towel draped over his shoulders. Carly repressed a smile, but appreciated the view. He waved and yelled, "Come on in, and feel free to tell the obnoxious pupsketeers to settle their furry selves down."

Carly walked in and went to the kitchen doorway. All of the puppies jumped up and put their front paws on the wood blocking the entrance. It was pretty clear that they'd be able to launch over the makeshift barricade all too soon.

Brent came up behind her and kissed her neck. A shiver ran down her spine, and she turned to face him, placing her palms flat on his bare chest. His skin was warm and irresistibly inviting. She leaned back from him in an effort to focus on why she was there. "So I probably already know where stuff is. What do I need to know to tend to this place?"

"The water pressure in the shower is terrible. That's why I sometimes wash my hair in the lake." He offered a lascivious grin. "I'd be happy to show you."

Carly laughed. "Although that sounds like fun, it's probably not a good idea. We can't catch a break, can we? Here you are running off to the city, and after you get back, I'll have to leave a couple days later."

He wrapped his arms around her. "Why don't you stay longer? You said you have a zillion hours of vacation time."

"It was only two weeks that I was in danger of losing because they have all these rules about rolling over your hours from year to year."

"How much vacation time do you have if you count everything?"

"Well, I'd have to look at my pay stub to be sure."

"Take a guess."

"Another six or seven weeks, maybe? It might be more. I'm not sure. I didn't take any vacation for five or six years. All the carrying over was starting to affect their profit and loss statement or something and the CEO noticed."

Brent pulled her closer, nibbled on her earlobe, and whispered, "That's funny and sad all at the same time. Tell them you want to use it all up."

Carly moved her head away. "I can't do that."

"Why not?" He brushed the back of his fingers across her cheek. "I'd like to get to know you better. A *lot* better. Without the distractions of your friends and puppies and everything else. That's not going to happen if you leave in a few days."

"A small detail is that the lovely place I'm staying in will be rented to someone else. Even if it weren't, I can't afford it or the dog boarding."

"So stay here."

"I can't do that."

"Why not?"

Carly stepped back from him but couldn't quite manage to remove her hands from his magnetic skin. "We talked about this before. We've only known each other for a week and I just broke up with Stuart. It's not fair to you."

"I already told you I'm dumb enough to be rebound guy. And that's my problem, not yours, isn't it?"

"I don't know. It feels really risky. I'm not ready for anything serious."

"Then don't be serious. Be casual. Relaxed. Whatever works." Brent leaned to kiss her. "I have to go. Think about it, okay? Maybe chemistry like this happens to you more often than it does to me, but you know how I feel. It's up to you."

Carly moved her hands up to his neck, enjoying the sensation of his skin under her fingertips. "It's going to be so strange staying in this cabin without you here."

He gave her another one of his now-legendary dizzying kisses and let her go. "You'll figure it out. This place is old. All I ask is that you don't burn it down or get all neat freaky on it. Let it remain its creaky, dirty self, and everything will be fine."

"I'll do my best."

Carly watched as Brent put on a t-shirt and sneakers and gathered his bags. After he closed the door behind him, she walked back to the kitchen. The typical puppy duties might distract her and keep her from thinking about what he'd said about the chemistry between them. Because he sure wasn't wrong about that. A fling was one thing. But was she supposed to simply forget that Stuart dumped her only a few weeks ago? She'd given her heart to him for years, and he'd stomped all over it. Why would she risk being hurt that way again?

After cleaning up the puppy area, Carly transferred the musketeers to their outdoor pen and spent most of the afternoon outside with them. The glorious weather was holding and Carly parked herself on a lounge chair with an old Dick Francis horse-oriented mystery novel that she'd found lying on an end table in the living room. Apparently the horse-racing world in the sixties was filled with quite a bit of action, adventure, and dastardly crimes.

The novel was a quick read, and when she was finished, she took the pups back inside, rummaged through the cabinets for food, and scrounged up some dinner. Afterward, she couldn't take it anymore. Because she was alone in the house without Brent there to observe, the urge to poke around the cabin was overwhelming. There was no one to talk to and nothing else to do, so she finally gave in to the urge to snoop.

Carly didn't think of herself as the type of person who crept around looking in other people's closets and bathroom cabinets. But after she set her toothbrush on the sink, she might have taken a peek in the medicine cabinet. She discovered that someone had treated poison ivy with calamine lotion a long, long time ago. Like maybe decades ago. The pink, crusty bottle might have been manufactured sometime in the early seventies.

The other contents of the medicine cabinet were fairly standard. Aspirin, soap, toothpaste, deodorant, and sunscreen. The vanity cabinet below the sink had toilet paper and standard-issue feminine hygiene products. Clearly women had been in the house at some point, since the products obviously weren't Brent's. On the dresser in the master bedroom where he was staying, she ran across an old bottle of Chanel No. 5, which she assumed wasn't his either.

She opened the bottle and took a whiff. It still smelled okay. Did perfume ever go bad? The bed was littered with Brent's clothes, and she picked up a t-shirt, fingering the soft cotton. Although she was trying to ignore her sappy feelings, she missed him more than she wanted to admit.

The puppies were still asleep, so Carly spent some time browsing through the living room, looking at the games and scanning through the books on the bookcases. She'd heard so much about Brent's family that now she was curious to find out what they looked like. Although the wood-paneled walls had quite a few paintings and ink drawings hanging on them, there weren't any photographs of people. There had to be an album or a box filled with snapshots somewhere. Every family had a cache of photos, didn't they?

The bookshelves were packed with books, but sadly no photo albums. Resigned to an evening of reading, Carly pulled a book that she'd read a million times off the shelf and settled onto the sofa. Anne, of Green Gables and Avonlea fame was one of the literary heroines of her youth along with Pollyanna, Heidi, and Pippi. Given Carly's quest for ideas to reinvent herself, Anne's story of working to build her dream life seemed appropriate.

She jolted awake at the ferocious barking coming from the kitchen. Ripley leaped over the wood, whooshing by the sofa toward the front door of the cabin. Carly lurched off the sofa, tripped on the coffee table, and stumbled onto the floor.

A tall woman with wild, wavy jet-black hair clad in a long colorful flowing robe waved her arms and shrieked, "What the mother…since when do we have dogs here? Get this animal away from me!"

Carly struggled to her feet and ran to grab Ripley's collar. "Ripley, stop."

The glare from the woman's unflinching round blue eyes was unnerving, and Carly smiled weakly. Burglars didn't usually dress like Stevie Nicks, did they?

The woman put a fist on her hip. "Who *are* you and why are you in my cabin?"

"My name is Carly and I'm taking care of the puppies."

"What puppies?"

Carly pointed at the small furry faces staring at them over the wood barrier. "The ones in the kitchen."

～

The woman didn't seem particularly thrilled by Carly's explanation. "Nice to meet you, Carly. My name is Rose and I still don't understand why you're here."

Carly grinned widely. "Brent told me about you. You're his aunt, right?"

"Where is he?"

"Los Angeles. He'll be back tomorrow." Carly pulled Ripley back toward the kitchen and her offspring, while Rose followed. They stopped at the doorway and Ripley deftly hopped over the wood, receiving an enthusiastic reception from the pups.

Rose reached down to pet one of the puppies. "Nothing's cuter than little puppies. Hey there, easy with the teeth, you little monster."

"They're chewing everything. People, toys, each other." Carly reached down to pet Aramis. "They're either chewing or sound asleep. There's no middle ground with these guys."

Rose straightened and gave Carly the once-over. "So Carly, how do you know my nephew?"

"My friends and I are renting the place next door and he helped us rescue the puppies. Our place doesn't allow dogs, so he's letting them stay here until we can get them set up with the Alpine Grove dog-rescue group, which will help find them homes."

"That's quite a story. God, I'd love a drink. Sobriety sucks." She gestured around the cabin, causing the sleeve of her robe to wave like a flag. "But it's sort of interesting to see what this place looks like without the purple haze."

"It's nice to meet you. Brent told me you're a musician and artist."

Rose settled into a spot on the sofa. "I'm embracing retirement at the moment. I came here because I'm thinking of getting my artsy side going again, and my nephew said he'd be here all summer painting."

"He is," Carly said. "Or he was, except for today. A lot of his paintings are in one of the bedrooms because he's using it as a studio."

"So are you his girlfriend or something? I still don't understand why you're here."

"I'm a friend now, I suppose. We have spent a lot of time talking and painting over the last week or so. He told me all about your parents. I wish I could have met them."

"He always got along better with them and me than he did with his own family. I think my brother is a throwback to some Prussian dictator or something."

"At the risk of being nosy, are there any pictures of your parents here?" Carly smiled. "I read through your mother's recipes and her comments made me laugh. I'd love to put a face to the lovely handwriting."

"So I guess you've learned how to cuss in French now?"

"Not really. But Brent said that's all the French he knows."

"That's probably the truth." She chuckled as she stood up. "I'm sure there's a photo album lying around here somewhere. Maybe someone threw it into the *merde* closet."

Carly followed her into the bedroom. "I think I know which closet that is. We were searching for yarn in there. It's like a junk drawer, but bigger."

"*Sans blague.*"

"What does that mean?"

Rose opened the closet door and an old shoe box rolled out, scattering about three hundred pink foam curlers onto the floor. "It means something like 'no kidding' or 'no joke,' more or less."

Carly picked up the box and started throwing curlers back into it. "I haven't seen these in years."

"I don't understand why we don't dump all this crap." Rose pulled a large, black leather album out of the detritus. "Found it!" She moved to the bed and sat down.

Carly sat down next to her and eagerly watched as Rose opened the cover. She pointed at a photo. "Looks like everybody got permed."

Rose groaned. "That was not an attractive phase. I don't know whose brilliant idea it was for Mom and me to get the same perm."

"So that's Claudette? She looks like she's laughing at something."

"Probably our reflection in the mirror. What were we thinking?" Rose flipped to the next page. "This was her big sixties hair. I called it the Coliseum."

"I see what you mean." Carly pointed at a snapshot of a little girl obviously having a temper tantrum on the ground while the adults looked on. "Is that you?"

"How'd you guess? I was always a bit emotional." She pointed at a young boy. "And there's Artie, wearing a bow tie. What ten-year-old wears a bow tie? Even in 1957 that was goofy."

Rose flipped to the next page. "Oh yuck. It's the dance photos. Here's a classy one of me. I look like I borrowed tights from Bigfoot. And I'm embodying extreme loser over here. Ugh. These are hard to look at."

"Who's that?" Carly asked, pointing at a photo of a towheaded boy on Santa's lap. "Kris Kringle doesn't seem too concerned about second-hand smoke."

"Even Santa was a chain smoker back then. And that's Misha. His hair was that white-blonde color when he was little, but it darkened as he got older."

"Who's Misha?"

"Brent. Who'd you think?" Rose flipped to the next page and pointed at a photo of the little boy in tights after what appeared to be a performance of *The Nutcracker*. "Here's when he got the nickname. After this performance, Artie said something about him being Baryshnikov and carped about Misha not being better at sports."

"But dancing is physically demanding. Ballet dancers have to be in incredible shape."

"I know! That's exactly what I told Misha. But it's not macho and testosterone-based like football or rugby." Rose thumped her palm on the album. "Arthur is such a jerk. I ended up having to talk that poor kid down off the ledge. After that, I always called him Misha. It was kind of an inside joke. I told the kid how athletic the real Mikhail Baryshnikov is and how his friends and I all call him Misha."

"Are you saying you've met Baryshnikov?"

"We crossed paths a few times in the seventies after he defected."

Carly wasn't sure what to say. After she saw the movie *The Turning Point*, she'd had a major crush on the dancer. "What's he like?"

"Oh I don't know. Russian. Artsy. I still think it's hilarious that Brent signs his paintings 'Misha.' I'm sure he did it just to piss off Artie."

"Wait a minute. At home, I have a whole book filled with his paintings. They're amazing. Brent is *that* Misha?"

"Well duh. I thought you said a bunch of his paintings are here."

"They're not finished, and he wasn't too excited about showing them to me. He hasn't been painting much wildlife since he's been here and I guess I didn't make the connection. I can't believe he didn't say anything."

Rose gave her a sideways glance and Carly gestured helplessly toward the studio with her hand. "He's upset about not being able to paint, and I was trying to give him some space."

"Since when does Misha *not* paint?" Rose demanded.

"That's why he's here. To try to get over his creative block. We spent some time painting outside and he painted a dragon that was brilliant. I'm hoping being here is helping him. He's actually thinking of giving up art entirely."

"He can't do that!" Rose slapped the photo album closed. "Painting is all he's ever wanted to do. Not to mention the fact that he's incredibly talented."

"I'm just telling you what he said."

"You seem to know an awful lot about Misha. How long have you known each other?"

"A little more than a week."

Rose raised her eyebrows. "You're more than friends, aren't you?"

"Maybe a little."

~

Carly made Rose a sandwich while Rose regaled her with funny family stories. When she finished eating, Carly took her plate. "I said this to Brent too, but I wish I'd met your mother. She sounds like she was a character."

"My rebellious genes come from her. We didn't always get along because we were too alike in a lot of ways, but I think she understood that too."

"Brent is using the master bedroom. Do you want me to make up the bed in the other bedroom for you?"

"I was going to sleep in the little back room, but I saw Misha filled it with his art stuff. You can barely turn around in there."

"His studio is a little crowded. I can take the couch."

"I'm not sleeping in that bedroom with Mona Lisa and the pink cows. Mona stares at me and it creeps me out."

Carly laughed as she took Rose's plate and took it to the sink. "You too? I thought it was just me."

"I'll shove the clothes on the floor and sleep in the master bedroom. Misha is such a slob."

"I noticed."

Rose took a sip of her water and returned the glass to the table. "You know, you don't seem like his type."

"What do you mean?"

"You're too nice."

"I don't know about that. I can be as unpleasant as the next girl."

"No. You're nice." Rose pointed at the sink. "I mean, you're cleaning up after me. Normally, Misha goes for women who trample all over him. The last one was a real shrew. And when she saw the numbers on his last licensing deal, she made a play to move in with him."

"I guess she didn't?" Carly tried not to sound too interested, but this was far more information than Brent had ever shared.

"Nope. He finally figured out she was an evil harpy. I mean sheesh, I told him that the moment I met her. She was mean to him. He's always been quiet and shy, and she used to dump all over him. He took it because he's too damn nice. He always does that and the whole thing infuriated me."

"That sounds terrible. Poor Brent."

"She was the latest in a string of venomous women. His poor choices in the romance department go way back." Rose pointed at the stove. "I suppose you cooked for him too?"

"Making you a sandwich isn't cooking. And yes, I offered to make something one day, but he turned me down. He also told me to relax my housekeeping standards a little." Carly sat down. "In fact, he specifically told me not to clean anything while I'm here. But I draw the line at the dishes. I'm sorry, but I'm going to wash them. It's unsanitary not to."

Rose smiled. "Fine by me. Maybe he's reacting to Arthur's proclamation that we not change anything in this place."

"Why not?"

"Who knows? Artie probably wants it to remain locked in time as a shrine to past glories. I have no idea. He's such a stuffed shirt, I never understand his reasoning."

"This cabin could be so cute if it were redecorated and restored a little." Carly gestured toward the ancient stove. "It wouldn't take much. Just a little TLC. If you don't put some work into it soon, things will start to really fall apart. I can't imagine anyone in your family wants that to happen."

"No, but we've been told in no uncertain terms not to touch anything."

Carly folded her paper napkin into a tidy triangle. "That's what Brent said too."

"It hasn't seemed worth it to make a stink about it, since we've just been renting it out. The location is so good and there are so few rentals that people overlook the problems."

"I still don't see why clean up or repairs would be a big deal, particularly since Brent moved his art stuff into the studio. Why wasn't that a problem?"

"Adding more crap isn't an issue, but removing stuff is apparently. I can't decipher the logic. Arthur has always been eccentric, and it seems like he gets more peculiar all the time. He and Misha can't stand each other."

"I got that impression. Brent said his father was a politician."

"Well that should tell you something right there." Rose widened her eyes. "It's like Arthur beamed in from another planet. He always says things like, "What would the neighbors think?" or "What would our relatives think?" Meanwhile, you've heard enough about my mother to know she didn't give a rat's patootie about what anyone thought. And it's pretty obvious I've never cared what anybody thought about my lifestyle or my personality.

"Arthur is unbelievably conservative and frankly, kinda odd. Over the years, he's become more obsessive and bizarre. I think spending too much time alone with his thoughts in that big house is making him weird."

Carly paused to absorb this information, examining her fingernails. Cleaning up after messy pups was hard on a girl's manicure. "Brent mentioned that his parents don't live together, even though they're still married."

"Yup. Like I said: weird. I don't know what happened, but something did. Whatever it was, Grace couldn't stand being in the same house with Artie anymore, and she moved to New York. I sure can't blame her. He drives me nuts."

True to her word, Carly did the dishes and then she and Rose said their goodnights. Rose disappeared into the master bedroom and Carly retired to the sofa. The puppies were rustling around in the kitchen and the sound of Ripley's claws clattering on the linoleum was jarring.

Carly had grabbed an ancient set of harvest gold sheets, pillows, and a blanket and curled herself up like a mummy on the old couch. The cushions sagged in the center, which indicated she wasn't the first to use it as a bed. So far, no one she'd met was willing to spend much time in the same room with the creepy painting.

She rolled over and watched shadows crawl across the old paneled walls. The strange environment in conjunction with the sounds of canines wandering around the kitchen made it difficult to relax. Sleep was elusive and Carly's mind wandered. Why was Rose here anyway? Carly hadn't thought to ask. Why now? Was something going on with the family that caused Rose to come check out the cabin? Or maybe some life event. Rose had talked a lot about other members of the family, but hadn't been particularly forthcoming about what was going on in her own life.

Carly rearranged the pillow under her head and then rolled onto her back, staring at the ceiling. What was Brent doing now in LA? Did he live there? If he didn't live in LA, where did he live? How could Carly not know this? She was falling for this guy and she didn't even know where his home was. How absurd was that? But she did know a lot about his family. Was that normal? Probably not. Normally you learned about the guy first. Then family.

Waitaminute…was she *falling* for him? Was she really thinking that? No. Maybe. A few sexy images fluttered through her mind. Okay, probably yes. But she was leaving in a few days. Getting any more involved with him was nuts. She needed to settle her hormones down, and focus on getting her life back together. So far she'd learned nothing about herself on this vacation. She was supposed to be finding herself, but the only discoveries she'd made were that she could still be infatuated with a man who was wrong for her and get into fights with her best friends.

At the sensation of something wet, Carly jerked her hand away from the edge of the sofa. She leaned over and found D'Artagnan's little paws next to her arm. He was wagging his tail furiously, eager for attention. Carly sat up and pulled the dog up onto her lap. "You are a naughty little thing, aren't you? It figures you're our first escapee." The puppy curled up and made happy, snorty noises as she stroked the fur on his head.

"So what do you think, D'Artagnan? Am I really falling for Brent? Is that completely crazy? I didn't even know he's a famous artist. He's *Misha*, and that floors me. I have books with his paintings at home, and I had no idea it was him. Sheesh, talk about close-mouthed. Rose said he's shy, but come on. I've actually been kissed by a guy in my art books. Hey, I guess that's kind of cool, isn't it?"

D'Artagnan didn't respond to the question and began to snore quietly. Carly giggled. "I know, I know. I'm over-thinking this, aren't I?"

D'Artagnan tapped his tail a couple of times, which Carly took as a yes. She sprawled out on the sofa again, cuddled the puppy to her chest, and joined him in slumber.

Chapter 12

Reframing

Carly was rudely awakened by a crashing noise. Fortunately, she'd returned D'Artagnan to the kitchen sometime in the middle of the night, or she'd have dumped him on the floor when she jolted upright. The dogs started barking and little D'Artagnan gracefully leaped over the wood and charged toward her.

She scooped him up into her arms and went down the hall to investigate. Rose was in Brent's studio setting up an easel that she'd apparently knocked over. Carly tapped on the door jamb. "Is everything okay?"

Rose straightened the legs of the easel and released it, holding her hands above the wood in case it decided to topple again. "Sorry if I woke you. I was looking around."

"Are you trying to find something in particular?"

"I found some paintings in the other bedroom and I wondered what was going on with Misha's work."

"Don't worry, the dandelions are mine. His brain would have to go all melty welty to create something that ugly."

Rose raised her eyebrows. "Melty?"

"All of his stuff is in here, I think." Carly walked in and moved a painting aside. "Did you see the one with the dragon? I think it's wonderful."

"I don't think so. It looks like he's started a bunch of stuff." Rose flipped through some canvases. "Lots of swashes of background color, but not much else."

"There was a wolf that was almost done, I think." Carly readjusted her hold on D'Artagnan and leaned over. "I don't see it though. He said he wasn't happy with it."

Rose dug through a pile of papers, pulled out a sketch pad, and flipped through it. "Here's some pen-and-ink stuff. Check this out—he drew the puppies. That's so cute. Not really his typical style, but still cute."

Carly moved next to her and looked over her shoulder. "Aww, they're adorable. Hey, D'Artagnan, if those spots are any indication, this one is you." She snuggled the squirmy puppy closer. "You're famous now."

Rose laid the pad aside and dug out another one. "More pencil sketches and a few more he inked. Here's one of you."

Carly moved the puppy so she could examine the drawing more closely. "Maybe on a good day that's me. Or me fifteen years ago. Once upon a time I might have looked like that, but not anymore."

Rose held the pad next to Carly's face. "Yep, that's you. And now I'm *sure* you're more than friends. A picture is worth a thousand words. This is a pen-and-ink love note if I ever saw one."

Carly didn't want to delve into this topic with Rose and hoisted D'Artagnan up above her hip again. What a wiggler he was. "I'm going to see if I can dredge up something for breakfast."

Rose nodded and continued to rummage around in the studio. Because she felt like it might be an invasion of Brent's privacy, Carly left her to it. When she'd snooped around the cabin, Carly had specifically avoided the studio. Family was allowed to be nosier than friends, and Rose owned the place, so she could do whatever she wanted. Plus, it was time for Carly to feed the pups, let them out, and set to work on puppy clean-up activities.

While the puppies ate their breakfast, Carly sat at the table leafing through Claudette's cookbook. The idea of writing in books was abhorrent to Carly, but with a cookbook it seemed like less of a violation because having notes about the results of recipes was useful. The poor old tome also was stuffed to the gills with newspaper clippings filled with still more recipes and random notes. Carly unfolded a few clippings, which were yellowed with age. She arranged them on the table by type of recipe, stacking them into neat piles.

Carly was carting Porthos to the outside pen when Lily walked out from the path through the trees.

Carly greeted her friend and pointed at the cabin, "Hey, could you help me bring the rest of them outside?"

Lily nodded and followed her inside. The table was covered with newspapers and Lily stopped to take a look. "What are you doing?"

"Organizing. I couldn't help myself." Carly picked up Aramis and handed him to Lily. "How was your evening without me? Did you and Ginger bury the hatchet?"

"More or less. We're on speaking terms again." Lily turned toward the door with her pup. "She talked to Nathan, who corroborated my account. It was nothing and a million years ago. Who cares at this point?"

"Well, she does."

"I suppose, but she's had kids with the man. It's not like I'm suddenly interested in Nathan fifteen years later. She can have him."

Carly picked up D'Artagnan and went back outside, followed by Ripley. "I think Ginger was more upset that you both lied for so long."

After securing the pups in their enclosure, Carly settled into a beach chair and Lily took the chaise lounge, perching on the edge. She pointed at the puppies. "Are you staying here all day until Monet gets back?"

"I guess I don't have to since Rose is here. Oh, and I found out something interesting. You won't believe it." Carly waved her hands in excitement. "Rose told me Brent is the artist Misha. His paintings are in my art books. I'm stunned."

"Who is Rose? And should I know who Misha is?"

"She's Brent's aunt and yes, you would know if you knew anything about art. He's famous. I knew I'd seen his work before. I *knew* it."

Lily made a wry face. "Okay, I'll take your word for it."

The two women turned at the sound of the screen door slamming. Rose was wearing another of her flowing, rainbow-colored caftans over her bathing suit, and the colorful fabric rippled in the breeze as she walked down the steps from the deck. She walked up to the women and Carly introduced Rose to Lily.

Rose sat on the chaise next to Lily and said, "So you're the lawyer who thinks my family is full of art thieves?"

Lily glared at Carly. "Not precisely. It was a theory I proposed, but it wasn't based on a large volume of factual evidence. My conjecture was based on the World War II markings on the back of the painting in your guest bedroom."

"And the French carving on the tree," Carly added. "It could be that there was a community of artists here and it was some type of an inside joke, like Brent said."

"My parents partied with a lot of artists. Some of their work is probably still at that gallery in town. I don't remember all their names, but the gallery used to have an area set aside for works by local artists."

Lily said, "Let's go! I have to go to town and use my cell phone anyway."

"Still no word?" Carly asked.

"When I checked my messages yesterday, I had nothing except whiny lawyers calling me." Lily stood up. "Today, once I find a signal, I'm starting a campaign of harassment."

Rose grinned. "I don't know what you're talking about, but you go, girl."

Carly turned to Rose. "Could you watch the puppies for a little while? They love it out here, and now that they've played, they'll probably pass out in the sun and snooze."

"Fine with me. I'm going to catch some rays and probably join them. I'm wiped."

Lily followed Carly inside and waited in the kitchen while Carly gathered her things. She leaned over the table. "Why are there names in this cookbook?"

"I don't know. I thought it might be people who liked the recipe."

"But they're numbered." Lily pointed at the page. "One, two, three. What's that supposed to mean?"

"No idea. Brent's grandmother put lots of editorial comments in there. Some of them are funny. They'd probably be funnier if I knew French."

Lily flipped through the pages. "Hmm. I think Grandma mighta been nuttier than a fruitcake. On this page the notes say 'end of the line' and over here it says 'she's home.' Who is home?"

Carly leaned over to read the notes. "I'm wishing again that I had taken French in school."

"I did, and it's not helping. Anyway, who cares about Grandma? Let's get outta here." Lily grabbed her hand. "I want that cell signal now!"

~

The gallery was located one street over from the main street that went through downtown Alpine Grove. Lily yelped when her cell phone indicated it had a signal, and Carly left her friend to make her calls from the privacy of her car. Lily promised to meet Carly inside after she was done badgering various medical professionals about her test results.

According to the plaque out front, the gallery had been a church that almost completely burned down in the twenties. A group of art lovers had purchased the derelict building and restored it. The walls of the open space had been painted white, and large white partitions were added to divide the area into rooms. Statues and carvings sat on white pedestals that were scattered throughout the space.

As Carly walked in, she was enveloped by a sense of peace. She'd forgotten how much she loved the clean, quiet space of an art gallery. She strolled slowly around the rooms, standing in front of paintings, feeling inspired. Viewing artwork always made her wonder about the artist. What was he or she trying to express? What was the story she was trying to tell? What was the artist thinking when she offered this gift of her imagination for others to enjoy? Did she select a small canvas purposefully, or was that particular canvas one that happened to be lying around? Carly pondered color choices and bold brush strokes versus delicate, controlled pointillism.

As she walked around the cool, serene room, she stopped in front of a painting with a style that seemed familiar. She leaned closer and squinted at the signature in the corner. The scrawl said Misha and she smiled at the fact that she knew without a doubt exactly who Misha was.

She turned at the sound of footsteps from the back of the room. A woman with short, bone-straight black hair cut in a severe blunt wedge walked around the partition and nodded at Carly. "Welcome to the Alpinista Gallery. I'm sorry I didn't see you earlier. I was in the back framing."

"Do you have new works you're putting up?"

"Not at the moment. We do custom picture framing on the side. It helps keep the gallery going." The woman held out her hand. "My name is Leslie and I'm the owner. And chief picture framer, bottle washer, and doer of everything else."

"It's nice to meet you. Please go back to what you were doing. I'm waiting for my friend to meet me here. This is such a relaxing and beautiful gallery. You've created a wonderful space."

Leslie smiled warmly. "That's so kind of you to say."

"Could I see what you're working on?"

Leslie waved toward the back of the gallery. "Sure. My workspace is over here."

The back room had hundreds of colors of mat board corners hanging on the walls, along with a vast array of frame corner samples. Wood, metal, and plexiglass frames leaned against the walls around the room, and a huge worktable sat in the middle.

Carly stopped in her tracks. "This room is like a candy store for me. Look at all the colors and variety."

Leslie gestured toward the walls, "Are you interested in having something framed? We have a wide selection of wood and metal moldings, colored, textured, fabric and archival matting, and regular, non-glare, conservation, and museum glass."

"Wow, that's great, but I, um, I'm definitely *not* an artist, so my framing needs are minimal." Carly tried not to cringe at the idea of framing her hideous dandelion paintings. Eek. "I'm more of an art appreciator. I volunteered at an art gallery when I was in college, and I did a little framing. I loved being around all the beautiful works of art."

"I was cutting some mat board for this print. It's going to be triple matted, with an antique frame that the customer asked me to restore."

"You do restoration work too?"

"We've been around for a long time, and if it relates to art, I'll give it a shot. We do custom frame designs, shadowboxes, photo restoration, and antique artwork preservation."

"That must be fascinating. How did you learn how to do it?"

"Mostly from my parents. I'm the second-generation owner of the gallery and frame shop. My father was a photographer and took lots of photos of the area. That led to opening the gallery, framing, and the rest of it."

Lily stopped in the doorway of the workroom. "Hey, there you are. I looked all over the place."

"Lily, this is Leslie, the owner of the gallery. We were talking about framing, and she's letting me observe while she cuts this mat."

"At school, you used to do that at the gallery, didn't you?" Lily asked.

"Yes, I almost flunked philosophy because I spent so much time at the gallery instead of doing my boring homework. Descartes and Locke were tedious, but framing was fun." Carly pointed at the print Leslie was working on. "Isn't that an amazing block print?"

Leslie said, "It's from a plate from the 1800s. That mill used to be on the lake."

"Leslie's family has owned this store for a long time," Carly added.

"So you must know all the local artists?" Lily said.

Leslie held up the X-Acto knife she was using to remove a strip of tape from a piece of glass. "If they've lived here in the last fifty years, probably."

"Did you know Roger and Claudette Michaelson?" Carly asked.

"Yeah, they were Misha's grandparents." Leslie gestured toward the door. "He was here yesterday picking up some stuff I framed for him."

Carly tried to suppress her surprise. Had he finished something? "Oh, that's interesting."

"He said he has some frames and mats, but he was in a rush, so he asked me to do it." Leslie said.

Lily interrupted. "We're curious about the history of a painting at the Michaelson's cabin. It's an old acrylic painting, but we think it might be oil underneath. It has markings that

I think are from World War II. Do you have any idea why that might be?"

Leslie shook her head. "No idea. But that place was a hub of the fine arts community for years. My father said they threw the best parties at their place on the lake."

"So we've heard," Carly said. "We're staying in the house next door."

"Are there any paintings here from that era?" Lily asked. "Or something from the Michaelsons' collection? I'm wondering if there's anything else from the forties that might have the same marking."

"Most of what we have isn't that old. My father opened the gallery in the sixties, and much of what we have is contemporary." Leslie shrugged. "I could look at it if you want and see if it seems familiar."

"It's not ours," Carly said quickly as she yanked on Lily's sleeve. "We were curious, that's all."

Lily raised her eyebrows at Carly, who shook her head. "Yes. Curious. That's us."

"Lily gets like a dog with a bone when she gets curious about something," Carly said. "We should really be going. Thank you for letting me watch you cut that mat. Your work is gorgeous."

They left the gallery, and the moment they stepped onto the sidewalk, Carly said, "So what did you find out? Don't leave me in suspense."

Lily grinned. "Negative. I think you're stuck with me for a while longer."

Carly launched into her friend's arms and squeezed as hard as she could. "I'm so relieved."

"Not as much as I am." Lily took Carly's hand and swung it between them. "And I want you to know that having this experience has led me to an inescapable conclusion."

"What's that?"

"I hate my job. Life is too short to fight about patents. I'm done. I called the firm, talked to my boss, and gave my notice. I reckon there's a bunch of lawyers all freaking out about now."

Carly dropped Lily's hand and turned to face her. "You can't be serious."

"Never been more serious in my life. I've got more money than I need, no kids, no man, and no attachments of any kind. What that means is I have no reason to sit at that desk if I don't feel like it. I'm at the point in my life where I want to do something completely different. I want to make a difference."

"Doing what?"

"I'm not sure yet. All I know is that it's not going to involve patents or lawyers."

Carly hugged her again. "I don't know what to say, other than that I'm so happy for you. Whatever you do next, I know it will be absolutely amazing. I think I'm going to cry."

Lily laughed. "I swear, you are *such* a softie. Let's get back to our vacation before you start bawling."

~

Carly had Lily drop her at Brent's cabin so she could relieve Rose from puppy duty. Carly requested that Lily share her good news with Karen and Ginger, and promised that she'd be back later for the big celebration after Brent returned from LA.

Rose was still out back, reading on the chaise next to the puppy enclosure. The pups interrupted their playtime to bark at Carly, who opened up the pen and let them romp on her, picking them up and hugging each one in turn.

Rose laughed. "They sure know a soft touch when they see one."

"They know I think they're completely adorable. It's going to be so hard to say goodbye to them." She held D'Artagnan up in front of her face. "Especially this guy. I know you're not supposed to have favorites, but..."

"But you're gonna have a new dog."

"I have Trixie, and I'm not in a good place in my life to take on another dog. Maybe Brent will adopt him."

"Nah, he travels too much."

"He does?" Carly paused for a second. "I, um, realized I never asked him where he lives."

"He rented a tiny loft in the arts district in LA, but he might have given it up." Rose shrugged. "I'm not really sure anymore. After our conversation about his witchy woman, I think he might have decided to share a little less about his personal life with me."

Carly put D'Artagnan back down. At least she wasn't the only one who had no clue. "I saw one of his paintings at the art gallery in town. The woman who owns the place is really nice."

"Leslie is great. Our families have known each other forever."

Carly picked up Aramis and tucked him under her arm. "I'm going to take them inside. Thanks for watching them."

"It was fun watching them play. If I didn't have an old curmudgeonly cat at home, I'd take one."

"Cats and dogs can get along, I think."

"Not this cat. Sheba is big and old and mean. Kinda like me."

Carly laughed and headed for the house. She needed to find a taller piece of wood, since D'Artagnan had demonstrated that leaping over the current barricade was no problem at all. After Carly carted all the pups inside, Rose settled in the kitchen to keep an eye on them while Carly ventured into the ever-so-creepy shed to find something larger to block the doorway.

It was dark and nasty inside the shed. Carly screeched and had a minor bug freak-out when she ran into a cobweb, but in the end, she emerged, otherwise unscathed, with an old, rusty chain-link gate. It would work to confine the pups, although getting in and out of the kitchen would be more of a production for the human members of the household.

She set up the new arrangement and locked herself in the kitchen with the pups. Rose proclaimed that she was going to go fight with the shower and see if she could convince it to do something more than spray a fine mist.

Having been awakened early by the puppies and recalling Brent's comments about the shower's feeble nature, Carly had skipped washing that morning. That's what ponytails were for, after all. She was looking forward to returning to the enormous shower and her bed at the rental house. Being here was a little too much like camping out and her compulsion to clean something was becoming difficult to ignore.

To console her inner neatnik, she returned to her task of sorting the newspaper clippings, which were still on the table with the cookbook. While the puppies cavorted and tumbled over each other, she carefully smoothed out the wrinkled scraps of newsprint and sorted the recipes by type. Some of the old ads were amusing, and she pondered the difficulty of making some of the dishes. Would Claudette really have had the patience to make these complicated recipes in *this* kitchen? It seemed unlikely.

She flipped over a recipe for hamburger pie that sounded tasty. The article on the back was about a World War II German war criminal who had been found traveling from Argentina. Hmm. Maybe Claudette had found that interesting. Was it possible she knew him? Carly was distracted from her musings by a crashing noise from the back of the house. What was Rose doing in there?

She got up and extricated herself from the kitchen. "Are you okay?"

Rose's reply was muffled, but Carly noted that Rose threw in an anatomically improbable statement for emphasis.

In the studio, Rose was sitting on the floor surrounded by paints. Carly stood in the doorway. "What happened?"

"I couldn't reach the shelf."

Carly moved around the room picking up tubes of paints and a few ancient stiff brushes. "Check it out. There was a hand-held mat cutter in this box. Leslie mentioned that Brent sometimes frames his own stuff."

Rose stood up and brushed dust off her caftan. "So much for the shower. After the misting, now the dust sticks to me better."

"It's filthy in here."

"I can tell you're itching to organize everything, but why don't you frame something instead? You said you know how, and it will keep you busy and away from scrubbing bubbles and other cleansers."

Carly smiled. "Is it that obvious?"

"There's tons of mat board over there. I'm sure Misha won't care if you use some of it. Knock yourself out."

"What should I frame? I don't think anything is finished. And what if I mess up? I haven't framed anything in years. I don't want to ruin Brent's artwork."

"Do the puppy pen-and-inks. Misha won't care because they're throw-away sketches to him. But I think they're cute. You can give them to the people who adopt them."

Carly clapped her hands together. "That's a brilliant idea! Who could resist having a picture of their own puppy, painted by a famous artist? When Brent gets back, I'll ask him if it's okay."

Rose smiled and patted Carly on the back. "Whatever you want. I'm meeting someone in town tonight, and I need to try to make myself presentable. At this rate, it might take a while."

Carly went into the studio, grabbed the sketchpad with the puppy images and returned to the living room, flipping through them as she settled onto the sofa. Because she'd spent so much time with the little canine monsters, she was able to recognize each puppy's personality from his expression.

She glanced up at the sound of the front door opening. Brent walked in and shut the door behind him. He gave Carly a half smile as he dropped his duffel bag on the floor. "I'm glad you're still here."

Something about the expression on his face made Carly's heart skip a beat and her insides melt into a puddle of emotional goo. She set the sketchpad on the coffee table and stood up. Her gaze locked with his and they moved toward each other. Brent put his hands on her shoulders and Carly looked into his gray-blue eyes. His face was so close that she could see the dark-blue ring around his iris. Carly was a sucker for blue eyes, and his were especially nice ones, the color of the sky in the heat of summer.

She said softly, "How was your trip?"

As an answer, he pressed his lips to hers. Carly might have uttered a tiny yelp as her heart rate shot into the stratosphere. He smelled like paint, which wasn't surprising, but it was mixed with the scent of warm summer breezes, which was intoxicating. As the kiss deepened, all Carly's late-night lectures to herself about being a responsible adult and saying goodbye to him evaporated into the ether.

He moved forward and mumbled, "I want..." Carly caught her foot on the leg of the coffee table and fell backward onto the couch. She clutched at him and they both rolled onto the floor with a thud.

Rose called from the bedroom. "Are you okay?"

Carly pushed Brent off her. "Fine. I'm fine. I just tripped."

Brent sat up looking dazed, and pulled his knees up to his chest. "Was that my Aunt Rose? What's she doing here?"

"I don't know." Carly shrugged and smiled feebly at Rose, who was standing over them with her hands on her hips. "Maybe you could ask her."

～

Rose stretched out her arms. "Hey, Misha. Long time no see."

Brent struggled to disentangle himself from Carly and the coffee table, stood up, and gave his aunt a hug.

Rose patted him on the back and stepped back. "So your girlfriend and I have been getting to know each other. She wants to frame some of your sketches, but she's afraid she might screw up because she hasn't framed anything in a long time. Are you going to freak out about it, or can she practice on your stuff?"

Brent looked down at Carly. "I guess so."

"Oh, and she wants to know where you live."

"Well, you know I had that furnished loft apartment in LA. Before I came here to Alpine Grove, I gave my notice and I moved the last of my art supplies out this morning. The lease runs out at the end of the month."

"Well, homelessness might not be the most desirable trait in a guy, but what can you do? There you go, Carly. Everything you wanted to know." Rose gave him another hug. "I'm glad that's settled. My work here is done. I'm meeting Jimmy in town. Don't wait up."

Rose marched out the door, shutting it behind her with an air of finality. Carly scrambled onto the sofa and sat perched on the edge, slightly stunned. Brent sat next to her and took one of her hands. "Well, now you've met my aunt."

"I like her. She's very, um, direct. And she tells great stories. Did you know she sang backup at Woodstock?"

"I knew." Brent put his arm around Carly's shoulders and pulled her back against him. "You're not about to run off, are you?"

Carly turned in his arms to face him and placed her palms flat on his chest. "I'm supposed to go back to the house to celebrate with my friends. Lily got some good news."

"Do you have to go now?"

"I said I would go over there once you got back from your trip."

"Maybe I got stuck in traffic." He kissed her and whispered in her ear. "LA has bad traffic, you know. *Really* bad traffic. Slow. Agonizingly, slow. Languorous. Prolonged. Relentless."

Given what he was doing with his hands, Carly was pretty sure he wasn't talking about cars anymore. With what was left of her rational mind, she pointed out that Rose had taken over his room.

"This place has more than one bedroom." He pulled her up off the sofa toward the hallway. Carly dug in her heels. "I'm not going in there with the turnips, cows, and bug-eyed Mona. Talk about a turn off. *Yuck.*"

Brent went into the room, grabbed the hideous painting from the wall, and leaned it against the wall in the hallway. "Fine with me."

Carly laughed and threw her arms around his neck as he kicked the door shut behind them. "Bye Mona."

Quite some time later, Carly was curled up next to Brent. Having explored various speeds, she had now settled on languid. She trailed a finger across his bare chest and he opened his eyes. "I need to go join the celebration next door. I should get up and take a shower."

"Good luck with that."

"Are you going to stop me?" Carly gave him a satisfied smile. "*Again?*"

"I meant good luck with the shower."

"I avoided it this morning." Carly reached up and felt the remnants of her now extremely tangled ponytail. "But my hair is a disaster. I can't go back over there like this."

Brent rolled onto his side and rested his chin on his palm. "I think you look beautiful."

"My hair is a filthy mess."

"There's always the lake. I have biodegradable shampoo and I wouldn't mind washing off the smog of Los Angeles, while we're at it."

"Are you saying you were actually serious about washing in the lake? But that water is freezing."

"I prefer to think of it as invigorating." He pulled her out from under the covers. "Let's go."

They stopped by the bathroom, he handed her a towel and a bottle of shampoo, and they went outside, across the deck, and down toward the lake. The sun had set, and the grass was wet and cold on her bare feet from the evening dew. She gazed up at the stars that were glittering above and shivered when she dropped her towel.

With a mischievous smile, Brent took her hand and they gingerly tiptoed into the lake. As she'd predicted, the water was cold, but it was also exhilarating. Soap and shampoo could be a lot of fun when shared, and the goosebumps on Carly's skin weren't only from the water temperature. Once her hair was finally cleaned and rinsed, Carly extricated herself from Brent and splashed at him. "Okay, now I *really* do have to go."

Back on the beach, he wrapped her towel around her and pulled her into his arms for one last lakeside kiss. "Would you be willing to come back over here later?"

"I might be convinced to return." Carly reached up and ran her fingers through his wet hair. "If you ask nicely."

Once they were inside, Brent gave her quite a few more reasons to return to the cabin that night but didn't aid in the getting-dressed process at all.

At the front door, she kissed him goodbye. "When I come back, you need to tell me what happened in LA."

"Sure, if you tell me why you suddenly want to frame stuff."

Carly looked into his eyes. "Because it's fun. I enjoy framing."

"You do?"

"Yes. I forgot how much until I went to the gallery today. Talking to Leslie, I realized it's a whole part of my life that I let go. When I walked into the gallery, it felt like home. I spent so much time at the gallery in college, talking about art, and framing pieces. I spent my days thinking about color and texture. I even skipped classes so I could spend more time there."

"*You* skipped classes? No way."

"Hey, I can be a rebel."

Brent pulled her close again. "Then stay here. Extend your vacation. I don't want this to end in a few days."

Carly's stomach clenched at the idea of saying goodbye. "I don't either."

"Then stay." He gestured toward the cabin. "If you don't want to stay here at the cabin, at least stay in Alpine Grove."

"I told you before. I can't. I'm already renting a crappy apartment with no furniture. And then there's Trixie. I just can't."

He leaned his forehead on hers. "It's probably way too soon to say this, but I'm falling in love with you, and we need more time."

Carly stepped back from him. "How can you say that? We've known each other for a *week*. I didn't even know where you lived until a few hours ago. Shouldn't we know things like that about each other?"

"Well, I don't live there anymore. I live here, at least for the time being."

"For the summer. But then what?"

"I'm not sure. I haven't figured it out yet."

Carly shook her head. "I'm one of those people who needs stability. I don't do uncertainty. I just rented a new apartment, after telling my new landlord how dependable I am. And I *am* dependable. My dog goes to the veterinarian once a year in March for her annual check-up. I get my teeth cleaned every six months. It's how I am."

"I know that. But sometimes life throws you a curve. Sometimes the guy you thought you were going to marry throws you out of the house you've lived in for years. Sometimes your creative muse flies out the window and you're considering chucking a career and a lifetime of training." He shrugged. "You can't control everything."

"But I *want* to." Carly paused. "I hate feeling like my whole life is out of control. And when you say something like you love me, I think that's completely nuts. We just met. There's no way you could love me or I could love you."

"Why not?"

"You're too young for me. Or I'm too old for you, depending on how you want to look at it. You're too famous and successful, and I'm completely lost. We don't know each other well enough yet."

"According to who?"

"Everybody."

"Who's everybody? And why do they get a say in this?"

Carly paused, wanting to shake him for twisting her words around. Finally she said, "I don't know. All I know is that I don't want to fall in love again. It hurts too much."

"Love doesn't hurt. Rejection hurts. Breaking up hurts. But love itself should feel good. Like this does." He took her hand and pulled her into his arms. "I understand what happened before, but that doesn't have anything to do with us. I don't see why you don't want to give this a chance."

Carly shook her head. "Because I tried so hard to be perfect and it wasn't enough. For fifteen years I tried and tried. And look how well it turned out. I can't go through that again."

"I don't want you to be perfect. I want you to be you."

"What if I don't know who that is?" she mumbled into his chest.

"Then you'll figure it out. Promise you'll come back later, okay?"

She squeezed her eyes shut, hugged him hard, and said softly, "I will."

Chapter 13

Discoveries

As Carly walked back toward the house, her mind was swirling with everything Brent had said. How could he possibly feel so strongly about her after such a short time? Rose had said he had terrible taste in women. Maybe she was the latest in a string of bad choices. And he was the latest in a string of *her* bad choices. They were quite a pair.

When she walked in the French doors, the party was in full swing. Karen came up to her and handed her a glass of wine. "Where have you *been?*"

Lily danced into the kitchen from the living room, swaying her hips in time to the music. "How come your hair is wet?"

Carly reached up to her hair absently. "I, uh, took a shower because we left so early this morning."

Lily swayed off, and Ginger handed Carly a bag of potato chips. "We're having a junk-food extravaganza."

Carly chatted and hugged her friends, but part of her wasn't feeling celebratory. By the time the CD changer ran out of CDs, the free-flowing wine had caught up with everybody and the party started to wind down.

Lily sat at the table nursing a glass of red. "So I guess Monet made it back from wherever he went. Must have been a long trip."

Carly nodded. "He said I could frame some of his stuff. There are some sketches he did of the pups that are adorable. If I frame them, we could give them to each of the adopters as a gift."

"Aww, that's so sweet. I love it," Ginger said.

Karen said, "At the end of the week, I can give them their last puppy shots, so they'll be good to go into their foster homes. Brigid left a message that she has someone lined up to foster them. I said we'll be able to drop them off with her on Friday afternoon."

"So everything is all set," Carly said with a touch of sadness. "I'm going to have a hard time seeing them go."

"Yeah, me too," Ginger said. "Not to mention saying goodbye to this vacation. Going home is going to be rough."

"I thought you talked to Nathan," Carly said. "Everything's okay now, right?"

"Not exactly. I told him some things need to change," Ginger frowned and glanced at Karen. "We've been talking, and I'm thinking I might try to go back to school."

Carly sat up straight. "*Really*? That's wonderful. Why do you look so glum?"

"It's hard." Ginger swirled the wine in her glass. "I'm not sure I can pass the MCATs at this point."

"You want to go to medical school?" Carly ran around the table and hugged Ginger. "That's fantastic! You're going to slay the MCATs. I'm sure of it."

Ginger laughed. "That's our Carly, always everyone's biggest cheerleader."

Carly sat back down. "Well, it's true. You'd be an amazing doctor."

"Certainly better than the losers that tested me every which way and then didn't give me results for weeks," Lily added.

"Plus, there are plenty of study guides and courses you can take," Karen said. "You only need to refresh your knowledge a bit, that's all."

"She's right," Lily said. "You were a total science geek, and I'm sure it will all come back to you."

"The other part is convincing Nathan. And telling my kids." Ginger rested her elbows on the table and set her chin in her palms. "Ugh."

"Hey, they'll get over it," Lily said. "You're their mother, not their slave."

Ginger sat up. "Then *you* can tell them their mom isn't going to be able to drive them to soccer and piano lessons anymore."

The conversation wound down, and after everyone retired to bed, Carly tiptoed out of the house, through the forest, and back to the cabin. She walked up onto the deck and tapped on the screen door. The puppies barked as if the world were ending, and Brent appeared from the hallway wearing nothing except an old pair of denim cut-offs. Carly loved his bare feet. Was it creepy to think that naked toes were sexy?

He opened the door and wrapped her in a hug. "You came back."

"Of course I did. I told you I would."

Taking her hand, he led her down the hallway to the studio. "I want to show you something."

"I think I've seen pretty much everything now, haven't I?" Carly said with a giggle. "Or do you still have etchings you haven't shown me yet?"

They went into the studio and he pulled a Polaroid photo off the desk. "I don't think you ever saw this after I finished it, but I sold it in LA. They want me to do a whole series of dragons because my agent has a line on a huge fantasy licensing deal."

Carly squinted at the photo. "I wish you'd shown it to me before you left, so I could see it better."

"I had to get it framed and take it down there before they changed their mind." He handed her another Polaroid. "I also finished this one, which is the first of a bunch of illustrations for a children's book about adopting puppies from animal shelters."

Carly held up the image. It was the painting of her with puppies, but the finished version was filled with details she hadn't seen. "I can't believe I'm going to be in a book."

"I hope you don't mind. Technically, I probably should have asked you to sign a model release."

"*Mind?* Why on earth would I mind?" She threw her arms around him in a hug and looked at the photo in her hand again. "This is amazing. I'm so thrilled for you. Your muse came back. She really did."

He unwrapped her arms from him. "That's why I need to stay here. I don't know why, but right now I need to be here to work."

"Please don't create anything like bug-eyed Mona, okay?"

"Do your friends still think my family is full of art thieves?"

"No, but…" Carly paused, recalling the notes in the cookbook. "I was talking to Lily, and then I thought of something. What if your grandparents were *saving* art, not stealing it? Your grandmother was involved with the Resistance. And her cookbook has names with numbers. Remember how Ginger said that there was some Burt Lancaster movie about art being moved on a train? What if your grandparents were involved in some type of artwork underground railroad?"

"Was there such a thing?"

"I'll talk to Lily in the morning. She might know from the reading she did. If not, we can try to find out at the library."

"I have to go to the post office tomorrow. Maybe Rose could watch the pups and we could do a few errands."

"Oh, I forgot to tell you. The pups go to foster care on Friday. And tomorrow is *Wednesday*. I felt like crying when Karen told me. How am I going to let them go?"

"I don't know." Brent pushed a curl of hair behind her ear. "If you have any ideas, let me know."

"I will." She took his hand and led him down the hallway. "But for right now, I think we should spend as much time together as we can."

~

When Carly opened her eyes, the sun was streaming in the window and Brent was no longer lying next to her. She dressed hurriedly and opened the door to the hallway. Ugly Mona was still leaning against the wall, and the cabin was suspiciously quiet. Where was everybody?

She padded down the hall to the kitchen. The puppies and Ripley weren't there, so she turned and walked to the screen door to the deck. Brent was outside wearing a towel around his waist, and the puppies were playing in their enclosure, jumping on each other while Ripley looked on.

Everyone seemed content, so Carly wandered into the kitchen. Brent had warned her about the coffeemaker, but she was willing to take a risk. They'd stayed up extremely late, so it would take a serious infusion of caffeine to jump-start her brain this morning.

Rose was standing in front of the machine and staring at it, as if she were willing the coffee to drip more quickly. She turned and pointed at it. "I tried to clean this thing yesterday, but it might be past saving."

"It's gross, but if you made extra, I'd love a cup."

The two women sat sipping their coffee, hugging the mugs as they sat in silent contemplation. At length, Rose said, "So are you moving in here with Misha?"

"What gave you that idea? I'm on vacation, and I have to go back to work next week."

Rose sleepily murmured something unintelligible and Carly raised her eyebrows in query. Rose said, "So this is all kind of a fling, huh?"

"No, of course not. Well, I don't know." Carly gazed down at her coffee. "But I have to go back to work."

"What do you do?"

"I'm an administrative assistant at a consulting company."

"That sounds, uh, interesting."

"You don't have to be nice. It's not." Carly sighed. "But I've worked there for years. So long, in fact, that I had to take this vacation. I've rolled over vacation hours for such a long time, I'd lose them if I didn't take time off. And that's like throwing money away."

Rose took a sip of coffee and a corner of her mouth turned up in a quasi-smirk. "Gee, I sure hate when I'm forced to take a paid vacation. That's rough."

"If it makes you feel any better, they were kind of jerks about it."

"Sound like a great job. What happens if you quit? Do you get the money for the rest of the vacation hours?"

"Yes, it's on the books that they owe me the money for the hours. If they don't pay, the accountants get angry."

"Don't piss off accountants." Rose tilted her mug toward Carly. "That's one of those life lessons I learned the hard way."

Carly figured there was a story there, but said evenly, "I'll take your word for it."

They looked up as Brent walked into the kitchen, still wearing only the towel. He pointed toward the door. "Could one of you keep an eye on the monsters? I need to get dressed, and D'Artagnan is acting like he wants to make a break for it."

"I'm on it." Carly stood up and went outside, thinking about what Rose had said. If she quit, she'd still have some money. Or she could extend her vacation. But there's no way they'd let her take another six weeks off. They'd need to hire a temp or a replacement. Or, more likely, they'd fire her for not being a "team player."

The apartment she'd rented was month to month, and she'd only been there two weeks. If she left, who would care? She'd told her landlord she was dependable, but there wasn't any type of long-term lease. Yet the idea of quitting her job felt way too huge. Good ole dependable Carly didn't impulsively bail out on her responsibilities. What would they do?

She sat on the edge of the lounge chair and watched as D'Artagnan stomped on Aramis. When Porthos jumped on Athos, the chase was on. She smiled at their happy yips. All of her friends had already boldly declared major new life choices. But Ginger and Lily weren't her. Karen wasn't exactly changing things up. She'd go back home, pick up Annie from camp, and return to work. And Carly would go back home. It was only a vacation, after all. If fifty percent of the women in the house had major life epiphanies, that was pretty good, wasn't it?

Brent sat next to her on the chaise and put his arm around her shoulders. He leaned to kiss her temple. "You look sad. Did Rose say something that upset you?"

"Nothing I haven't thought of myself. She has this way of saying in one sentence what's been spinning around in my mind forty-nine different ways."

"I know what you mean. She was the one who convinced me to go to school in London."

Carly looked up at him. "Really? What did she say?"

"'Opportunities like this don't happen every day. You're an idiot if you miss this chance to study at one of the greatest art schools in the world.'" He gave her a wry grin. "I may have only been a stupid teenager, but even *I* realized the truth of that statement."

"What if I did stay here? What would I do? I can't loaf around like I'm on vacation forever."

"You can do whatever you want to do. You said you like framing. That's the first thing you've ever mentioned that you enjoy." He glanced back at the cabin. "Well, other than cleaning toaster ovens, I guess."

"Should I stay?"

"You know how I feel about you, but what you do next is your decision, not mine. All I know is that I'm going to be here for the rest of the summer. Once it starts getting cold, I need to live somewhere else or I'll freeze to death. But I'll figure that out later."

Carly shook her head. "I don't know how you can live with such vague plans. I have so much baggage and so many questions, but at this point I'm sick of my own circular thoughts. Maybe a blistering hot shower will help. I need to go back to the house and take a real shower. I'll be back in a little while, and then we can go to town."

"I'll be here."

When Carly returned to the cabin, Brent and Rose were outside hanging out with the puppies and chatting. The sound of his laughter gave her a happy flutter in her tummy. You could tell how people felt about each other by how they laughed. It was obvious Brent and his aunt had a special bond.

Brent stood up when she approached and pulled her into his arms, and Carly resisted a little. Getting all touchy feely in front of Rose felt funny, even though she was obviously aware they'd spent the night together.

Rose took a sip from her coffee mug and waved them off. "Get going and don't forget to get my mini-donuts. I don't like the big yucky ones. Make sure you get the little ones that have the powdered sugar. My morning coffee isn't the same without them."

Carly followed Brent to the front of the house and got into his truck. She peered at the debris strewn throughout the cab and then looked at him. "You really are a confirmed slob, aren't you?"

"I just returned from a road trip." He turned the key in the ignition. "And then when I got back I had other things on my mind. Namely you."

Carly couldn't argue with that. "I suppose that was a good thing."

"Very good."

Carly leaned over and rested her head on his shoulder. "You're right. It was very good. I don't care one bit about your trashy trucky."

Carly was quiet during the drive to town. It was beautiful here, which, along with the sexy man sitting next to her, would make it that much more difficult to leave. Creative people like Brent and Rose were accustomed to continuous change and letting events unfold organically. No one became an artist or musician because they yearned for job security, after all. But Carly was just an average person, not extraordinary, brilliant, or talented at much of anything at all. What if she couldn't find a job? Alpine Grove wasn't exactly rolling in job opportunities. Even Leslie had to have both a gallery and a framing business to survive.

Making decisions wasn't exactly one of Carly's strengths, and throwing away her entire work life seemed too monumental to consider seriously. She wasn't that brave. What if Brent suddenly had a change of heart like Stuart had? She couldn't go through that again.

The fact was, Carly was afraid. She stared out the window, watching the scenery go by and wishing she had more time.

Even though she knew leaving this beautiful place was the right thing to do, at the same time it also felt impossibly hard to say goodbye.

~

When Carly had asked Lily about stolen artwork in World War II, Lily said that she thought she'd read about people who had worked to save art from the Nazis, but nothing specific. So the first stop in town was the Alpine Grove library. Lily claimed the librarian was a researching machine.

Brent parked in front of the library, which was a pretty two-story brick building with concrete accents around the windows and doors. According to the historical plaque on the front, it had been built in the 1920s and restored in the seventies for use as the town library. Carly and Brent went inside and stopped by the front desk, where a woman with curly, reddish-blonde hair sat going through a pile of papers. She put down what she was reading and asked if she could help them.

Carly said, "We have a painting that we think has markings from World War II. We're trying to find out if there were people who saved paintings from the Nazis."

"Yes, there were. I'm Jan, by the way." The woman walked around the desk and shook Carly's hand. "Someone was asking about something similar the other day. I gave her some information, but I found it so interesting that after she left I kept reading. Have you ever heard of the Monuments Men?"

"Nope." Carly glanced at Brent, who shook his head.

The librarian reached to pull some papers from the stack. "I printed out more information about it because I was curious, and I thought the person who asked might come back. In 1943, the Allied armies established The Monuments, Fine Arts, and Archives program. The MFAA had about 400 members, who were mostly museum personnel, artists, and historians. They were known as the Monuments Men."

Brent said, "At around that time, my grandfather went on some mission that he never talked about. It was near the end of the war, before he brought my grandmother to the United States."

"The Monuments Men worked to locate art that had been damaged or stolen during the war, and then preserve the items as best they could in the field," Jan continued. "As I understand it, many works were rescued. Although some major works of art were never found, over the course of six years or so, more than five million pieces of artwork and cultural items stolen from wealthy Jews, museums, universities, and religious institutions were recovered."

"Maybe now we know what your grandfather was up to," Carly said. "Do you think they smuggled that painting out of the country to keep the Nazis from getting it, then disguised it with ugly paint?"

"It's possible. I can imagine both he and my grandmother being appalled at the looting of art throughout Europe. I have no idea why they'd disguise it though."

Carly smiled. "Maybe because no one would think something that ugly could be valuable."

"I suppose so." He sighed. "Rose doesn't seem to know anything about it, but my father might, I guess."

Carly said, "I found a clipping in the cookbook about a Nazi war criminal. Maybe your grandparents were keeping it hidden from someone in particular."

Brent shrugged. "Could be."

Carly thanked Jan, who returned to her stacks of papers. Carly put her hand on Brent's forearm. "When I was at the gallery, Leslie told me that she does restoration work. Do you think she'd be able to tell if the ugly painting is worth something?"

Brent said, "If not, she'd know an expert we could talk to about it."

"If it's an important work and not grandpa's creepy cows and turnips, I'd like to get it back to the rightful owner if we can."

"I would too, although the idea of talking to my father about it doesn't sound like fun."

Carly squeezed his arm gently. "Sorry."

"It's okay. I'd like to find out what happened."

"Me too."

Next they stopped by the gallery, and Leslie promised to make a few calls to see if she could find experts willing to evaluate the painting. Afterward, they headed to the post office. Brent handed Carly a nine-by-twelve envelope. "I wish I'd thought to buy stamps to mail this contract when I was in LA. You can kill hours waiting in line at the Alpine Grove post office. If I had stamps, I'd put seven or eight on there and call it good. It beats waiting in line and watching Ethel move in slow motion."

"It's no big deal," Carly said. "We're not in any rush. Rose seems to like hanging out with the puppies."

Brent had parked across the street from the post office, and through the glass windows Carly could see that the line was meandering out the interior door and slithering off into the area where the rows of PO boxes were located. Mailing this contract was likely to take a while.

A bald man had been smart enough to bring a lawn chair. He sat with his package in his lap, chatting with the guy next to him in line. He thumped the chair sideways whenever the line slowly crawled forward. Carly felt like an outsider. It seemed like everyone in this town knew everybody else.

Brent leaned back against the metal boxes. "Do you know any word games we could play to pass the time?"

"Well, there's the alphabet game. Karen and I used to play that on long car trips. Find something here that starts with the letter A."

"The guy with the cooler is eating an apple. Score one for me."

Carly scrutinized the area, searching for something that started with the letter B. "Got it. You're wearing a blue t-shirt."

Brent lurched off the wall and stumbled. Startled, Carly grabbed at him. "Are you okay?"

"Cindy."

"Names don't count. I don't know anyone in this town, so you could make up names for anyone and I'd never know. Although I suppose you could use Carly for C. That wouldn't be too big of a cheat."

"No, Cindy is *here*. That woman with the kid." He pointed and bent over, putting his hands on his knees.

"Okay, I guess I can give you that one, since I've met her." Carly smiled at the woman she'd encountered at the kennel, with the little boy who had been in a time out. "She came by when I dropped off Trixie. Cindy is Kat's sister-in-law."

"What's she doing here?"

"Getting mail, I suppose. I got the impression from Kat that she lives here in town. I can tell you that she and Kat don't seem to get along."

Brent stood up. "She lives *here*? Jeez, what are the odds?"

Cindy was walking toward the end of the line and jerked, doing a double take at the sight of Brent. She grabbed her son's hand. "Let's go, Johnny. Hurry up. We're going over there."

Johnny yanked his hand out of Cindy's so he could wave at Carly. He ran up and skidded to a stop in front of her. "I remember you! You have the fat dog."

Carly said, "Hi again. Trixie prefers to think of herself as pleasantly plump. This is my friend, Brent."

Cindy and Brent stared at each other in shocked silence. The color had drained from Brent's face, and he was so pale that Carly wondered if he was about to be sick.

Finally, he said, "How have you been, Cindy?"

Cindy appeared to be as horrified to see Brent as he was to see her. "I thought you were in Europe."

"That was a long time ago."

Johnny looked up at them. "I'm Johnny. I'm eight. My teacher Mrs. Detweiler says I'm imaginative. But she's not my teacher anymore. I'll be in a different class in September."

Carly stifled a giggle. That poor teacher was probably counting her blessings. Johnny had grayish-blue eyes and sandy, dark-blonde hair that was exactly the same color as Cindy's.

Carly glanced at Brent, who was still glaring at Cindy. "So how do you two know each other?"

"We met here in Alpine Grove many years ago." Brent said.

Johnny tugged on the leg of Brent's jeans. "Did you know Mommy when she was little?"

Brent studied the boy and then cast his gaze back to Cindy. "I'm not that hard to find. You could have called and *told* me."

"It's complicated." Cindy ran her hand through her short hair. "You might want to talk to your father."

"I'd rather talk to *you*."

Cindy's angry expression crumpled and she grabbed Johnny's hand. "This line is too long. We've got to go."

Johnny was clearly confused, but waved goodbye to Carly as Cindy dragged him out the door. "Say hi to the fatso dog!"

Brent leaned back against the wall again and slid down to the floor. He pulled his knees up to his chest and wrapped his arms around them, watching as Cindy and Johnny fled the building.

Carly sat on the floor next to him and put her hand on his arm. "Is she the woman you told me about?"

"Yes."

"Is that little boy your son?"

"I think so, unless nine years ago she managed to sleep with another guy who looks exactly like me."

He rested his forehead on his knees. "Why don't they have a stamp machine here? What post office doesn't have a machine? It's like Ethel wants a monopoly."

"We should go." Carly tugged at his arm. "We should talk about this."

"I don't want to talk. I need to go somewhere and think. But I have to get this stupid contract in the mail."

Carly opened her purse and took out her wallet. She whipped out a ten-dollar bill and stood up. She held up the bill and waved it as she walked in front of the line of postal patrons. "Okay people, the first person to give me ten stamps gets ten bucks."

Women scrabbled for their purses and men reached into their pockets. An older woman wearing a light-blue jogging suit set down her package and raised her hand so aggressively she was practically jumping up and down. "Right here!"

Carly performed the transaction and returned to Brent with her prize. "Let's get out of here."

After dropping the stamped envelope in the outgoing mail slot, they got into the truck and headed back to the lake. It was a quiet drive back. Carly made a few feeble attempts at conversation, but it was clear from his monosyllabic responses that Brent wasn't kidding when he said he didn't want to talk.

∼

When they got back to the cabin, Carly followed Brent to the back of the house, where Rose was still hanging out with the puppies.

Brent stalked up to his aunt. "Did you know about Cindy?"

Rose squinted up at him, shading her eyes with her palm. "Who is Cindy?"

He waved his arms in exasperation. "The girlfriend I had the summer after I graduated from high school. The one that my father was so desperate for me to get rid of that he sent me to London."

Rose sat up. "I know Arthur wanted you to go to college. And that he was afraid you'd run off with that girl and ruin your chances at a career."

"Did he know she has a kid who looks a lot like me? Did *you*?"

Rose placed her hand on her chest. "I had no idea. I swear I didn't. Are you saying you have a child? How did that happen?"

Brent made a disgusted noise, whirled away, and started down to the beach. Rose looked at Carly in alarm. "Where is he going?"

Carly shook her head and turned to run after him because she had a pretty good idea where he was headed. She caught up and grabbed his arm. "Don't go up there alone. I'll go with you."

Brent's expression relaxed. "I know that you're trying to be nice, but I'd really rather be by myself for a while."

"I understand that you're upset, but everything will work out okay. You'll see."

"Thanks for the Pollyanna vote, but you have absolutely no idea how I feel right now. I mean, have you ever had everything you thought was true in your life suddenly get thrown out the window?"

"A few weeks ago, I was asked to leave my own house by the man I thought I loved. So yes, I do."

Brent regarded her for a second, then pulled her into his arms and hugged her. "All right. Let's go."

Carly followed him, huffing and puffing her way up the trail. Leave it to her to find a guy who could only manage to think at a scenic overlook at the top of an extremely steep hiking trail. It was going to be hard to be appropriately sympathetic if she was busy having a heart attack.

At last, Carly stepped through the final craggy pass and out onto the flat slab of rock that hovered over the lake. She stumbled over to the rock that resembled a chair and leaned back, grateful that she'd survived the climb. It might be time to consider getting into better shape. This was ridiculous.

Brent walked out to the end of the promontory, sat down, and let his legs dangle over the edge. He sat motionless with his arms folded across his chest, staring out at the lake. Carly wasn't sure what to do. If she walked over there, she'd probably tip over and fall right off the edge. Even the idea of being that close to the edge gave her the willies.

After pausing for a moment to consider her options, she got down on her hands and knees and slowly crept along the granite, looking down at the rock rather than at the lake three gazillion miles below. When she got close enough to Brent to touch him, she flattened to the ground, rolled over onto her back, and gazed up at the sky.

He leaned over and gave her a kiss. "You really aren't good with heights, are you?"

"Not really. Let's not talk about it. The sky is pretty today. Look at those clouds." She reached her hand over her head and placed it on his thigh. "Are you okay?"

"No." He pulled his legs in from the edge and rearranged himself so he was lying next to her on the rock, looking up at the sky. "You're right, the clouds are pretty."

"Is there anything I can do?"

"Turn back time and buy me a box of condoms?"

Carly laughed and covered her mouth with her hand. "I'm sorry. That wasn't funny."

"It's okay. I think anyone who has been young and in lust probably can relate."

"When I was that age, I was terribly in lust with Greg Kincaid. He didn't know I was alive though. But if he'd paid any attention to me, I'd probably have a kid by now too."

"As you know, I've gotten more cautious in my old age."

"True. I'm glad you have come to appreciate the wisdom of safe sex." Carly rolled over and propped herself up on her elbows. "I need to ask you something."

"Go for it. My secrets are an open book. Even secrets I didn't know I had."

"How do you feel about Cindy? Is she the girl you've pined for over the years? According to you, she's Juliet to your Romeo."

"And look how well that worked out for them." He closed his eyes. "Although Cindy and I aren't dead, it's a miracle we didn't kill each other. We had fights like you wouldn't believe. They were…well…let's just say that things were said that can't be unsaid. No one has ever made me that angry before or since. At the time, I swore up and down to my father that we were passionate artists who were destined to be together, but I know now that we never could have made it work. I've never regretted saying goodbye to her."

"I guess that means you're not going to be her knight in shining armor, sweeping her off her feet and riding off into the sunset with your new happy family?"

Brent rolled onto his side, propped himself up on an elbow, and looked at her. "That sounds like a movie. Wait. How many times have you watched *Pretty Woman?* Or *Officer and a Gentleman?*"

"Too many." Carly put her hand on his shoulder. "I like sweepie feetie movies. But I'm serious. How do you plan to approach this situation?"

"Well, first, Cindy would have to talk to me, which, given her reaction today, might be a problem."

"She said to call your father."

"I know. If he knows about this, I don't think I can ever forgive him. I mean, Cindy and I had been fighting and had more or less broken up anyway. But maybe he caused that." Brent lay flat again and put his arm over his eyes. "God, what a mess. I don't know what to do."

Carly sat up, pulled his arm away, and gazed down into his eyes. "You'll do the right thing."

"Which is what?"

"You don't know yet. But you'll find out."

"How do you know?"

"Because I know you. You're an amazing listener. You'll let Cindy tell you what she wants and you'll listen."

Brent pulled her close and gave her a kiss. "You're not so bad at listening yourself, you know. Thanks for coming up here with me."

Carly rested her head on his chest. "I don't suppose you'd like to crawl with me over to that rock over there, would you?"

Brent took her hand, pulled her upright, and put his arm around her waist. He then slowly led her away from the edge. "Sorry I made you confront your fear of heights."

Carly sat down on the chair-shaped rock and gazed out at the lake. It was a brilliant blue, and from the safe distance she could again appreciate the breathtaking view. "I've been afraid of a lot of things for a long time. Afraid of making decisions. Afraid of upsetting Stuart. Afraid of taking risks. Afraid of how I feel."

"How *do* you feel?"

"Happy." Carly turned to face him. "I mean, I'm not happy that you're upset about everything that's happened. But I'm happy being here with you."

"That's good to hear."

"It's true. I've come up with every excuse in the book for why I shouldn't care about you and why I shouldn't stay here. And they're all meaningless. What matters is that I love you. *There.* I said it. After you told me how you felt, I've been afraid to say that to you. To admit how I really feel."

He kissed her. "You know I love you too. And you're right, everything will work out. It might take a while, but it will. And I'm sorry I called you Pollyanna."

"We have a lot of calls to make." She tilted her head. "Wait. You do have a phone at the cabin, don't you?"

"Of course I do."

"I've never heard it ring."

"I may have a phone, but that doesn't mean I've told anybody the number." He smiled. "I came up here to get away from business and people pressures. I wanted to be left alone to paint."

Carly laughed. "Well, that didn't work out too well. You ended up with a house full of barking dogs, relatives, and neighbors traipsing all over your privacy."

"I suppose. But maybe that was exactly what I needed." He ran his hand across her hair, brushing it back from her face. "If it weren't for those stray puppies, I wouldn't have met you."

"Maybe you should adopt D'Artagnan as a thank you."

"Maybe I should."

Chapter 14

Decisions

Carly spent most of the next morning at the cabin with Brent, framing his pen-and-ink drawings of the puppies and dreading making the phone call she knew she needed to make. Brent kept putting off calling his father while she put off calling her boss. Both conversations were likely to be unpleasant, so power procrastination was in order.

It turned out that the telephone was located in the art studio buried under piles of art supplies, which Carly found amusing. The reason Rose had been rummaging around in there so much was because she was trying to find the telephone. Rose was once again relaxing lakeside with the puppies, leaving Brent to work and Carly to practice her framing techniques.

Carly was mentally berating herself for being a chicken until she finally couldn't stand the little nagging voice in her head anymore. Brent was painting in his studio and she tapped on the door jamb. "We can't put this off any longer. I'll call my boss now, if you call your father afterward."

"All right. I guess we should." He leaned down and dug the phone out from its hidey hole. "The cord is really long. It reaches into the bedroom if you want some privacy."

Carly took the phone and wandered slowly down the hall, trying to figure out what she was going to say. "Hi. Remember me? I want to take more vacation." Yeah, that would go over well. With a sigh, she sat on the bed, picked up the handset, and dialed. A voice she didn't recognize answered, and Carly said, "Yes, I'd like to speak to Mr. Henderson, please."

Her boss's deep voice came on the line. "Jerry Henderson."

"Hi, this is Carly. How are you doing?"

"Looking forward to having you back. The last two weeks have been hellacious. The Werner proposal is due on Tuesday and we need you to finish assembling it."

"Well, about that...I'm calling because I may need to take a bit more of my vacation time."

"*What*? You said two weeks."

"HR said that I had to take two weeks or I would lose the hours. I actually had a total of three hundred and forty-eight hours. I've taken eighty, so I still have two hundred and sixty-eight left to use."

"Only with management approval."

"I'm calling for management approval now. It turns out I have some things I need to take care of here. We found some..."

"I don't care *what* you found. I want you back in the office and at your desk first thing Monday morning."

Carly gulped. Uh oh. "I'm sorry, but I have some..."

"*Nothing* is as important as you getting back to work. That Werner proposal is sitting on your desk and we need it out the door. In fact, we should have had it to them yesterday, but we got an extension until Tuesday. The courier needs to pick it up Monday afternoon."

Carly had known this would happen and that they'd never agree to let her extend her vacation. She had to go back to work. But she'd been hoping to have a few more weeks in Alpine Grove. She *needed* more time. She couldn't leave now, with so much still to figure out. She rubbed her eyes, listening to Jerry go on and on about the tedious details of the proposal. She dropped her hand and said, "What was that? I'm sorry but I can't hear you. This must be a bad connection. I'll call back. Bye."

She slammed the phone on the cradle and walked to the studio. Brent looked up from his sketchpad. "How'd it go?"

"About like I expected, but it's your turn now. Time to chat with dear old Dad."

"I have no idea what I'm going to say to him." Brent appeared to be distressed, but a deal was a deal, and he followed the phone cord down the hall and disappeared into the bedroom.

While he was on the phone, Carly amused herself by sorting through more of Brent's sketches. He'd been playing around with dragons again and some of them were amazing. She sat cross-legged on the floor and kept finding more and more pieces she wanted to frame. These things should be in a gallery so everyone could enjoy them, instead of hiding in a random sketchbook in the depths of this messy studio.

Brent strolled in carrying the phone and sat down cross-legged next to her on the floor.

Carly set the sketchbook aside. "What happened? What did he say?"

He shook his head. "Talking to my father always feels futile. I don't know where I got these listening skills you mentioned, but it's not from him. He claims that he had no idea Cindy had a child."

"Do you believe him?"

"I don't know. He said what he always says. He wanted me to get away from 'that girl,' get an education, and become a productive member of society."

Carly tugged on his t-shirt. "Society might not look too kindly on the fact that you're homeless at the moment though."

"Sure, rub it in. Maybe you can support me, since I've become a drain on the system. After the chat about Cindy went nowhere, I mentioned I was going to have the ugly painting evaluated and he freaked."

"What do you mean *freaked?*"

"He said the cabin wasn't mine to tamper with, and I don't know what else. It was a whole long tirade." He shrugged. "It pissed me off enough that I told him I was going to clean out this place and start throwing away stuff."

Carly pressed her palms to her chest. "Oh, be still my heart."

"He got all pissed off, said he had a meeting, and hung up on me. But I've been thinking about it, and there's no reason I can't live here year-round. It wouldn't take that much to winterize this place. The paneling is horrible, and if someone pulled that nasty stuff off, they could redo the walls and put in a bunch of insulation. And maybe fix the pathetic shower while they're at it."

"I think this place has a lot of potential. I was telling your aunt that it could be really cute if it were fixed up a little."

"Technically, I'm one-third owner of it, but if Rose goes along with the idea, we outvote Dad."

"After listening to her complaints about the shower, I think she'll be okay with the idea of making a few improvements and repairs."

He leaned over and whispered in her ear. "So would you be willing to help?"

Carly thought about the fact that they'd only known each other for less than two weeks and how she'd ended up "helping" Stuart for fifteen years. But she tossed it out of her mind. Brent wasn't Stuart, and this was more about him acknowledging and accepting her neaty freaky tendencies than it was about indentured servitude. She giggled at the tickling sensations. "Hey, cut that out. You're trying to lure me with the potential of cleaning and organizing, aren't you?"

"Maybe. Is it working?"

"It might be. What you're doing now isn't hurting either."

"Okay, let's go talk to Rose."

"Wait." Carly pushed him away. "I have a confession to make."

"What? You want to rip off all my clothes?"

"Well, that would be nice, but it's about the call I made to my boss."

"Oh yeah, I forgot to ask. How much vacation time can you take?"

"None. I have to be back in the office on Monday."

He moved to lean against the wall and rubbed the back of his neck. "So you're leaving?"

"I hung up on him."

Brent jerked his head up with a grin. "You're kidding. *Really?*"

Carly looked into his eyes. "While I was on the phone, I realized that if they refused to give me more time, I'd have to have to quit. And I couldn't do it. I chickened out."

"Leaving a job is a big decision."

Carly was tired of being a coward. She deserved more out of life. "Could I borrow your phone again?"

"Of course." He leaned over to give her a hug. "Good luck."

Carly dragged the phone back to the bedroom and dialed her office. When Jerry came on the line, she said, "I'm afraid I'm not able to come back to work right now. If you can't give me the vacation time, I'm going to have to tender my resignation."

"You can't do that," he exclaimed. "We need you here on Monday."

"I'm sorry, but that's not going to happen. I'd like you to mail my final paycheck and vacation pay to me. I know I gave HR the address for my new apartment, but I need you to mail it here to Alpine Grove instead."

Jerry blustered and threatened, but Carly held her ground. Finally, he gave up and she rattled off Karen's address. After she hung up the phone, she flopped back onto the bed with her arms spread wide. It was official. She'd actually quit, and now she was really and truly unemployed.

She sat up again and scanned the room. The world hadn't come to an end. Nothing had changed. It was okay. She let out a sly giggle. In fact, so far, unemployment felt pretty good. Really good.

She leaped off the bed and ran to the studio. Brent turned from his canvas and she announced, "Guess what? I'm not a member of the workforce anymore."

With a smile, he set his brush down and opened his arms wide. "Congratulations!"

As Carly hugged him, she knew she'd done the right thing. Although she never would have guessed it, quitting a job you didn't like was more than a little exhilarating.

Maybe taking a few risks wasn't so bad, after all.

～

The next morning Carly went back to the house and related the events of the previous day.

"You quit your *job*? This is the most un-Carly-like thing you've ever done!" Lily set her juice glass down on the table with a thump. "But I like it. Those trolls didn't deserve you."

"Is this about you jumping into a relationship with another man?" Ginger demanded. "Because that *would* be Carly-like. Given that you're strolling in here all happy, we know what's going on. We're not dumb. It's pretty obvious you didn't sleep here last night."

Carly shook her head. "It's not like that. You all know Brent. He's completely different from Stuart."

Karen said, "That's for sure."

"Even if I try to make him a sandwich, he tells me he'll do it himself. And he needs time alone. Whenever I was around Stuart, I felt like it was my job to entertain him." Carly shrugged. "It's hard to explain, but they are extremely different people."

Ginger's fierce expression relaxed slightly. "Okay, I think I see what you mean. Monet isn't likely to let you turn into his personal maid."

Carly laughed. "He won't let me clean anything."

"It's not just you. I don't think anyone has cleaned anything in that cabin for a long time," Lily quipped.

"Well, that's about to change. *Both* of us made some phone calls." Carly gestured toward the path to the cabin. "Brent has some things going on right now, which mean he needs space to paint. He also wants to stay in Alpine Grove for a while to deal with family issues. And I still need to figure out my life."

"Well, that's vague," Lily said. "You quit your job. What are you going to do all day?"

"I'm not sure," Carly said. "I have a few ideas though."

Ginger said, "I suppose you're moving in with Monet, aren't you?"

"Maybe at some point, but not now. I need to find a place. He's going to have a bunch of work done on the cabin, so it will be a construction zone."

"I thought he wasn't allowed to change anything." Karen said. "It was some rule in his family."

"He tried talking to his father, but it didn't go well, so Rose talked to him. Apparently, Brent's grandfather told his father not to mess with anything in the cabin because there was something valuable in there. Brent and I think it might be the painting," Carly said. "We think that his grandparents smuggled it out of Europe at the end of the war. There was a whole group of people who worked to save art that had been looted by the Nazis, and we're guessing Brent's grandfather was involved. But I think it went on long after the war, and that's what the notes in the cookbook mean. They may have been part of some type of network, returning lost art. The lists have entries like 'she's home,' which implies items were returned."

Lily said, "So they *were* art thieves, after all?"

"Sort of, but in more of a Robin Hood kind of way," Carly said. "We took the frame off and you can see the edges of the canvas that weren't painted over. We both think the color and brush work is similar to Degas."

"Is it possible it's a *real* Degas?" Lily asked.

"Brent talked to the gallery owner, Leslie, and she wants to see it. She already called around to find some experts to look at it too," Carly said. "If it's real, we'll get it restored, figure out the provenance, and get it back to the rightful owner. It could be from a museum or collector. It will take some research to figure it out."

"Discovering a long-lost Degas is mind-blowing, but how did Brent's father or his aunt *not* know about this?" Lily said.

"Nobody told them." Carly shrugged. "I found a newspaper clipping and was wondering if Brent's grandmother had saved it because that Nazi had a special interest in the ugly painting. He was captured in the seventies. By the time this guy surfaced, both kids were off living their own lives."

"And they never told Brent either?" Karen asked.

"Apparently not. His grandfather died suddenly, and maybe by the time his grandmother died, she figured it didn't matter anymore because everyone who knew about the painting was dead." Carly said.

"That seems a little lame, but who am I to criticize the keeping of family secrets? Sometimes they last a long, long time." Ginger picked up her mug and took a sip and then raised her eyebrows. "Do you realize we might have helped solve a fifty-year-old mystery? That's pretty cool."

Karen stood up. "Okay, ladies, I don't know about you, but I need to start packing. I'm picking up Annie early tomorrow, so I'm going to head home tonight. On my way back to town, I'm going to stop by the clinic and give Brigid the pups, so please say your goodbyes today."

Carly raised her hand as if she were in school. "Brent is adopting D'Artagnan, so it's no big deal if the pups stay for another night. Brent and I can drop them off tomorrow."

Karen put her hand on Carly's shoulder and gave it a squeeze. "I'm glad I'm not the only sucker. Because of my schedule, I can't adopt a puppy, but I already told Brigid that I'm taking Ripley. That dog is a total sweetheart, and Annie is going to be completely thrilled. She's wanted a dog for years."

"I've become attached to little Porthos, but I can't take him." Ginger stared down at her mug. "There's no way I can deal with studying for the MCATs and housebreaking a puppy, along with tending to the endless needs of my kids and Nathan. But Karen said Brigid already has families lined up to adopt. Apparently, she's got ten people on a waiting list to meet the musketeers."

"I'm considering joining the Peace Corps or AmeriCorps, so I'm not really in a good situation to adopt a puppy either," Lily said. "But over the last two weeks, I discovered I like dogs a lot more than I thought. I'm going to miss those pups."

"I'm sure Brent will let you visit D'Artagnan whenever you want," Carly said. "And Karen will let you visit Ripley too."

Karen nodded her agreement. "I can't believe our vacation is practically over. Carly was right that I needed some time away from work. I feel more relaxed than I have in years. And for the record, I'm thrilled that you're moving here, Carly. It's been great spending time with you again."

Carly jumped up and gave her sister a hug. "I know! We'll get to see each other more than on Thanksgiving or the random national holidays when I could get away from work."

Lily held up her glass. "I suggest that we not wait until one of us has some terrible life crisis to do this kind of thing again."

"Let's make a pact to keep in better touch. I promise that even with medical school, I will not wait so long to visit you people in person again," Ginger said.

The other three women raised their coffee mugs high. "Here, here!"

Carly set down her mug. "I'm going to miss you guys. I know we argued, but you know I love you all. Thanks for coming here and joining me in my summer vacation."

"It's not over yet, baby." Ginger said. "I'm going in that water. Naked. If Monet can do it, I can do it."

"After you adjust to the cold, the water isn't as bad as you might think," Carly said.

Lily laughed, "Did you go skinny dipping? Because that's another un-Carly-like thing to do."

"I *did*. And I dare you all to join me right now."

All four women looked at each other for a moment and stood up. Carly ran for the door, hopping as she pulled off her shoes. "Last one in is a rotten egg!"

~

The next morning, Brent and Carly put the puppies in their enclosure so Rose could keep an eye on them while she reclined on the chaise with a steamy romance novel. She made a shooing motion with both hands. "Go and say goodbye to your friends. That scoundrel Lord Reginald is about to make a move on Princess Isolde, and I have to find out what happens."

Carly took Brent's hand. "I can't believe I'm really staying. It feels like a dream."

"I hope it's a good dream."

"Really good. I don't want to wake up and find myself back in my depressing apartment getting ready to go to work at my crummy job."

He gave her hand a squeeze. "Once you find a place to live here and move your stuff, everything will feel more real."

They emerged from the trees and walked around to the front of the house. Lily was carrying a suitcase out to her car. She dropped it on the ground and waved. "Hey dormie roomie, get over here and say goodbye!"

Carly let go of Brent's hand and ran to give her friend a hug. "I'm going to miss you so much."

"It feels strange to be going back. So much has changed. I have to wrap up my life as a lawyer."

"You're really doing it?"

"I really am. In fact, I think now I've started a movement, since you quit your job too. I feel like a trailblazer."

Carly laughed and hugged her again. "Here's to whatever is next."

"Hey, it's about time you showed up." Ginger walked up and held up a key. "Karen says you need to give this to Tracy at the clinic when you hand off the puppies to Brigid."

Carly took the key and stuffed it in her pocket. "Are you both all packed and ready to go?"

Ginger launched into Carly's arms. "You behave yourself and call me the moment you find a place to live. I'll need your new phone number stat."

Brent was standing quietly off to one side and stepped backward when Ginger charged forward and threw herself at him for a bear hug. "You make sure to take care of our Carly."

When Ginger stepped back, Lily gave him a more sedate embrace. "We'll come and jerk a knot in your tail if you don't treat her right."

Ginger said, "Don't think we won't, Monet."

Carly watched as her friends drove off, and then she and Brent went into the house to collect the last of her things. Carly couldn't resist doing a little final straightening up as well.

Brent held her suitcase as she locked the front door and put the key back in her pocket. She turned to look into his eyes. "The end of vacation is always melancholy, but this is worse because we have to say goodbye to the puppies too. I hope I don't end up weeping all over this Brigid person. I don't even know her."

Brent leaned over to give her a kiss. "Alpine Grove is a small town, so I bet you'll see those dogs again."

After dropping off her stuff at Brent's cabin, they grabbed the hideous cow painting and placed Athos, Porthos, and Aramis into the plastic carriers that Karen had let them borrow from the clinic for the journey.

Carly picked up D'Artagnan and snuggled him to her. "I promise we'll be back soon with a new friend. You met Trixie briefly, but now you'll get to know her."

Brent picked up a carrier. "Leslie and Brigid are waiting so we should get going."

Carly handed D'Artagnan to Rose, who said, "Don't worry, I'll play with him, so he won't have a chance to get lonely."

They stopped by the gallery first to drop off the painting, which gave Carly time to pull herself together. Leslie expressed interest in adopting a puppy and Carly gave her Brigid's name, but warned her that there was a waiting list.

On the way to the clinic, Carly kept telling herself that she must not cry. She must *not* because there was no reason to be sad. The puppies had people waiting in line for them. They would live great lives with families who would love them. But every time she visualized handing over the carrier, another tear slipped out.

When they arrived, Carly got out of the truck and lifted a carrier from the floor of the cab. She held it up in front of her to peek inside. "Okay Porthos, get ready for your new life."

Brent took the carrier from her and she handed him another. "I don't suppose you were able to get through to Cindy, were you?"

"Nope. Since she hung up on me, she's been letting her machine screen her calls. Technically, I must have legal rights to see that boy. But I don't want to go about it that way."

"I know." She opened the door to the clinic. "It will work out."

Kat Stevens was standing in the waiting room, talking to a short woman with curly red hair. At the sound of the door, the two women turned and Kat said, "Hi Carly. This is Brigid Fitzpatrick, the Alpine Grove goddess of canine rescue."

Brigid laughed. "I'm not a goddess of anything. I'm a sucker for furry critters."

"Aren't we all," Kat said with a smile.

Carly set her carrier on the floor and Aramis whimpered. She gulped down the sob that wanted to leap from her throat and managed to squeak, "Me too."

Brent set down his carriers and held out his hand. "I'm Brent Michaelson. As Karen probably mentioned, the puppies have been staying at my place."

Carly took a deep breath and crouched down. "This is Aramis, that's Porthos, and Athos is over there. Thank you for finding them homes."

Brigid crouched next to Carly and held her hand out to the grate, so Aramis could sniff her fingers. "It's not going to be hard. They're adorable, aren't they?"

"Yes. I'm going to…" Carly stood up and covered her mouth quickly. No crying. None. *Don't.*

Brent said, "She means she's going to miss them."

Brigid turned to Kat, "Thanks for meeting me and handing off the newsletter. I should get going."

Brent picked up a carrier. "I'll help you with them."

Carly waved a feeble goodbye and Kat touched her arm. "Brigid is really good at this. Don't worry. They'll have homes quickly."

"I'm not worried. I'm really not. It's just there have been a lot of changes. I think I'm having a little meltdown."

"Nothing bad, I hope."

Carly offered a watery smile. "No, exactly the opposite. I think I told you about the old creepy painting at Brent's cabin."

"Wasn't it old—like from World War II?"

"Yes, and it turns out it might be valuable. We dropped it off with Leslie at the gallery in town. She has an expert who is driving up from LA, who is going to evaluate it."

"I guess anything becomes valuable if it's old enough."

"We think the ugly painting was painted over something much more interesting. But the best thing is that I might have a job lead."

"Are you staying in Alpine Grove?"

"I quit my job, and I'd like to be closer to my sister and Brent." Carly brushed away a final tear. "It feels like everything is working out. Leslie hasn't had a vacation in years, and she's been thinking about getting someone to help out in the gallery for a while.

"She was hoping one of her kids would be interested in taking over the gallery one day, particularly after her daughter moved back home. But after working for a while, her daughter decided she wants to try going back to school, after all. That means the space behind the gallery where she was living is also available for rent."

"That sounds great," Kat said, glancing at the door.

"I'm sorry, I'm just going on and on. But it's been a big day." Carly stopped short and stared at Kat for a moment. "You're Cindy's sister-in-law."

Kat's attention returned to Carly. "What? Yes. Although she's convinced that Joel and I are getting divorced any minute now."

Brent walked back into the clinic and took Carly's hand. "The puppies are safely in Brigid's care. Are you ready to go home?"

Carly pointed at Kat. "She's Cindy's sister-in-law."

Kat smiled. "Is there something I should know? Her car didn't break down again, did it? Joel will have a fit."

Brent raised his eyebrows. "That means we're sort of related. By marriage or something. Are we in-laws? I'm not sure."

Kat said to Carly. "I'm confused."

"Brent is Johnny's father," Carly gestured at him. "It's obvious once you know."

Kat gave him the once-over, uttered an incredulous, blasphemous expletive, and covered her mouth. "Sorry but…I can't…I mean, whoa! You're right. It's like seeing my nephew twenty years from now."

"I don't suppose you have any advice for getting Cindy to talk to me, do you?" Brent jammed his hands in his pockets. "She won't answer my calls. I'd like to get to know Johnny. My father was never around, and it bothers me that this kid doesn't even know who I am."

Kat pursed her lips. "I have an idea. How do you feel about walking dogs?"

"It's fine, I guess." He pulled his hands out of his pockets and clasped them in front of him.

Carly added, "Brent can out hike me any day."

"Joel and I are on nephew-sitting duty in July, and Johnny is staying with us." Kat widened her eyes melodramatically. "I'll ask Joel to clear it with his sister first, but maybe you'd like to come by and walk a few dogs that week."

Brent grinned. "I'd like that."

Chapter 15

Epilogue

A couple of weeks later, Brent and Carly were in his truck, driving out to the Wag On Inn to drop off Trixie and D'Artagnan with Kat. Trixie was sitting between them looking officious, while the puppy dozed on Carly's lap.

Brent had agreed to a road trip in his truck to help Carly move the boxes from her studio apartment up to Alpine Grove. Although Trixie had shown herself to be a good traveler, going that many miles with an unruly puppy was more than Carly wanted to manage. Because Trixie and D'Artagnan had become fast friends, it seemed easiest to let them spend a little time at doggie camp, rather than drag them along. Having lots of alone time with Brent wouldn't be so bad either.

Carly was dying to meet Kat's husband and Cindy's brother, Joel. Although Brent had spent a lot of time sneaking off with Joel's sister the summer after high school and had heard lots of disparaging words about the guy from Cindy, he'd never laid eyes on him.

At this point, it was a little odd, since they were related. Maybe this was why everyone knew each other in small towns. If you lived in a place long enough and a bunch of people got married or reproduced, eventually you could be distantly related to a large percentage of the population.

Brent turned at the sign and they made their way down the long, meandering driveway toward the kennels. D'Artagnan stood up in Carly's lap and raised his nose toward the window, frantically sniffing the fragrant pine-scented breeze wafting into the truck.

At the kennel, Brent parked, they got out, and Carly placed D'Artagnan on the ground, holding tightly to his leash. The pup still hadn't quite figured out that his leash was designed to restrict his movement and ran behind Carly, wrapping the leash around her legs. Carly bent over to try to disentangle herself. Kat was going to have fun trying to walk this little beastie weastie.

Carly stood up at the sound of the door slamming at the house. Kat and Joel walked down the driveway, hand in hand. He'd obviously said something funny because she was laughing.

They walked up and Kat crouched in front of the puppy. "Oh my gosh, look at this guy. He's absolutely adorable." She picked him up and cradled him in her arms.

Joel introduced himself to Brent. "It sounds like we'll see you again in July."

"Thanks for talking to your sister. She drives a hard bargain," Brent replied. "But I finally convinced her that I should get to know Johnny."

"I heard," Joel said.

"At length. Repeatedly." Kat volunteered, gesturing toward Brent. "I think it may take Cindy a while to adjust to the sight of you. So this works out well. She doesn't have to see you and you can go on thousands of dog walks with us while Johnny is here."

"Tiring Johnny out is a good thing," Joel added.

"You know that I had nothing to do with the money my father gave her, right?" Brent said. "He paid her to keep her from contacting me and luring me from college."

Kat cuddled the puppy closer. "We know. Once she realized your father wasn't going to come and hunt her down and take her house, Cindy calmed down a little."

"We're glad to know what really happened," Joel added. "She always said you left after Johnny was born and she bought her house here."

Carly said, "Actually, Brent was in England then."

"From my perspective, Cindy more or less disappeared." Brent said. "I had no idea Johnny existed until I saw them at the post office."

Kat said, "I've learned first-hand that you should expect the unexpected at the PO. There's nothing to do, so people talk. Gossip is exchanged. Secrets are revealed."

Carly pointed at the puppy in Kat's arms. "Have you heard how D'Artagnan's siblings are doing?"

Kat ruffled the puppy's ears. "According to Brigid, the families are in love with them. In fact, a bunch of foster dogs got adopted too. Now we have a backlog of people who have filled out adoption applications and waiting to adopt. Brigid is thrilled."

Carly clapped her palms together, "That's wonderful. I knew all the floofie woofies would get homes."

"Yes, they weren't even in foster care. Those pups went straight from you to Brigid to their forever homes. So what happened with the painting?"

Carly smiled. "It's real. It turns out that Brent's grandparents were part of a secret group called Pink Cow."

"Better known as *Vache Rose* in French," Brent said. "Apparently, they saved and returned many paintings after the war. This was the last one, and now it has finally made it home, thanks to all the research Carly and her friends did."

"I love happy endings." Kat put D'Artagnan down and glanced at Joel. "This little guy might need to be special dog for a while."

"I figured," Joel said.

Carly asked, "What's special dog?"

"A dog who spends time in the house with Kat." Joel said. "The honor of being special dog happens more than you might expect."

"But he's adorable," Kat said.

Carly smiled and handed Kat Trixie's leash. "We'll see you in a week."

"Drive safely," Kat said, handing the leash to Joel so she could pick up the puppy again. "Call if you need anything."

Carly and Brent climbed back into the truck and Carly looked behind her to catch a last glimpse of Kat cuddling the puppy. Joel was leaning over and stroking the fur on D'Artagnan's head.

Carly turned back to Brent. "I don't think we need to worry about D'Artagnan missing out on affection while we're gone."

"It doesn't seem like it will be a problem." He put his hand on her arm. "Are you still feeling good about moving?"

She leaned against him and placed her palm on his chest. "It feels right. I keep thinking about that quote your grandmother liked from Goethe. 'As soon as you trust yourself, you will know how to live.'"

"So are you trusting yourself?"

"For the first time in a long time. I think I am. I really am."

"Me too."

Thanks for Reading

Thank you for dedicating some of your reading time to *The Last Train to Barksville*. I hope you enjoyed the adventures with Carly and Brent. I'll be writing more books that will feature Kat, Joel and various other residents of Alpine Grove who bring dogs to the boarding kennel, so keep your eye out for the next book in the series.

If you would like to be notified by e-mail when I release a new book, you can sign up for my New Releases e-mail list at SusanDaffron.com.

I know that not everyone likes to write book reviews, but if you are willing to write a sentence or two about what you thought of *The Last Train to Barksville*, I encourage you to post a review at your favorite book vendor site or share a message with your social networking friends.

If you would like to share your thoughts about the book with me privately, you can reach me through the contact page on the SusanDaffron.com web site.

I look forward to hearing from you!

~ Susan C. Daffron

Acknowledgements

Writing a novel is never easy and I'd like to thank my husband James Byrd for his support and encouragement throughout the publishing process.

I'd also like to thank my alpha and beta readers for their eagle-eyed reading and great feedback.

About the Author

S usan Daffron is the author of the Jennings & O'Shea series and the Alpine Grove romantic comedies, a series of novels that feature residents of the small town of Alpine Grove and their various quirky dogs and cats. She is also an award-winning author of many nonfiction books, including several about pets and animal rescue. She lives in a small town in northern Idaho and shares her life with her husband and three really cute dogs.